Wanderlust & Wild Horses

Riverbend Valley Book 2

Tara Baisden

STERLING RIDGE PRESS LLC

Copyright

Cover designed by Sterling Ridge Press LLC

Published by: Sterling Ridge Press, LLC www.sterlingridgepress.com

ISBN: 978-1-966093-12-1 Printed in the United States of America

First Edition: March 2025

For permissions, contact: tara@tarabaisden.com or visit www.tarabaisden.com

Dedication

To those who embrace the courage to love despite the shadows of the past.

To the steadfast souls who find strength in family, both born and found.

And to every wandering heart that discovers a place to call home.

This story is for you.

With gratitude and love,

Tara

About Riverbend Valley

Welcome to the fictional town of Riverbend Valley, Montana!

Nestled in the shadow of the breathtaking Sapphire Mountains, Riverbend Valley is a place where life flows as peacefully as the rivers winding through it. Surrounded by rolling ranch lands, dense forests, and the rugged peaks of Montana's wilderness, this picturesque valley is the perfect setting for tales of faith, love, and second chances.

<u>A Rugged Heritage</u>

Founded in the late 1800s by homesteaders drawn to the fertile land and expansive views, Riverbend Valley began as a ranching settlement. Riverbend Valley's roots run deep, forged by generations of ranchers and cowboys who've worked the land with grit and determination. This is a place where faith has always been a cornerstone, guiding its people through hardships and celebrating their triumphs. From the well-worn pews of Riverbend Valley Community Church to the lively gatherings at the rodeo grounds, Riverbend Valley's traditions reflect a steadfast commitment to God, family, and the land.

<u>A Community of Faith</u>

Riverbend Valley offers a refuge for weary souls and a chance to rediscover the beauty of life's simple pleasures. Whether it's through a quiet moment of prayer along the river, a moonlit ride under Montana skies, or the laughter of a community united in celebration, this is a place where hearts are mended, faith is renewed, and love abounds.

<u>The Essence of Small-Town Life</u>

With a population of just over three thousand, Riverbend Valley retains its small-town charm. Main Street is lined with family-owned businesses, from the Bluebird Café, famous for its huckleberry pies, to the General Mercantile, where locals gather to swap stories and stock up on supplies. Seasonal festivals bring the community together, from the Spring Rodeo to the Fall Harvest Festival, celebrating the rhythms of life in this ranching town.

<u>A Haven for Visitors</u>

Visitors to Riverbend Valley are captivated by its rustic charm and natural beauty. Whether it's horseback riding through the foothills, fishing in the Deer Run River, or stargazing from Silver Bluff's iconic overlook, there's something for everyone to enjoy.

Experience the Heart of Riverbend Valley

Here, under the endless skies and among the resilient people of Montana, you'll find stories of redemption, second chances, and unwavering faith. Riverbend Valley isn't just a setting—it's a celebration of the rugged heritage and timeless grace that make this place unforgettable.

Welcome to Riverbend Valley, where faith is strong, family is everything, and love always finds a way.

I hope you fall in love with its enduring spirit.

Contents

Chapter 1

Sadie Beaumont gripped the reins and leaned forward in the saddle. Daisy, her high-spirited chestnut mare, shifted beneath her, ears flicking toward the breeze. The morning sun cast long shadows over the east pasture, its light catching the rugged lines of weathered fence posts and the uneven plains. Sadie's sharp gaze zeroed in on the problem—a section of fence leaning at an awkward angle, its wood post scarred with deep gouges. A bull's temper had left its mark, plain as day.

"Figures," she muttered, brushing a stray strand of blonde hair from her cheek with the back of her hand. She clicked her tongue, an instinctive sound passed down from her father, as Daisy snorted and pawed at the dry ground. "Easy, girl," Sadie murmured, patting the mare's neck absently before pulling a pair of well-worn leather gloves from her back pocket. Her fingers slid into them with practiced ease. This wasn't her first repair job, and it wouldn't be her last.

Her gaze drifted to the horizon, taking in the rugged mountain peaks in the distance and the endless expanse of sky above. The view was a steadying presence, even when the land itself pushed back. Out here, nothing came easy, but the hard work felt honest. The midsummer heat hung heavy over Riverbend Valley, painting the horizon in a shimmering haze. The air carried the dry tang of sun-baked soil mingled with the sharp scent of sagebrush—a fragrance of survival. Eagle's Nest Ranch, her family's legacy, bore the weight of the season's relentless drought. The creek that once flowed clear and steady now trickled weakly, its banks cracked and dusty. Pastures were brittle underfoot, and every choice seemed like a gamble with history, livelihood, and survival at stake.

Sadie shook off her thoughts and refocused on the task at hand. "Guess you had your fun, didn't you?" she said, as if the absent bull owed her an explanation. Tugging the brim of her Stetson lower to shield her eyes from the glare, she slid off Daisy's back and landed lightly on her boots.

She gave Daisy a quick pat. "What do you think, girl?" The mare snorted, pawing at the ground again, and Sadie chuckled. "Yeah, that's what I thought, too. We've got our work cut out for us." The fence repair would take at least an hour, maybe more. She glanced toward the radio clipped to her saddle as it crackled to life.

"Sadie? You out there, honey?"

"I'm here, Dad. East pasture, checking that section of fence you were worried about."

"How bad is it?" Jack Beaumont's voice carried the gravelly tone of someone who'd already been up for hours.

"Nothing I can't handle, but it'll take some time. The bull did a number on it."

"That ornery beast," Jack muttered. "Need help?"

"No, I've got it. But I'll be late getting to the north pasture check."

"Don't worry about that. Mitch offered to ride up there this morning."

Sadie felt her stomach give the faintest squeeze at the sound of his name. Mitch Monarch had always been a steady presence in her life. A dependable ranch hand at Eagle's Nest and the older brother of her best friend, Laura. Their dynamic had always been straightforward, framed by years of familiarity and mutual respect, but lately, something had shifted. The easy camaraderie they once shared now felt muddled, weighed down by an unspoken tension that neither seemed ready to confront. Sadie wasn't sure what had changed, but she could feel it in the way Mitch's eyes lingered a little too long when he thought she wasn't looking, and in the awkward silences that crept into conversations that used to flow effortlessly. Whether or not she wanted to admit it, the change unnerved her more than she cared to let on.

"Tell him thanks," she said, keeping her voice neutral. "I'll catch up with him later."

"Copy that," Jack's voice came steadily over the radio. "How's the pasture looking?"

"Bone dry, Dad," Sadie answered, her gaze sweeping the brittle grass stretching endlessly beneath the Montana sky.

The radio crackled before his response came through. "And the creek?"

"Pretty much the same—just a thin trickle," she replied, her voice tinged with worry.

A sigh carried through the static. "Not good. Not good at all. Guess it's in the Lord's hands now. Don't push yourself too hard out there, honey. I'll see you when you when you get back."

Sadie hesitated, concern settling deep in her chest. "Will do, Dad," she said, before clipping the radio onto her belt.

Sadie rolled up her sleeves and got to work, adjusting the stubborn fence post. The rhythmic flow of physical labor was a welcome antidote to her restless mind, each hammer strike and twist of wire helping to settle the whirlwind of thoughts she couldn't seem to shake. Running a ranch was no small feat. It demanded wearing countless hats: repair worker, animal caretaker, business manager, problem-solver, and a handful of other roles she never had the luxury of shedding. Most days, she thrived on the constant hustle, finding joy and pride in managing the land her family had cultivated for generations. The Beaumont ranch wasn't just her livelihood; it was her legacy. Deep in Montana's Riverbend Valley, it stood as a testament to her ancestors' grit and determination, a piece of history she carried forward with every fence mended and every herd tended.

Still, no amount of sweeping mountain views or the familiar cadence of ranch life could keep her true desires from creeping into her thoughts when the pace slowed. What started a few years ago as a creative outlet, her self-published series of cowboy romance novels following the fictional lives of ranchers in a remote Montana valley, had unexpectedly blossomed into something more recently. Readers had fallen in love with her vivid storytelling. The pressure to meet her next self-inflicted book deadline gnawed at her, even now, as she worked the stubborn post back into position.

As the sun edged higher in the sky, warming the surrounding landscape, her mind wandered further away from the job at hand. The fence before her blurred, replaced by visions of her protagonist in the latest novel she was writing, a fiery, determined rancher named Amelia Keys, facing a storm both literal and metaphorical. Amelia had been grappling with her place on the Keys' family ranch while navigating a burgeoning romance with her best friend-turned-business partner.

Sadie allowed herself a small smile as she tightened the last wire. Life has a funny way of mirroring art.

Rusty, her faithful Australian Shepherd, appeared from around a bend in the fence line, probably done investigating whatever fascinating scent had caught his attention earlier. He trotted over, tail wagging, then suddenly froze, ears perked toward the distant tree line.

"What is it, boy?" Sadie followed his gaze but saw nothing unusual among the grove of trees. Rusty barked once, then took off running. "Rusty! Get back here!"

The dog ignored her, racing toward whatever had captured his interest.

"Probably chasing a rabbit," Sadie muttered.

Her thoughts drifted back to the looming deadlines she could no longer ignore. She had assured her readers that the next book in her series would be in their hands by late-summer, a promise made with more optimism than foresight. But the way things were going, she'd be fortunate to have the manuscript finished by fall. The realization gnawed at her, sending a deep pang of guilt cascading through her chest. She hated the idea of disappointing the people who believed in her work, yet the clock seemed to tick louder with every passing day, mocking her dwindling progress.

"Your timing needs work, Lord," she murmured, then immediately felt bad for the complaint. Her mother always said God's timing was perfect, even when it didn't make sense to human understanding.

The rest of the fence repair went smoothly, muscle memory taking over as she worked. By the time she finished, the heat of the day was amping up. Sadie packed up her tools, satisfied with the repair, but knowing she'd need to check it again tomorrow. That bull had a tendency to test his boundaries.

As she rode back toward the ranch yard, she spotted Mitch near the main barn. He was leading his horse, Thunder, his movements efficient and practiced. Their eyes met across the yard, and he raised a hand in greeting.

"Fence all fixed?" Mitch called out as Sadie approached.

"For now," she replied, brushing a stray strand of hair from her face. "Thanks for covering the north pasture check."

"Anytime." He hesitated, a weight behind his words, before adding, "How's the east pasture holding up?"

"Dry," she said with a sigh.

"Same with the north," he said, his brow furrowing. "I left some extra hay for the cattle, but your dad wants me to take the water truck out and fill the troughs. The drought's getting worse, Sadie."

"Yeah, it is." She offered a faint smile, though it didn't quite meet her eyes. "The creek in the east pasture's down to just a trickle. When you're delivering water to the north, be sure to swing by the east and top off the troughs there, too."

"Will do," Mitch said with a sharp nod. He paused, longer this time, as though wrestling with something unspoken. Finally, he looked back at her. "Hey, Sadie... you got plans for dinner tonight?"

The question caught her off guard, and a flicker of irritation crossed her face before she tempered it into a curt reply. "Yeah, Mitch. I plan to eat dinner at home and work on my book, like always." She gave him a polite but firm smile, her tone making it clear the conversation was over.

Madge Carter's voice rang out from the kitchen door of the main house. "Sadie, breakfast is about ready!"

Grateful for the timely interruption, Sadie called back, "Coming!"

As Mitch reached for Daisy's reins, his fingers brushed against hers, sending a jolt of awareness that Sadie wasn't prepared for. Quickly, she let go and took a small step back. "Thanks," she murmured, avoiding his eyes.

Sadie turned for the house, refusing to let herself look back, though she could feel the weight of his eyes following her the entire way.

The kitchen hummed with its familiar morning rhythm, alive with bustling energy. Harriet Beaumont stood at the stove beside Madge, cooking eggs in a cast-iron skillet. Harriet was never one to leave the ranch cook to manage the kitchen by herself. She took pride in rolling up her sleeves, stepping into the heart of the action, and lending a hand wherever she could. Madge deftly flipped pancakes with practiced ease. The soft strains of a country gospel song floated from the radio in the corner of the kitchen.

"There she is," Madge said, handing a loaded plate to Sadie. "Sit. Eat. And tell me why you look like you've got more on your mind than ranch work this morning."

Sadie slid onto her usual stool at the kitchen island. "My thoughts are on the drought right now. That's about it, Madge."

"Mm hmm." Madge's knowing look suggested she wasn't buying it.

The kitchen door swung open, and her father stepped in, bringing with him the sharp scent of leather and horse liniment. He kissed Harriet's cheek, nodded to Madge, and settled on a stool beside Sadie.

"Fence all fixed?" he asked Sadie.

"Yes, sir."

"Good." Jack's said. "Pete mentioned seeing tracks in the south pasture yesterday. Might want to check the fencing down there as well."

"What kind of animal do you suspect?" Harriet turned from the stove, concern creasing her brow.

"Probably just deer or elk, nothing out of the normal," Jack assured her.

Harriet set a steaming mug of coffee in front of Sadie, adding an extra splash of cream, just the way Sadie liked it. "Jack," she said, her tone light but edged with a hint of challenge, "surely one of the ranch hands can check the south pasture. Sadie might have other plans this afternoon."

Sadie wrapped her hands around the cup, feeling the warmth seep into her palms. She shot a small, grateful smile in her mom's direction, wordlessly appreciating the subtle nudge on her behalf. Her mom's steady support for Sadie's dream of becoming a full-time author was a lifeline on days when her father's expectations felt particularly heavy. Jack Beaumont, however, saw things differently. To him, the idea of his only child pouring her efforts into writing novels was just a fleeting interest, something she'd grow out of. In his mind, Sadie's future was as clear as the Montana sky above them: head of operations at Eagle's Nest Ranch, carrying on the family legacy. Anything else was a distraction.

Jack cleared his throat. "I could probably have Mitch take a look at it."

"Thanks, Dad," Sadie replied, though a ripple of guilt tugged at her chest.

Madge chimed in, her eyes sparkling mischievously. "By the way, I checked Amazon this morning. Your latest book's hit the top 100."

"Well, now, isn't that something!" Harriet exclaimed, her proud gaze bouncing between her husband and daughter. "Did you hear that, Jack? Our daughter's making waves out there. Her book is selling like hotcakes."

"I heard," Jack said with a measured nod. "That's nice, Sadie. Sounds like your little hobby's coming along." His voice was calm, maybe even kind, but Sadie couldn't miss the faint edge of dismissal woven into his words.

Her fingers tightened around the handle of her mug, but she managed a steady smile. "It's more than a hobby, Daddy," she hesitated, weighing the options of her next words against the look on her father's face. "My books are doing well, better than I ever expected." She paused again. "And... I feel it, Dad. Writing—it's not just something I do on the side. It's in my bones. The same way ranching is. I want to give more of my time to it."

The kitchen fell into an awkward silence. Sadie glanced down at her coffee, feeling the battle within her heart, the desire to honor her father's expectations while chasing the dream that wouldn't let her go.

Jack pushed back from the table. "Well, best get back to it. The ranch won't run itself." He paused at the door, looking back at Sadie. "You know I'm proud of you, right? With everything you do here on the ranch, and..." he gestured vaguely, "all that writing stuff, too."

The words struck a chord deep within her, and her voice wavered under the sudden swell of emotion. "Thanks, Dad," she managed, her tone soft but earnest, as he pulled the door closed behind him.

Harriet reached across the kitchen island and squeezed Sadie's hand. Her hazel eyes, so similar to her daughter's, were filled with understanding. "Give him some grace, sweetheart," Harriet said, her voice steady with encouragement. "He's trying. It's just... hard for a man to come to terms with the idea that the dreams he's always had for you aren't the same ones you have for yourself."

Madge stepped closer and nodded in agreement. "Pray on it, sugar," she said, her tone equal parts sage wisdom and no-nonsense pragmatism. "Men like Jack? Their hearts get tied up in their land, their work, every corner of their lives is built on the hope that they'll pass it along to someone who loves it like they do. That kind of realization, accepting it might look different, it takes time."

Sadie let out a slow breath. "I know," she said, her voice soft but resolute. "I'll be patient, and I'll keep praying. But I believe I can honor this ranch, the legacy he's built, and still find a way to chase my own dreams. I have to. There has to be room for both."

Harriet smiled gently, pride flickering in her expression.

"Well, if anyone can figure it out, it's you, Sadie Beaumont," Madge said with a wink. "Strong women make space where men can't even see a door."

Chapter 2

Gage West eased his battered Ford pickup onto the gravel drive of Eagle's Nest Ranch, the truck's worn engine grumbling like the storm of doubts rolling through his mind. A wooden sign loomed ahead: Eagle's Nest Ranch—Established 1892.

Pulling to a stop near the main house, Gage slid out of the driver's seat and took in the ranch laid out around him. The place seemed like something out of a postcard: an enormous red barn stood proud against the rolling landscape, its roof gleaming faintly where sunlight struck the tin just right. Sturdy corrals held horses that flicked their tails lazily in the midafternoon breeze. The distant lowing of cattle echoed softly across the open plains. The Montana mountains rose with unassuming grandeur all around, their forested slopes stretching skyward until they dissolved into a sea of endless blue.

The view stretched out before him, a canvas of untamed beauty that seemed to pull the sky down to meet the earth. Gage wouldn't have admitted it out loud, but it was the kind of sight that could stop a man in his tracks if he let it. The rolling hills dipped and climbed like the rhythm of a song you couldn't help but sway to, sprawled beneath a backdrop of rugged mountains that stood tall and unyielding against the horizon. The expanse of the land was so vast, so resolute, it felt as if time itself had decided to linger here.

He shifted his stance, rocking back on his heels, trying to shake off the feeling of steadiness and belonging he felt. Only then did he realize his breaths had been shallow ever since he drove through the front gate. The towering trees and mountains, the sturdy fences weathered by years of storms and sun, and the main ranch house standing proud and steadfast, it all whispered things he wasn't ready to hear. Things about belonging, about staying... family.

This place was more than land. It wasn't just cows to herd or fences to mend; it was a story written across generations, stitched into the very soil. Every blade of grass and every beam of the barn seemed to carry the weight of a thousand sacrifices. This was the sort of place people poured their lives into, the sort of place that asked for everything and more. The type of place that stayed steady and true, whether you did or not.

Gage shoved his hands deep into his pockets. For someone like him, a man who had always been ready to move on before the dust could settle, it was nerve-wracking. This wasn't just a ranch; it was a legacy, inheritance, and rich history. And those things, he'd learned long ago, came with expectations so heavy they could anchor a man to the ground before he even knew it. That kind of commitment had always been something he'd avoided like wildfire.

"Just another job," Gage muttered under his breath. "Get in, earn some cash, get out. Simple."

The logic was sound, at least on the surface, but the words rang hollow, like boots against an empty wooden floor. They had for years now, though he'd perfected the art of brushing off the ache, burying it somewhere that even he couldn't reach most days. Yet as he walked closer to the sprawling ranch house, its log exterior shining in the afternoon sun, something heavier pressed against him. Memories—always showing up uninvited.

Tommy Martinez's lopsided, gap-toothed grin pushed its way to the front of his mind, hitting him like a stray gust of wind. Tommy had been his bunk mate in one of the countless foster homes where Gage had hung his hat as a child. For six months, when Gage was twelve, the two of them had built the kind of brotherhood that only came from whispered plans under threadbare blankets and stolen comic books traded like treasure. Tommy had declared they'd always be best friends, no matter what. Gage, desperate for a connection, had believed him.

Then Tommy's aunt had shown up out of the blue. A woman who smelled like lilacs and talked excitedly about homemade breakfasts and family traditions. She'd come to take Tommy home. Not a temporary home, but a real one, where pictures hung on the walls and the silverware matched.

Gage remembered that day in excruciating detail. The screech of tires as a navy-blue station wagon had stopped in the driveway. The sound of Tommy's favorite sneakers slapping against the linoleum floor as he dashed out the door, barely glancing back. Gage had stood at the upstairs window of that drafty, dirty house, fingers curled tightly around the dingy curtain. He'd watched until the car became a speck in the distance. The sinking feeling in his chest was as vivid now as it had been then, like something had been yanked clean out of him and replaced with hollowness.

That gap-toothed grin and those whispered promises might have left him all those years ago, but the lesson hadn't: nothing good stayed. Permanence was a mirage, something meant for other people. People like Tommy, not Gage West.

He clenched his jaw tightly, willing himself to shove the thought aside, as though it were just another stubborn layer of dust that clung to his boots after a hard day's work.

As Gage ascended the wide wooden porch, the boards beneath him creaked in subtle protest, a testament to age and countless footsteps before him. Before he could knock, the front door eased open, revealing a tall, stocky ma. His black stetson cast a shadow across his face, but it couldn't hide the sharp, intelligent eyes beneath it, studying Gage with quiet intensity. Without a word, the man's steady gaze swept over him, not cold exactly, but assessing, as if he were sizing up both the stranger on his porch and the purpose that had brought him here.

"Mr. Beaumont?" Gage straightened, removing his stetson and squaring his shoulders.

"Jack's fine." The ranch owner's handshake was firm but not challenging. "How can I help you?"

"Gage West, sir. Heard you might need an extra ranch hand."

Jack nodded toward the barn. "Walk with me."

They fell into step, Jack's pace unhurried but purposeful.

"You any good with horses, ever worked cattle," Jack asked as they entered the barn.

"Done my share of breaking and training horses. Worked mostly quarter horses, some thoroughbreds. Worked most of my life around cattle."

A horse whinnied from one of the stalls, and Gage automatically turned toward the sound. A beautiful bay mare watched them with intelligent eyes.

"That's Lightning," Jack said. "Been giving us trouble. Previous owner mishandled her—now she's got trust issues."

Something in Jack's tone made Gage glance sharply at him, but the older man's expression revealed nothing.

"Mind showing me how you'd approach her?"

Gage moved toward the stall. Lightning's ears flicked forward, then back—interested but wary. He kept his movements slow, deliberate, speaking in low tones.

"Hey there, beautiful. No need to worry about me."

He extended his hand, palm up, letting her catch his scent. After a moment's hesitation, she stretched her neck, nostrils flaring as she investigated him.

"Good girl," he murmured. "That's right. Nobody here's gonna hurt you."

Jack watched the interaction without comment, though Gage sensed the man was seeing more than just his horse-handling skills.

Jack studied Gage with his usual penetrating gaze, his expression unreadable. "You know your way around cattle, then?"

"Yes, sir," Gage replied, his tone steady and sure.

Jack nodded once, but his sharp eyes didn't waver. "Are you reliable?"

The muscles in Gage's jaw tensed, but he answered without hesitation. "As reliable as the sun coming up each morning."

Jack leaned back slightly, arms folded across his chest. "How long were you at your last job?"

"Six months," Gage said curtly.

"And the one before that?"

"Four months."

A furrow appeared on Jack's brow, though he said nothing at first. He held Gage's gaze long enough to make the air between them feel heavy with unspoken thoughts. Finally, Jack spoke, his voice level but firm. "I expect my ranch hands to stick around. Folks who work here tend to stay. That's how we get the job done right."

"Yes, sir," Gage replied evenly, meeting Jack's scrutiny head-on. "I understand."

"Eagle's Nest Ranch isn't just a patch of land to work. It's a family, both the kind you're born into and the kind you choose. I need to know if that's something you can handle," Jack said, his voice steady and firm. "We run a family operation here. My daughter Sadie is one of the ranches foremen, my wife, Harriet, pitches in whenever she's needed. Every evening, we have dinner together, ranch workers included. Breakfast and lunch are your responsibility. Dinner is served in the main house every evening, six sharp. On Sundays, we do our best to rest. I encourage my ranch hands to attend church. There's no cussin' or taking the Lord's name in vain on my ranch. I catch you doing it, you're gone. Understood"

Gage shifted his stance, an unfamiliar tightness stirring in his chest. "Yes sir. I'm here to work hard, sir. Do the job, earn my pay, plain and simple."

Jack's sharp blue eyes stayed fixed on him, the silence stretching just long enough to feel uncomfortable. "Sometimes, son," he said evenly, "it's not that simple."

Before Gage could reply, the sounds of boots crunching on gravel and distant voices floated in through the barn door. The ranch was alive with the rhythm of the day. Jack's gaze lingered for another beat before he turned his attention toward the commotion outside.

"Bunkhouse is around back. I'll have one of my ranch hands show you the ropes. Five hundred dollars weekly salary." He paused. "And Gage? My daughter Sadie, you'll listen to her. She's got a good head on her shoulders. Strong woman. You have to respect her. Have a problem with that?"

"Won't be any trouble," Gage assured him.

"Good." Jack headed for the door, then stopped. "One more thing. Sunday services at Riverbend Valley Community Church start at ten AM sharp. You're welcome to join us."

"I appreciate the offer, but—"

"Just putting it out there." Jack's smile held no judgment. "The Lord has a way of finding folks when they're ready."

Gage stared after him, unease prickling at the edges of his thoughts. He'd worked countless ranches over the years, but there was something about this one that gnawed at him. It felt different, not just the sprawling land or the quiet hum of activity, but something deeper. It was dangerous in a way he couldn't name, yet strangely grounding all the same.

Lightning nickered softly, and he reached over the half door, giving the horse a reassuring pat.

"Church ain't for me," he grumbled to the horse. "But a good daily meal at the main house? Now that's something I can handle."

A burst of laughter and lively chatter drifted in from outside, pulling Gage from his thoughts. Curiosity sparked, he strode toward the noise and spotted a group of ranch hands gathered by a ranch truck, their easy camaraderie evident as they worked together to unload the heavy sacks of feed.

Gage was greeted by a friendly shout. "You must be the new guy!" The voice belonged to a younger man with a laid-back grin that matched his easy demeanor. "Name's Ross. This guy here is Pete—don't let his scowl fool you—and this is Julie, pretending to look busy." He waved toward a rider approaching on horseback. "And coming up now, that's Mitch, another ranch hand."

"Pretending?" Julie shot back, tugging off her gloves with a pointed glare. "I've done more work this morning than you'll get done all week, Ross."

"Children," Pete grumbled. Though his tone carried the weight of a reprimand, there was an unmistakable warmth beneath the gravelly delivery. "Some of us actually have work to do."

Ross just grinned wider. "Don't mind him. He has the disposition of a wounded grizzly."

"Ya'll need to get back to work and quit foolin' around. I don't have time for your nonsense." Pete's look cast their way was colorful enough to make Julie laugh and Ross feign shock.

"Ahhh... Pete," Ross clutched his chest dramatically, "a little fun mixed with work is a good thing. Helps pass the time."

Gage almost smiled. The easy banter between the ranch hands was unusual, but not unwelcoming.

"Bunkhouse is that way," Julie pointed. "Hope you don't mind country music, 'cause Ross thinks he's the next George Strait."

"Hey, I have a gift," Ross protested.

"Yeah, the gift of making cats jealous of your singing."

Gage left the sound of their laughter behind as he strode toward the bunkhouse. Stepping inside, he took in the space—a no-frills setup, but clean and organized. Bunks lined the walls, each showing hints of the personalities who occupied them. It was familiar territory for him, a functional place for work-worn men and women to recharge. Nothing fancy, just a spot to sleep, whip up a quick meal, or catch a show on an old TV when downtime allowed.

"This'll do," he muttered, turning on his heel and heading back out the door.

Chapter 3

Gage returned to his truck and grabbed his few belongings. It didn't take long, twenty minutes, maybe, to settle into his quarters, his entire life packed into a couple of battered duffels. Changing out of his road-weary clothes, he pulled on his sturdy work jeans, a faded flannel, and his scuffed boots. Practical. Durable. Ready.

Stepping back outside, the sweep of Montana's breathtaking expanse took hold of him. The Sapphire Mountains loomed in the distance, steadfast and eternal, their rugged peaks piercing the boundless expanse of blue sky. The pastures stretched wide, the parched earth making the drought plain to see. Scattered cattle grazed in pockets, their movements slow under the weight of a relentless sun. Nearby, horses gathered around hay bales, their coats glinting faintly in the afternoon light.

Even after years of roaming, Montana had a way of stopping a man in his tracks. Something about the land, raw and unyielding, seemed to echo the parts of himself he'd long kept hidden.

"Pretty, ain't it?"

Gage turned to find Pete watching him, the older man's weathered face unreadable.

"It'll do," Gage said neutrally.

"Right. Well, come on then. Boss wants you working with that new string of horses we got in. Figure we'll see what you're made of."

As they walked toward the training corral, Pete filled him in on the ranch's operations. Eagle's Nest was known for its cattle, but they also did significant business in horse training and breeding. The new string of horses had come from a ranch in Wyoming that was closing down—good bloodlines, but most needed work.

"The main thing you need to know," Pete said as they approached the corral, "is that we do things right here. No shortcuts, no rushing. These animals are more than inventory. They're family."

"Everything's about family here, isn't it?" Gage couldn't keep the edge from his voice.

Pete gave him a sharp look. "Got a problem with that?"

"No problem. Just making an observation."

"Mmm hmm," Pete jerked his chin toward the corral, where a striking black gelding paced nervously. "That one's been giving us fits. Show me how you'd handle him."

Gage studied the horse's movement, noting the tension in its muscles, the way it kept one ear constantly trained on them. Fear behavior, but not panicked. This was a horse that had learned to expect the worst while hoping for better.

He knew the feeling.

Moving slowly, he entered the corral. The gelding's pacing increased, but Gage just stood quietly, letting the animal grow accustomed to his presence. After a few minutes, he began speaking in low, even tones.

"Easy now. Nobody's in a hurry here. We've got all day to figure each other out."

Pete watched from the fence as Gage worked, gradually earning the horse's trust through patience and consistent gentleness. By the time the sun was setting lower in the sky, the gelding was allowing Gage to approach, even accepting brief touches along its neck.

"Not bad," Pete admitted. "Though you might want to watch that left shoulder. He's got a tendency to swing it out when he's fixing to bolt."

"Noticed that. Previous owner probably came at him too strong on that side."

Pete's expression softened slightly. "Yeah, well, most folks carry their hurts somewhere. Horses ain't so different from people that way."

The words hit closer to home than Gage liked. He busied himself with checking the gelding's hooves, avoiding Pete's knowing gaze.

"Dinner's at six sharp, don't forget," Pete said. "Madge doesn't tolerate tardiness, so don't be late. Woman's got a wooden spoon, and she ain't afraid to use it."

"Madge?"

"Ranch cook. Been here longer than most of us. Makes the best chicken and dumplings this side of heaven, but she runs her kitchen like a drill sergeant."

As if on cue, a bell rang from the direction of the main house. The sound carried across the ranch, bringing work to a momentary halt.

"Better wash up," Pete advised. "Madge can smell horse on you from a mile away, and she won't have it at her table."

Gage trailed behind the others toward the washhouse, then followed to the side entrance of the main house. It opened into a spacious dining room that connected seamlessly to the bustling kitchen and offered a glimpse into the family's expansive living room beyond. The warm, inviting scent of freshly baked bread mingled with something rich and savory, causing his stomach to grumble in protest.

The kitchen was alive with the clink of silverware and the hum of conversation as workers lined up to fill their plates from steaming pots on the counter. At the center of the bustling scene stood a tall woman with silver-streaked hair, her sharp eyes taking in every detail with quiet authority.

As Gage stepped closer, she turned her attention to him. "You're the new hand, aren't you?" she asked, her tone brisk but not unfriendly.

"Yes, ma'am," he replied, nodding politely.

She gestured toward the food. "Well, go on then, grab a plate and pile it high. Can't have you collapsing out there for lack of a decent meal."

"Thank you, ma'am," he said, his voice steady but grateful.

The woman's eyebrows lifted, and a wry smile tugged at the corners of her mouth. "'Ma'am,' huh?" She gave him a pointed look. "Call me Madge, honey. 'Ma'am' makes me sound like I just hit seventy-five and started collecting cats."

Ross, already seated at the long dining table, grinned. "You are old, Madge."

"Watch it, boy, or you'll be eating bread crusts for a week."

The threat only made Ross's grin wider. "You love me too much for that."

"Lord help me, I do." Madge turned back to Gage. "Sit. Eat. And don't mind this bunch—they may act like hooligans, but they're good people."

Gage found a spot at the table, half-listening to the conversations around him. The easy familiarity between the workers stirred something in his chest, longing, maybe, or regret. He pushed the feeling aside as he waited and watched the scene unfold before him.

Jack sat at the head of the table, flanked by two women.

"Let's say grace," he began. "Lord, please bless this food we are about to eat and thank you for all your blessings. Amen."

For Gage, this was all uncharted territory. He had never been on a ranch where the hired hands were expected to join the owners for dinner. He sensed that the Beaumonts and perhaps even the other ranch workers were a very spiritual bunch, something he hadn't encountered during his previous stints on other ranches. As a child in foster care, he had brushed against religion and held a small belief in God, but in recent years, he felt God had little use for him. Prayer had all but evacuated his life, and he hadn't set foot in a church since he was a boy.

"Gage..."

Gage snapped back to the moment, realizing Jack was trying to catch his attention.

"Yes, sir?" he replied.

"This is my wife, Harriet," Jack introduced, gently patting her hand. "She manages all the paperwork here on the ranch, so be good to her; she's the one who signs your paychecks."

"Pleased to meet you, ma'am," Gage said, offering a respectful nod.

Harriet smiled warmly and nodded in return.

Jack then turned to the woman seated on his left.

She was beautiful, not in the conventional, delicate way of magazine models displayed in truck stop diners, but strikingly so in her own right. Her blond wavy hair was pulled back in a simple ponytail, with wisps framing her face perfectly. Her hazel eyes sparkled with amber flecks, and her natural beauty compelled Gage to sit up a little taller.

"And this is my daughter, Sadie," Jack said, resting a hand on her shoulder. "She's our ranch foreman. Respect her, and she'll respect you."

"Ma'am," Gage said, nodding in acknowledgment.

Sadie returned his nod, then tilted her head slightly, her expression curious. "So, what brings you to Eagle's Nest?"

"Work," he answered shortly.

"Man of many words, I see." She shared an amused look with her father. "Well, you'll fit right in with Pete, then. He's fluent in grunt."

"I heard that," Pete called from another table.

Chapter 4

Morning came with an efficiency that only Montana could deliver. The ranch buzzed to life not long after the sun crept over the hills. Sadie stood in the barn, ready to delegate tasks and keep the sprawling operation running smoothly. The barn was a scene of orderly chaos, with ranch hands joking and teasing as they gathered near an old wooden tack trunk that served as their impromptu meeting hub. Sadie had long since grown used to the good-natured ribbing and talk of the day's work. Even so, she had to nudge them into focus.

"All right, folks," Sadie said, her voice carrying a calm authority that cut through the commotion. "We've got a full day ahead of us. Pete, you're tackling the calf barn today—looks like we've got nine new arrivals that need tagging, and the pens need cleaning before this afternoon's vet visit."

Pete grunted in acknowledgment, his leathery face unreadable as he adjusted his hat.

Ross, standing beside him, muttered, "Pete loves his quality time with the calves."

"Careful, boy," Pete shot back, his tone dry. "Might just have to ask Sadie to assign you as my helper."

Sadie smirked, but kept them moving. "Ross, you'll be in the north pasture with Mitch. He's already headed that way with the water truck. On your list, replace the gate latch near the creek, and check on that heifer dad mentioned yesterday. She might need closer monitoring. Take down a load of hay, and make sure all the water troughs are filled throughout the day."

"Julie," Sadie said with a warm but no-nonsense tone, "I'm putting you in charge of the storage barn inventory. Make sure everything's accounted for before the hay delivery gets here at the end of the day today."

Julie gave a brisk nod, determination flashing in her eyes.

Sadie shifted her gaze to the new ranch hand leaning casually against a barn post, his arms crossed over his chest as if he had all the time in the world. Gage wore an expression of bemused detachment, though his stormy blue-gray eyes gave nothing away. He'd only been at Eagle's Nest for a day, but there was something about him that Sadie couldn't put her finger on—a tension behind the sharp edges, like a man who'd been through too much and trusted too little.

"Gage," she said firmly. "You're with me today."

A low whistle rippled through the group like an incoming breeze, accompanied by chuckles and a few not-so-subtle grins. Ross leaned closer to Pete. "How'd he earn that honor? Last I checked, new hands had to put in a few weeks of grunt work before riding with the foreman."

"Careful, Ross," Pete replied, as deadpan as ever. "You're gonna get yourself assigned to manure pit duty if you don't quit running that mouth."

Gage, unbothered by their banter, raised an eyebrow at Sadie. "Something special lined up?"

"Fences in the south pasture," she replied crisply. "Fences here need constant checking. We have issues with deer and elk."

"Fences," he said with a wry twist of his mouth. "Exciting."

"It's hard work," Sadie quipped, "but if that's too much for you, I can assign you something lighter. Like sweeping the barns."

He didn't bite. She was trying to needle him—not overtly, but enough to set the tone. Gage, however, stood unmoving, like a mountain against the wind. "I'll leave the sweeping to someone else," he said.

"Good. Grab a fencing toolkit from the corner there," she said, nodding toward the barn's neatly organized shelves. "We'll saddle up and head out in ten. Meet me out front and don't keep me waiting."

"I wouldn't dare," he said, his sarcasm as light as air but unmistakable.

Sadie didn't bother dignifying that with a response. She turned sharply, heading toward the tack room. The sooner she got this day started, the sooner it would be over.

***

The sound of hooves trailed along the dirt path leading out to the south pasture as Sadie rode Daisy, with Gage keeping pace beside her on an older chestnut gelding named Bandit. Rusty, the ranch dog, trotted ahead, nose sniffing everything in his path, as though the fate of the day rested on his findings. The landscape was quintessential Montana, rolling hills undulating toward the distant embrace of the Sapphire Mountains, their rugged peaks etched against the horizon.

Yet, the stark imprint of the drought lingered, casting a sobering shadow over the otherwise breathtaking view.

Sadie had no time to appreciate the scenery. Her attention was fixed squarely on the man riding next to her.

"You ride like it's second nature," she remarked, breaking the silence that had stretched for most of their ride. She wasn't sure what prompted her to say it, some combination of vague curiosity and an unwillingness to let the quiet linger any longer.

"I've had plenty of practice, most ranch hands do," Gage replied, his tone as unreadable as his expression.

"So, have you worked on a lot of ranches in the area before?"

"Yep. Here and there."

Sadie glanced at him, her eyebrows lifting. "Here and there, huh? That's not exactly a map."

He shrugged loosely, the reins in his hand held with a practiced ease that only came from years of working cattle or rounding up stock. "Never stayed anywhere long enough to need one."

Sadie didn't respond immediately, her hazel eyes searching his face for a flicker of something—anything—that might tell her more about him. But Gage's features remained guarded, as though carved from the same unyielding stone as the cliffs in the distance.

"Well," she said, her tone steady but firm, "just so we're clear, this isn't the kind of place where you can melt into the background and take it easy. Eagle's Nest runs on everyone, pulling their weight."

His lips quirked in an almost-smile. "Thanks for the heads-up, boss."

The title, said with a drawling, almost teasing tone, set her teeth on edge. She focused back on the trail ahead. Maybe assigning herself to ride with Gage wasn't her wisest move, but if there was one thing Sadie took pride in, it was knowing her crew. And she wanted to figure this man out, if not for curiosity's sake, then for the sake of the ranch and her own sanity.

They reached the first stretch of fencing near the far edge of the south pasture, a long line of posts running parallel to a shallow creek. As they dismounted, Sadie spotted a section of fence that sagged.

"Looks like the deer or elk were busy," Sadie said, pointing to the tangled wire. She crossed her arms, watching as Gage stepped closer to the damage. "Think you can handle it?"

Gage didn't reply right away. He crouched by the post, running a hand over it with ease. He might talk like a man unconcerned, but his movements told a different story—calculated, competent, and steady.

Without pausing, he grabbed pliers from the tool kit and began cutting away the mangled sections of wire. "Looks like the post is sturdy enough," he commented. "Just needs proper re-stringing."

Sadie watched carefully, keeping her arms crossed.

The corner of his mouth tugged upward as he glanced at her. "You don't trust me, do you?"

Her eyes narrowed. "No, not yet."

He chuckled low, the sound barely there but not lost on her. "Fair enough, Boss."

She let the comment slide, though her irritation flickered again. Boss. It was a word Gage used just enough to sound respectful, but she couldn't help feeling it also carried a whisper of mockery. So when he flicked her another look, as though daring her to challenge him further, she pointedly stepped closer, standing her ground just within his space.

For a moment, neither moved. Her hazel eyes met his blue-gray ones, and for the first time, she saw something beneath his cool exterior—something quiet, sharp, and not entirely unwelcome. It lasted only a second, but it left her unsettled. His eyes sent little fireworks through her, and it made her nervous. She stepped back and let him work.

"So," Gage said after a stretch of silence, his tone lighter, "do you supervise every new ranch hand, or am I just special?"

Sadie arched a brow and offered him a measured glance. "Only when it's necessary."

"Then I'd better tread carefully."

"Good," she shot back with an even tone, but just a hint of amusement in her eyes. "Eagle's Nest doesn't do anything halfway, and neither do I."

Gage let out a low chuckle, the sound warm and unexpected, as though it surprised even him. "Noted, boss."

"Quit calling me boss. It's irritating," Sadie said, her voice tinged with exasperation as she brushed loose strands of hair out of her face.

Gage glanced at her, the corner of his mouth twitching with suppressed amusement. "Got it, Sadie," he replied. As he straightened himself, brushing the dirt off his weathered gloves before packing the tools neatly back into the saddlebag.

Sadie swung into the saddle, settling easily atop her horse. With a soft nudge of her heels, she urged the mare forward. "Let's go, girl," she murmured, her voice warm and reassuring. The horse obeyed with fluid grace, her tail flicking rhythmically with each steady step.

Gage swung up onto his horse with practiced ease and urged it forward, the steady rhythm of its hooves eating up the ground between them. Within moments, he pulled alongside Sadie, matching her pace effortlessly.

"So, tell me something," he said. "Why do your ranch workers sit down with your family for dinner? I've worked on plenty of ranches—big ones, small ones, all kinds in between—and I've never seen the hands set foot in the main house, let alone share a meal."

Sadie turned her head toward him, her eyes sharp as they studied his face. "It's just how we've always done things," she said, then paused, letting her gaze drift toward the horizon. "I mean, sure, it started as a necessity when my great-grandparents first built the ranch. The dining table was where they made plans, hashed out their problems, and prayed for whatever little they had to stretch just a bit farther. It's become a tradition since then."

"Tradition, huh?"

"Yeah," Sadie said, her tone softening. "My dad always says ranch life isn't just about cattle, horses, fences, and bills—it's about people. Relationships. You can't build something as lasting and special as Eagle's Nest without community, without trust in the people who work alongside you. Sharing meals together—it's a tradition, sure, but it's also a reminder. Everyone here matters. There's no divide between those who own this ranch and those who work it. We're all family."

Gage wasn't used to this type of talk, most ranch owners he'd worked for treated their employees more like gears in a machine than people with names.

"Seems..." He hesitated, squinting as if the sunlight might burn through his discomfort. "Seems like y'all take things pretty seriously here, but kind of laid back at the same time."

"I'd say so."

He cleared his throat. "So, what happens if someone doesn't fit?"

Sadie shot him a sidelong glance. "What do you mean?"

"You've got a tight-knit thing here," he said, gesturing loosely toward the ranch in the distance. "Seems like everyone's expected to play along with the family dynamic. What if someone doesn't? What if they keep their head down, do the work, but don't play along with fitting in or whatever?"

"Are you asking out of curiosity… or asking because you're already planning how to exclude yourself?"

"Just curious," he said evenly, though the flicker of defensiveness in his voice was unmistakable.

"Look, nobody's forcing you to stay here. My dad's got a soft heart when it comes to his employees, and he obviously felt you were worth a shot. The only thing I ask for while you're here is respect. Respect the work, respect the animals, respect the people. Do that, and what you call 'fitting in' tends to take care of itself," she said with quiet certainty, then urged Daisy into a brisker pace.

Her response hit him square in the chest, sharper than he'd expected. The quiet stretched between them as they rode along the fence line, the rhythmic clink of reins and the soft creak of the saddles filling the space. Respect, he could handle that. But the idea of connection, of this whole "family thing" she and her father both spoke of? That twisted his insides into knots. Yet, despite himself, her words lingered, leaving an imprint he couldn't quite shake.

Chapter 5

Sadie's pencil hovered above the blank page, motionless, while the untouched coffee on the kitchen island grew cold. Usually, this was her refuge—a quiet pocket of time carved out of the chaos of ranch life, a moment to focus on her writing. But today, her thoughts refused to cooperate. They kept drifting, circling back to the same infuriating subject.

Gage West.

No matter how much she tried to shove him out of her mind, the morning she'd spent riding fences with the new ranch hand replayed in vivid, exasperating detail. His steady, methodical work on the fences had earned a grudging respect. But his words, the casual, almost smug way he'd asked about "fitting in", still rubbed her raw. What had he meant by that? And why did it bother her so much?

She hadn't realized how long she'd been sitting there motionless until Madge's voice broke through her thoughts.

"Sadie, honey, you've been staring at that notebook like it owes you an apology."

The older woman stood at the sink, scrubbing dishes, her tone as warm and teasing as ever. Nearby, Harriet sat, flipping absentmindedly through a well-worn cookbook.

"Just thinking," Sadie murmured.

"Uh-huh. Thinking about what? Or who?" Madge pressed, her grin sly.

"Thinking," Sadie repeated, closing the notebook with a decisive snap. "I'm just trying to get a few words down before I head back out to work."

"Need some inspiration? I'd say you've got a mystery man around here who fits the bill nicely."

Sadie frowned, her brow furrowing. "What are you talking about?"

"You know exactly what I'm talking about," Madge said, wiping her hands on a towel. "The new hire. What's his name again? Gabe? Greg?"

"Gage," Harriet supplied without looking up.

"Gage West," Madge said, shooting a knowing glance in Sadie's direction. "Seems like an interesting one. Could even make a good character in one of your stories."

Sadie rolled her eyes, a defensive heat creeping along her neck. "Madge, if you're waiting for me to turn his arrival into some kind of great love story, you're going to be disappointed. He's been here all of a day, and besides—" She stopped abruptly.

"Besides what?" Madge prodded, leaning forward eagerly.

"Besides," Sadie said, her mouth tightening, "I suspect he's a drifter. He's here for the paycheck and won't think twice before packing up and leaving. That's not exactly 'heartwarming romance' material. He's hard, edgy... has a smart mouth, too."

Harriet looked up then, fixing her daughter with a pointed gaze. "Now, Sadie, labeling him a drifter doesn't do any good. He may just surprise you."

"He doesn't need to surprise me," Sadie said quickly. "He just needs to do his job."

Madge smirked, clearly entertained. "Boy oh boy, he sure does have you fired up now, doesn't he?"

Sadie shot her a withering look, though the warmth spreading across her cheeks betrayed her. "I'm not 'fired up.' I'm... cautious. That's all. We don't know anything about him."

"Other than the fact he looks like he just walked out of a cowboy calendar," Madge quipped with a grin, earning a chuckle from Harriet.

"I hadn't noticed," Sadie said flatly, reaching for her cold coffee.

"Come on, Sadie," her mom said, her tone soft but probing. "What's really chewing on you? You've been bristling like a cat in a rainstorm all afternoon."

Sadie hesitated, her fingers tightening around the mug. "It's nothing—just... nothing worth talking about."

"Now, don't think you can fool me," Madge said, leaning on the counter with a playful glint in her eye. "I've been running this kitchen and keeping an eye on you Beaumont's—longer than you've been tying your boots. Something's stirring in that head of yours. So, out with it. Ranch troubles? Or," her smirk deepened, "if I were a wagering woman, I'd say it's Gabe getting under your skin."

Sadie groaned, pressing the heels of her hands to her temples. "Oh, stop. It's not him." She paused and tilted her head. "Okay, maybe it is a little him."

Madge chuckled knowingly. "Thought so. So what'd he do? Or better yet, what didn't he do?"

Sadie sighed, the words tumbling out before she could stop them. "He's just... impossible. He's good at the work—too good, honestly—but his attitude? Ugh. It's like trying to wrestle a tumbleweed. And don't even get me started on this morning. He kept calling me 'boss' like... like he thought it was funny or something!" Her voice rose with frustration. "It drove me crazy!"

"'Boss,' huh?" Harriet asked with a raised brow. "And why exactly does that rub you the wrong way?"

"I don't know, it just does," she huffed. "He's arrogant, infuriating, and... I don't know. He's just annoying, okay?"

"Mmm-hmm," Harriet said with a quiet smile. "And yet, here you are, letting him take up space in your head."

Sadie opened her mouth to respond but thought better of it, closing it with a frustrated sigh.

Madge shook her head, chuckling. "Oh, honey, you've got it bad. The harder you try to push him out of your mind, the more that cowboy's gonna stick like burrs to a horse's mane."

"Madge," Sadie groaned. "He's just a ranch hand passing through, and I'm too busy to get tangled up in whatever it is he's doing."

"As if you're not tangled up already?" Madge raised an eyebrow, daring Sadie to deny it.

Sadie scrubbed her face with her hands, groaning again. "Why do I even tell you these things?"

Harriet patted her arm, her touch gentle. "Because, sweetheart, you know I'm going to get it out of you one way or another."

Sadie sighed, standing abruptly. "I'd better get back outside before Daddy comes looking for me."

Madge's voice followed her toward the door, laced with teasing affection. "Sure thing, boss. But if that cowboy shows up looking for a partner in the fields, try not to scare him off. He might just need a Beaumont nudge to set him straight."

Sadie didn't bother turning around to retort.

Chapter 6

The bunkhouse, while not luxurious, provided everything essential for the ranch hands. Comfortable beds for resting after long days, a simple yet functional kitchen for meal preparation, and a living room where they could unwind. There was also a television for entertainment and a bathroom that met their basic needs. Overall, it was a practical and welcoming space that served its purpose, a home for those who worked on the ranch.

The four ranch hands—Pete, Ross, Julie, and Gage—gathered around the sturdy oak table that dominated the kitchen for lunch, its surface scarred with the wear of countless meals and stories shared.

Julie sat absorbed in her task, meticulously slicing an apple with her trusty pocketknife. Pete chewed thoughtfully, his silvery streaked mustache twitching every now and then as he silently observed the lively exchange between his friends. Ross, the natural entertainer of the group, filled the air with grandiose tales. His voice was animated, punctuating his stories with gestures that painted vivid pictures of adventures that danced on the edge of reality and exaggeration. Gage leaned back in his chair, a grin on his face, thoroughly enjoying the banter and camaraderie that filled the bunkhouse.

"...and so there I was, holding onto that cranky bull's rope with one hand and waving the other like I was trying to flag down a plane," Ross was saying, his grin wide as he leaned back in his chair, balancing it precariously on two legs. "Course, the bull didn't think it was so funny. Tossed me higher than popcorn in a skillet. I nailed the landing, didn't I, Pete?"

Pete, who had heard this exact story about fifty times before, didn't even look up from his sandwich. "Sure, kid. If landing flat on your backside counts."

Ross groaned and dramatically clutched his chest. "You wound me, old-timer."

Pete raised an eyebrow, unimpressed. "Cut the dramatics. You'd be lucky if that bull hasn't told the story better than you by now."

Julie grinned, shaking her head as she started chewing a slice of apple. Ross's antics were expected, and Pete's no-nonsense responses typically provided the perfect foil for the younger ranch hand's mischief. It was the rhythm of the bunkhouse, an easy give-and-take that kept the tough work of ranch life just a little lighter.

Gage, for his part, might as well have been a fence post for all he contributed to the conversation.

"Hey, Gage," Ross said, "you're awful quiet. Did Sadie wear you out this morning fixing fences?"

"She didn't wear me out," Gage replied, his voice low and steady. "I'm just listening to you rattle on. A man can't get a word in edge-wise with you around."

"Oh, so you've got a sense of humor hiding underneath that calm exterior?" Ross said.

"Careful, Ross. Poke too much, and you might just regret it," Pete cautioned, his tone half-serious, half-teasing.

"Let the man settle in Ross." Julie said, glancing between the two men, her expression playful. "Some of us appreciate a little silence now and then."

"Please, if we left it up to y'all, these meals would be quieter than church before the choir starts up." He shifted his attention back to Gage, his grin not slipping for a second. "Seriously, though, Gage. What's your deal? What brings you to our little piece of Montana paradise?"

All eyes shifting toward Gage. Even Pete had stopped chewing, apparently curious whether this line of questioning might coax the new guy into actually opening up. Julie, however, didn't look quite as expectant, returning to slicing her apple with focused disinterest, a sure sign she was listening intently.

Gage took his time answering, finishing the bite of food he'd just taken. Eventually, he shrugged. "What brings anyone to a ranch?" he said, casually brushing crumbs off his jeans. "Same thing that brings 'em to whatever job's hiring at the time. It's work."

Ross looked momentarily deflated. "That's it? Just... work?"

"What were you expecting?" Gage replied. "An outlaw running from the sheriff?"

Ross perked up, snapping his fingers. "Now, wouldn't that be something? Can you imagine?"

"Cut it out, Ross," Julie said, though her smirk betrayed her amusement. "He doesn't owe you his life story just because you're nosey."

"Thanks," Gage muttered, tilting his head toward Julie in understated gratitude.

"What do you think of the bosses' daughter?" Pete asked, folding his arms across his chest.

Gage raised an eyebrow. "Sadie?"

Pete nodded. "The one and only. She might not look it, but that girl's as tough as barbed wire when it comes to running things."

"She's not bad," Gage admitted cautiously. "Knows what she's doing. Pushes hard, but she's fair."

"Fair?" Julie repeated, eyeing him shrewdly. "I don't think I've ever heard anybody describe Sadie Beaumont as just 'fair.' You've got to have more of an opinion than that."

Before Gage could respond, the door swung open, revealing Mitch as he stepped inside. Mitch exuded a calm, composed demeanor, yet there was an undeniable sense of self-importance about him. He reminded Gage of someone who was constantly involved in the affairs of others, all the while pretending to be indifferent to anyone else's issues. The word arrogant seemed to fit Mitch perfectly.

"Don't let me interrupt the conversation," Mitch said with an approving nod. "Just thought I'd come meet our new ranch hand."

The subtle shift in the room didn't go unnoticed by Gage. He'd have to be blind not to recognize Mitch wasn't just the friendly neighborhood ranch hand the others painted him as, at least, not entirely. Mitch's tone was friendly enough, but there was something else, unspoken and intentional. Mitch was sizing him up.

"Gage?" Mitch asked, leaning against the wall at the opposite end of the table.

"That's me," Gage answered.

"Nice to meet you. I'm Mitch Monarch," Mitch said as he stretched out a hand. "Been working Eagle's Nest on and off my whole life. Feel like part of the family, you know."

Gage shook his hand, feeling the firmness in Mitch's grip. "Nice to meet you, Mitch."

"So, how're you liking it here so far?"

"It's a job," Gage replied, leaning back slightly, keeping his words neutral.

Mitch chuckled softly, but the sound didn't quite reach his eyes. "A job, sure. But a ranch like this doesn't feel like work if you do it right. You crop up from around here?"

"Nope," Gage said simply, meeting Mitch's gaze evenly.

"Hmm," Mitch said, the gears turning behind his calm expression. "So you just passin' through?"

"That's usually how it works," Gage replied with the faintest shrug. "You finish one job and move on to the next."

"Maybe for you, but most of us stick around," Ross said.

Gage glanced toward Mitch again. "What about you?" he asked, turning the line of questioning back around. "All the other ranch hands stay in the bunkhouse, but you don't."

Mitch's expression didn't falter. "I live nearby. Family land, just close enough to see the ranch lights at night if the wind blows right."

Gage held that detail in his mind, not responding.

"So where ya from?" Mitch asked.

"Here and there," Gage replied, his voice steady. "Spent some time all over, but the last few years, I've been in Wyoming."

"Ah, cowboy country for sure," Mitch nodded appreciatively, "bet that was a real experience. A solid background for ranch work. Must have some good stories from there."

"Nothing a bunch of ranch hands haven't heard before," Gage said, a hint of a smile tugging at the corners of his mouth.

"Let me guess," Mitch said, his expression scrutinizing, "you've wrangled horses and bulldogged some steers?"

Gage chuckled, recognizing the challenge in Mitch's tone. "More like trying not to get thrown off 'em. Horses and steers have a way of reminding you who's in charge."

"Sounds like a chip on your shoulder about it," Mitch said, genuinely cocking an eyebrow at him, leaning forward slightly. "Thinking we might see you at the rodeo later this month?"

"Maybe," Gage replied slowly, not wanting to appease Mitch too easily. "Depends on the work schedule. If we've got time off, I might roll on by."

"Make a night of it, why not? It tends to get lively, more stories to tell," Mitch pressed, his interest waning into suggestiveness.

Pete interjected, sensing the growing tension. "The rodeo's fun, but it's nothing like a late-night bonfire at Birdsville Creek. That's where the real laughter is, isn't it, Julie?"

Julie nodded with a conspiratorial grin. "Nothing beats sitting around a good fire after a long day's work."

Gage leaned back in his chair, musing over their camaraderie, a fleeting sense of warmth in the shared atmosphere, but Mitch persisted, his focus and intent clear.

"Just remember," Mitch said, "you need to pull your weight around here. We don't take kindly to slackers."

"Not planning on slacking," Gage replied evenly. "But I appreciate the heads-up."

Mitch's eyes narrowed, as if weighing Gage's resilience. A beat of silence stretched between them. "Good," he finally said. "We watch out for our own here, especially when it comes to the boss's daughter."

Gage felt Mitch's words sink in, a subtle warning cloaked in casual conversation. The tension in the air flickered briefly, but quickly dissipated as Ross, ever the peacemaker, clapped his hands together and leaned forward, eager to change the subject.

"Alright, alright! Enough of this serious talk. Gage, my man, how about a little competition? You up for showing us what you're really made of before we get back to work? A little roping practice?" Ross's eyes glinted with mischief, clearly relishing the idea of adding some excitement to their lunch hour.

Gage smirked. "Sounds tempting, but I have to warn you—my roping skills might surprise you."

"Surprises, huh? I'm intrigued," Ross said, leaning forward in his seat. "Let's see if you can match that wit with some genuine skill."

"Alright," Gage relented, the spirit of camaraderie igniting a flicker of competitiveness within him. "But let's set some rules. Winner gets bragging rights."

"Deal." Ross said.

Mitch, still leaning against the wall, observed with a mix of intrigue and skepticism. "You sure you can handle it? Ross's been known to get a little rowdy with these roping competitions."

"Bring it on," Gage replied with an air of confidence, a determined glint in his eye. "What about you? Are you in for this challenge?"

Mitch smirked, leaning back casually. "No, I think I'll just sit this one out and enjoy the show as you try to prove yourself."

"Whatever, man," Gage said, as he brushed past Mitch and stepped out the door, ready to take on whatever adventure awaited him outside.

Chapter 7

Ross twirled his rope casually, showing off with an elaborate overhead spin. "Let's set the stakes high, folks. Winner gets full bragging rights for the week and," he grinned, "treated to a meal at the Bluebird Café in town."

Gage nodded as he checked his saddle cinch, eyes scanning the corral. He had yet to attempt a single dramatic flourish with his lasso, but the look of steady precision etched on his face made it clear he wasn't planning to lose. For him, winning wasn't playful posturing. It was a test of his control, something he could measure against the restless churn in his chest.

His rope coiled neatly in his hand, Gage ignored the cheerful back-and-forth around him. His thoughts darted momentarily to the morning's brisk exchanges with Sadie. Her words were still stuck in his mind, and those eyes... "Focus...," he reminded himself.

From across the yard, Mitch leaned against the fence post, casually observing with a smug air. "Looks like you've got some competition,

West. Think you can keep up without tripping over that chip on your shoulder?" Mitch's tone was light, but the barb was unmistakable.

Gage's jaw tightened, but he didn't bite. He simply swung the rope once to test its weight, meeting Mitch's gaze with a calm that belied the heat simmering beneath his stoic demeanor. "Guess we'll find out," Gage replied evenly, his voice low but steady, carrying just enough grit to make it clear. This was about more than roping.

Julie whistled sharply, redirecting the group. "Alright, are we talking or roping? Let's see what you've got, boys. I don't have all day." She glanced playfully at Ross, who rolled his eyes as he adjusted his own stance, spinning his lasso into a confident loop.

With a shouted cue, the competition began. Each participant took turns charging at the roping dummy on horseback, aiming to throw their rope cleanly around its horns. Ross was first managing a decent toss that caught the dummy squarely before his horse slowed to a halt. "Boom!" he crowed, throwing his arms up in victory. "That's how you start a competition!"

Julie's turn followed, her lasso cutting through the air almost gracefully as she skillfully looped the rope over the dummy. She raised an eyebrow at Ross and smiled.

Pete went after Julie, his years of experience showing in the way his cast was solid and precise, though he didn't bother celebrating the way the younger hands did. He simply tipped his hat. "Still got it," he grunted.

All the while, Mitch leaned against the fence, his critical gaze flicking between the riders and, occasionally, over toward the barn—waiting. Watching.

Finally, it was Gage's turn. He spurred his horse forward, the steady rhythm of hooves against the dusty ground pounding in sync with the concentrated thrum in his chest. The rope slid through his hands like an extension of his arm, and when he cast it, the loop sailed cleanly over the dummy's horns. He pulled the rope taut, stopping his horse neatly, the dummy jerking slightly from the force.

"Whoo!" Ross hollered, leaning forward to clap his hands. "Now that's what I'm talkin' about! Quiet cowboys got some skill!"

Julie smirked from atop her mare. "About time someone shut you up, Ross."

"Well, kid," Pete said, "I'll be danged. You've got yourself a steady hand."

Gage gave a small nod of acknowledgment, his lips twitching into the faintest smirk. He coiled his rope back up neatly, more focused on the task than the applause. The win felt good, sure, but he wasn't about to let it inflate his ego, especially with Mitch still loitering by the fence, looking like he had plenty to say.

As Gage lined up for another round, he caught movement out of the corner of his eye. Sadie was approaching, her blonde hair tied back in a loose braid that swayed with each confident step. She carried an air of authority that came naturally to her, yet it was softened by her smile as she surveyed what was clearly an unplanned break in the day's work.

"What's all this ruckus about?" she called out, her voice carrying easily over the sounds of hooves and laughter.

Ross was the first to answer, puffing out his chest like a rooster. "Just a little friendly competition, Ma'am. Gage here's showing off for us."

Sadie raised an eyebrow at Gage, her lips quirking into a bemused smile. "Gage, showing off? Now that I'd like to see."

Gage felt the warmth rise at the back of his neck, but he masked it with a smooth nod and a tip of his hat.

Her gaze lingered on him a beat longer than necessary before she turned to the group at large. "Who's winning?"

"Well, right now, Gage," Ross said. "But you're just in time to see Mitch throw his hat in the ring—right, Mitch?"

The fence creaked as Mitch pushed away from it, his expression shifting into something more eager, more performative. "I suppose I could show you all how it's done," he said, his tone light but pointed as he glanced toward Sadie. "But only if the boss's daughter sticks around to watch."

Sadie's smile faltered just slightly, the shift so subtle most wouldn't notice. But Gage did. He watched as she forced politeness back into place, though her fingers twitched at her side like she was itching to escape Mitch's attention.

"How generous of you, Mitch," Sadie said, deftly sidestepping his pointed comment. There was an edge to her tone that she likely thought no one could detect, but Gage caught it. He wondered just how often Sadie had to fend off Mitch's self-satisfied charm.

Mitch mounted his horse with exaggerated confidence, tipping his hat toward Sadie with what he probably thought was roguish flair. "Don't blink, Sadie," he said, spinning his rope in a tight circle. "You won't want to miss this."

Gage tightened his jaw, silently willing himself to stay out of it. Whatever history or familiarity Mitch and Sadie shared, it wasn't his concern. And yet, it didn't escape his notice that Sadie didn't seem particularly invested in Mitch's attempts to impress her. Despite himself, Gage's gaze flicked her way as Mitch took his first run, curiosity getting the better of him. He wasn't sure what he was expecting to see—approval, amusement, or maybe even indifference—but whatever it was, he was more intrigued by her reaction than Mitch's performance.

Mitch's throw wasn't bad. He hooked the dummy, but his timing with the horse was off, and the rope jerked awkwardly as he pulled it taut. "Got it!" Mitch crowed, casting a quick glance toward Sadie to gauge her approval.

"Not bad," she said, though her voice lacked the enthusiasm Mitch was clearly fishing for.

"Alright, who's next?" he asked, though his tone had taken on a slight edge, as if daring someone to outperform him.

Pete nudged his hat back, a small smirk playing at his lips. "Tell you what, Mitch—why don't you pair up with Gage for the next round? Let's see how you two fare as a team. Think you can handle it?"

The challenge hung in the air like a gauntlet, and Mitch's quick glance toward Sadie made it clear he wasn't about to back down. "Sure," Mitch said with a forced laugh. "Let's see if the new cowboy can keep up."

Gage didn't look at Mitch. He didn't need to. He could already feel the tension radiating off him as they lined their horses up side by side, preparing to rope the dummy that Julie would now pull behind a four-wheeler at a steady trot. The makeshift setup was standard ranch practice, but the stakes felt unnaturally high as the two men prepared their throws, their horses shifting restlessly beneath them.

Gage coiled his rope methodically, his fingers steady and sure, betraying none of the simmering irritation Mitch seemed determined to provoke. He'd dealt with plenty of men like Mitch before, guys who needed to prove something, usually to themselves, more than anyone else. But the way Mitch was angling for Sadie's attention had a distinct edge to it, one that pricked at Gage.

"All right, boys," Ross called out, pacing a few steps ahead of the four-wheeler like a rodeo announcer gearing up a crowd. "Remember: it's all about coordination. You've got to cast fast and work together.

No lone heroes." He shot a pointed look at Mitch, grinning as if he were enjoying the prospect of watching this partnership dissolve into chaos.

Sadie had moved closer to the action, her arms loosely crossed, an unreadable expression on her face. Gage could feel her gaze brushing over him, and it steadied him. Then Mitch's voice cut into the silence, snapping the tension taut.

"You ready, partner?" Mitch asked, the sarcasm barely veiled as he kicked his boot lightly against his stirrup. His tone twisted the word "partner" into something sharp, almost mocking.

Gage didn't take the bait. He settled his weight in the saddle and nodded, his voice even. "Let's get on with it."

Julie revved up the four-wheeler, and the dummy jerked forward, dragging behind it at a pace that mimicked the slow, determined trot of a calf. The horses moved in unison, their riders adjusting their speed as the target came into range.

Mitch, true to form, rushed his cast. His rope flew wide, missing the dummy's horns completely and slapping uselessly against the dirt. Gage, however, held back just a fraction of a second, his rope spinning with precision before snapping out cleanly. The loop landed perfectly over the dummy's horns, drawing tight with a satisfying tug as he pulled his horse to a stop.

The stillness that followed was punctuated only by the low hum of the four-wheeler idling in the background. Mitch pulled his horse around with more force than necessary as he retrieved his failed rope. The cheers erupted, with Ross whooping loud enough to startle a few birds out of the nearby brush.

"Nicely done!" Pete called, his voice steady and approving. "That's what I'm talkin' about. Clean, sharp, and no fuss."

Julie leaned lazily against the four-wheeler, a gleaming grin splitting her face. "Guess our new ranch hand knows what he's doing after all," she quipped, eyes sparkling with humor as she shot Gage a wink.

Gage gave a brief nod, his expression calm but his chest a drumbeat of conflicting emotions. He was satisfied with the win, sure, but the heat of Mitch's glare boring into the side of his head was a reminder that this competition wasn't just about roping. Gage coiled his rope with practiced ease, keeping his gaze fixed on his horse's mane to avoid looking in Mitch's direction. He couldn't trust himself not to smirk.

Mitch's voice broke through the moment, every word layered with forced nonchalance. "Lucky shot, West. Don't let it go to your head."

Gage didn't respond immediately, taking his time as he swung down from his horse and looped the reins over the corral rail. When he finally spoke, his tone was measured, deliberate. "Luck doesn't catch calves, Monarch. Practice does."

That earned a low "ooooh" from Julie, who, despite the obvious tension in the air, couldn't resist stirring the pot from a safe distance.

Sadie, still standing near the gate, took a step forward. Her expression was amused but closely guarded, as though trying to read between the lines of the exchange without letting anyone notice. "Alright, boys," she said, her tone light but firm, "I think we've had enough showboating for one day. Gage, nice work. Mitch…" She paused just long enough to let the air hang. "You'll get 'em next time."

The chuckles that followed were good-natured from almost everyone, that is, except Mitch. He moved closer to Sadie, the easy charm sliding back onto his face like a mask. "Next time," he drawled, "I'll make sure there are actual stakes involved. Maybe something worth winning." His eyes flicked toward her for half a beat longer than they should have, his suggestive words clear to everyone within earshot.

Sadie stiffened, though she quickly smoothed her expression into one of polite disinterest.

Before Mitch could add anything further, Jack Beaumont's voice cut through the hum of voices, firm and deliberate, as he strode into the scene. "Sadie! Gage! Mitch! Need you—now."

The levity in the group evaporated, replaced by the sharp alertness only ranchers understood. Something was wrong.

Chapter 8

Sadie sprinted toward the barn with urgent determination, her boots kicking up small clouds of dust as she moved with the kind of focus born from instinct. Her braid trailed behind her, the sunlight glinting off its honeyed strands as she closed the distance between herself and her father in no time. Gage followed closely, his long strides purposeful but measured, his eyes scanning the horizon for any sign of what might have caused Jack's summons. Behind him, Mitch trailed with a hint of less urgency, his pace just fast enough to avoid being left behind.

By the time they reached the barn, Sadie was already standing in front of Jack, her chest rising and falling from her brisk pace. Her father, usually an unshakable figure of calm, now stood with his hands planted firmly on his hips, his frame taut with tension. His weathered face, lined with years of ranching and resilience, held an expression of worry, precision, and quiet authority. Whatever was happening, it wasn't routine.

"What's going on?" Sadie asked, her voice steady despite the flicker of unease rising in her chest.

Jack didn't immediately answer, his sharp gaze flicking between her, Gage, and Mitch as they gathered in front of him. His stout frame radiated the kind of energy that commanded attention without the need for theatrics. Jack Beaumont was a man whose actions always spoke louder than his words.

"Follow me. It's Starfire," Jack said urgently, as he strode toward the row of stalls in the barn. His gait was brisk, the set of his shoulders signaling this was no time for delays. The mare's muffled, restless sounds grew louder as they approached, her hooves scraping frantically against the wood.

Inside the stall, Starfire, a striking chestnut mare with a coat gleaming even under the dim light, pawed at the ground with restless determination. Her ears twitched erratically, her sides heaving, and her wide, rolling eyes were edged with white—a clear sign of distress. Every muscle in her body bunched and quivered, a coiled spring just waiting for the right moment to snap.

"She won't settle," Jack explained, his voice gruff but edged with unmistakable concern. "I think it's colic. We need to get her moving out in the pasture before she gets worse and hurts herself."

Gage's chest tightened instinctively at the word colic. He'd been here before, that helpless knot in his gut, the sound of hooves striking against hard stalls, the delicate mix of urgency and patience that could mean the difference between recovery and disaster. Memories of lost horses surged unbidden, but he shoved them aside. This wasn't the time to get tangled up in ghosts.

"Stay back," Gage instructed firmly as he stepped toward the stall gate. The others froze, their gazes locked on him.

Sadie's hand hovered near the latch, a flicker of uncertainty crossing her face. "She's spooked," she said, her voice low yet insistent. Beneath it was something else: concern, trust, or maybe a conflicted mix of both.

Gage didn't rush. His movements were measured, his response steady. "I've dealt with colicky horses before," he reassured her, his blue eyes meeting hers for a fleeting moment. "Just give me space."

Something shifted in her expression, the lines around her brow softening. She nodded, taking a cautious step back, though her arms crossed over her chest like she was bracing herself. Mitch, standing a yard or two behind Sadie, stuffed his hands into his pockets. He looked ready to jump in if needed, but Gage could feel the skepticism radiating from him.

Gage didn't spare either of them another glance. His focus narrowed entirely on Starfire as he eased into the stall. The mare's head jerked upward, nostrils flaring as her sides rippled. She edged deeper into the corner, her back hoof stamping a sharp warning into the straw-covered ground.

"Easy, girl," Gage murmured, his voice dropping to a low, calming register. Each word was deliberate, his tone carrying an unhurried calm meant to wrap around the horse like a warm blanket. He took another slow step forward, keeping his body angled slightly away, non-threatening but present, letting her sense the steadiness radiating from him. "No one's gonna hurt you."

Starfire's ears flicked toward him briefly, an acknowledgment, as her adrenaline spiked again. Her chest shuddered as she let out a high-pitched nicker, scraping her hoof as if to challenge the oppression of the stall's walls or the twisting discomfort in her gut. Gage pushed aside the rising urgency clawing at him. Rushing her now would only make things worse.

Sadie lingered near the stall door, her fingers clutching the top rung. She watched every movement Gage made, her lips lightly pressed together. Mitch stood, shifting from foot to foot. No one broke the fragile silence in the barn except for Starfire's snorts and the muffled rustling of the hay below her hooves.

Gage took his time as he closed the distance between them inch by inch. "That's it," he said softly, his eyes firmly on hers, his tone as steady as the rhythm of a windless night. "Just me and you, girl. We'll take this slow."

He knew better than to reach for her too soon. Skittish or distressed horses could react in ways that were as unpredictable as they were dangerous. One wrong move—a hand moving too quickly, a step coming too close—and she could rear up or lash out before anyone had time to react.

"Breathe, Starfire," he whispered, more to himself than to her. Matching his breath to the slow rise and fall of his chest, he made sure to keep his energy grounded. Horses could read people far better than most gave them credit for, and this mare didn't need to feel his own simmering emotions.

He extended his hand slowly, palm open downward, as he let her catch his scent. As his fingers neared her nose, she flared her nostrils wide, her breath coming in short, high bursts against his skin. "Atta girl," Gage murmured when she didn't flinch. His words seemed to hum like vibrations, soothing the edge of her wildness. "We're getting there."

When her body gave the faintest of trembles, signaling the tiniest release of tension, Gage dared a little closer. His other hand reached for the lead rope hanging on the stall wall. His grip on the leather length was sure but gentle as he eased it toward her halter. One loop—not too tight, not too sudden—secured in place, and Gage let out a long breath of relief. He gave the lead rope the lightest tug, testing her willingness to follow, though he wasn't about to force her into it. Cooperation had to come on her terms.

"That's it. Steady now," he coaxed. Starfire's hooves shuffled hesitantly, her trembling weight leaning forward just enough to let Gage move toward the stall door with her in tow. His movements were seamless, a slow dance of understanding between man and horse. Each step was deliberate, calming the fire simmering just beneath the mare's skin.

"Easy now," Gage said, not taking his eyes off Starfire as they moved together toward the stall exit.

Sadie's hold on the gate tightened, her shoulders stiff even as she backed away to give them room. Mitch's stance stiffened too, though it was clear his patience and perhaps his ego were wearing thin. Gage felt their presence like static electricity in the background, but he didn't let it distract him.

Once outside the stall, the openness of the barn aisle seemed to sit uneasily with the nervous mare. Her hind legs kicked back once, tapping against the wooden boards. Gage didn't flinch. He simply steadied his footing, his hand on the lead rope remaining firm yet unyielding. "You're alright, Starfire. Let's keep moving."

By the time they reached the outer doors of the barn, a breeze hit them both. Starfire inhaled sharply, her nostrils wide as she took in the open air of the early afternoon. Gage felt her tension diminish ever so slightly, her steps less clumsy as she finally began to stretch her legs.

"Let's get her moving," he said over his shoulder, his tone even. "The motion will help settle things."

Sadie fell in step just behind him, watching as Starfire began to follow Gage's lead, her head still high, but her movements no longer jerking or erratic. "You did good, Gage," she said. There was a note of admiration there as she said it.

Gage didn't look back. He simply nodded once, running a hand along the mare's neck with the same steady rhythm. "Starfire just needed someone to tell her it's alright. Sometimes that's all it takes."

Sadie walked forward to unfasten the paddock gate, her movements deliberate and calm, to avoid startling the mare. Gage kept his steady pace, not stopping until they were both inside the enclosure, giving Starfire plenty of space to stretch out and settle.

Sadie joined Gage in the paddock, latching the gate behind her. She stood quietly a few steps away. Together, they watched as the mare began to pace, her tension melting away bit by bit.

"Thanks for stepping in," she said, her voice carrying a mix of gratitude and worry. "Do you think she'll be alright? Should we call the vet, or give it a little time and see how she does?"

"Just part of the job," Gage replied, his gaze steady on Starfire. Then, after a brief pause, his expression softened. "But... you're welcome. I'd say let's wait this out and see how she does."

Sadie glanced up at him, catching his gaze for the briefest second before looking away. "Well..." She cleared her throat. "Guess you're good for more than just fixing fences."

Gage grinned, amused by the hardness creeping back into her tone. "Guess so."

Sadie turned toward the gate, then hesitated, glancing back over her shoulder. "See you at the Bluebird tonight," she said, her voice laced with a teasing edge.

"The Bluebird?" Gage asked, a flicker of surprise breaking through his usually steady tone.

She tipped her head, a playful smirk curving her lips. "Winner's privilege, remember? I heard the wager earlier. Dinner at the Bluebird

Café is on us." Her gaze lingered on him. "I'll see if Mom, Dad, and Madge feel like joining, too. Should make for an interesting evening."

Without waiting for a reply, she strode off, braid swaying in rhythm with her confident steps, leaving Gage watching after her with a smile tugging at the corner of his mouth.

Chapter 9

Sadie pushed open the door to the Bluebird Café, holding it wide for the group behind her. The warm smell of fresh bread, coffee, and the faint, sweet swirl of pie greeted them. The bustling cafe wasn't exactly packed. Riverbend Valley rarely boasted enormous crowds, but a handful of tables buzzed with conversation, the hum of community life rolling effortlessly beneath the surface.

Lillian Hawthorne, the cafe's owner and unofficial small-town ambassador, turned from her spot behind the counter. Her wild, gray-streaked curls were tucked loosely beneath a polka-dot scarf, and her bright turquoise earrings jingled with every movement. She placed her hands on her hips as soon as she spotted the crew, her mischievous smile stretching wide across her face.

"Well, look at this! The Beaumont ranch hands out on the town, enjoying a social evening like regular folks!" her voice boomed, carrying over the chatter in the cafe like a cheerful thunderclap.

Sadie grinned at the greeting used to Lillian's animated ways. "HeyLillian," she said, tipping her head. "Any chance you've got room for this crew?"

Lillian propped one elbow on the counter, narrowing her eyes with mock suspicion. "Sadie Beaumont, are you telling me you've dragged these poor souls in here to corrupt my nice, quiet cafe with your ranch madness?"

"I couldn't help myself," Sadie replied, the teasing lilt in her voice mirroring Lillian's energy.

"Well, come on in and sit yourselves down wherever," Lillian said, waving them toward one of the long tables near the window. "I'll bring over menus before you can lasso a wild chicken."

The crew filed in, each claiming a seat at the wooden table that seemed perfectly suited to a group of their size. Ross immediately dropped into a chair with the enthusiasm of a man settling in for a long moment of relaxation. Julie tugged at the chair next to him, plopped down, and leaned back, as though mentally preparing herself for whatever was to come. Pete grumbled something about chairs being softer when he was younger, but took a seat with the air of a man who knew he could survive one more evening with these young folks.

Mitch lingered for just a moment, waiting until Sadie sat down before sliding into the chair beside her, making sure his position at the table was as close to hers as propriety would allow. Gage, who had been more than content to hang back unnoticed, quietly claimed the chair across from Sadie, a choice that didn't go unnoticed by Mitch, whose jaw tightened ever so slightly. Sadie caught the brief tension flitting between the two men, but she refused to acknowledge it, focusing instead on straightening her napkin and keeping the conversation light.

"I've earned myself a slice of Lillian's huckleberry pie, no doubt about it," Ross declared, his voice dripping with anticipation.

"Oh, really?" Sadie said, her tone skeptically amused.

"Hey, it was a long day filled with hard work, grit, and sweat," he said.

Sadie couldn't help but grin. "Hard work and sweat, huh?" she said, leaning forward.

"That's what I said, and I'm sticking to it. You know I always work my tail off," Ross said.

Sadie let out a low laugh, shaking her head. "Sure, Ross. Whatever helps you sleep at night."

The group's laughter echoed, and Gage leaned into it, his lips quirking into a quiet smile. It was strange, this ease they all seemed to share. He couldn't remember the last time he'd felt content enough to sit in the middle of something like this—with noise, teasing, and camaraderie swirling around him like an endless tide. He kept his head down, letting them take the lead as he listened with quiet attentiveness.

"Alright, alright," Lillian interrupted, sweeping toward the table with her usual burst of energy. In one arm, she balanced a tray of water glasses and coffee mugs. "Coffee for Pete, Julie, Ross and you, Sadie. Water to go around for everyone. Mitch, I'd offer you a cup, but we both know you've got enough jittery energy to power this cafe 'til Sunday."

Mitch chuckled politely as Lillian began setting mugs and glasses in front of them, but his sharp gaze was less humored, landing on Gage and lingering just a heartbeat longer than necessary. Gage barely looked up from his glass of water, letting Mitch's watchful irritation slide past him as effectively as water off a duck's back.

"Well, well, a new face," Lillian said, her eyes sparkling with curiosity as she zeroed in on Gage. "Tell me, young man, are you a coffee drinker?"

"This is Gage West, Lillian. He's our newest ranch hand," Sadie said.

Gage rose from his chair, extending a hand toward Lillian with an easy confidence. "Pleasure to meet you, ma'am."

Lillian took his hand, giving it a firm shake as her gaze swept over him, a mischievous grin tugging at her lips. "Well now, aren't you a fine-looking addition to the Beaumont ranch?"

Gage sat back down, brushing off the playful comment without missing a beat. "Thank you, ma'am. I'd be happy to take you up on that cup of coffee."

"That I can do. Now, what'll it be tonight?" Lillian asked, producing a pen with the flair of a magician pulling a rabbit from a hat. "Same ol' same ol', or are we feeling adventurous? Sadie? You starting us off?"

Sadie opened her mouth to respond, but she was cut off by the jingle of the bell above the door as it swung open. All heads turned toward the entrance, where Laura Monarch stepped into the room, her leather purse slung easily over one shoulder, cheeks glowing.

"Well, speak of the devil!" Lillian exclaimed. "If it isn't Riverbend's favorite librarian. Laura, your timing's perfect. Looks like your brother needs help holding down his corner of the table before he explodes."

"Always glad to be of service," Laura shot back with a playful grin, making her way over to the group. "Sadie called for backup."

Sadie pushed her chair out slightly to make room, nodding toward the seat beside her. "Backup, a little sanity—take your pick. Mitch has been brimming with all kinds of, uh... energy today," she added, leaning in for a quick side hug with Laura as the latter dropped into her seat.

"Oh, he's always full of energy," Laura teased, winking at Mitch as she slipped her purse to the floor. "You look wound tighter than Grandpa Monarch's fishing lines after his run-in with that pelican."

"You gonna order, or are we skipping ahead to story hour?" Mitch muttered, his tone good-natured but visibly fraying.

"Relax, Mitch," Sadie interjected with a smile as she passed Laura a menu. "You'd think sharing a meal was more stressful than ranch work with the way you're acting."

Lillian beamed at the chance to steer them back to the task at hand. "All right, folks, make a decision; the cook isn't getting any younger."

As choices were made and orders handed off to Lillian, conversation flowed in waves. Ross entertained the group with his fourth retelling of a wildly exaggerated calf-rearing incident. Pete counterbalanced the talk with well-timed sarcasm. Sadie mostly listened, taking it all in. Somewhere in the middle of it all, her gaze met Gage's as he pushed his glass aside.

And briefly, without words, it was like the rushing noise of the café folded inward. For just a second, she saw something there, something steady but uncertain, like distant thunderstorm clouds that hadn't yet decided when or where they'd break. But just as quickly, Gage looked away, hiding behind the familiar mask of a lopsided, mysterious cowboy grin. The moment was soft and fleeting, even so, it nestled itself into Sadie's chest.

"So," Laura began, her tone warm and laced with curiosity as her green eyes danced with interest. She leaned slightly forward, as she gestured toward Gage. "Sadie tells me you're the new ranch hand... Gage, isn't it?"

"Yes, ma'am," he answered, his voice steady and polite.

Laura's face lit up with amusement as she waved a hand dismissively. "Oh, no need for the 'ma'am.' You're making me feel ancient here, Gage. Laura is fine." She tilted her head with a playful grin. "I'm Sadie's oldest and dearest friend," she added, nudging Sadie with her elbow. The gesture betrayed the easy familiarity of a friendship that had weathered everything from childhood mishaps to adulthood's complexities.

Sadie gave an exaggerated roll of her eyes at Laura's theatrics, but the faint smile tugging at her lips suggested she wasn't entirely annoyed. "She's also the town's self-appointed welcoming committee," Sadie quipped, her tone dry but affectionate. "You'll find she has an uncanny knack for making newcomers spill their life stories."

Laura gasped dramatically, clutching her heart. "Now, that's just unfair, Sadie! I prefer to call it being 'community-oriented.'" Turning her attention back to Gage, she leaned in slightly, her eyebrows raised in exaggerated curiosity. "So? How are you liking the Beaumont ranch so far, Gage? Not too rough around the edges for you?"

Gage took a moment before answering, his calm demeanor giving nothing away as he set his coffee mug down on the table. "It's good," he said. "Hard work's never been a problem for me, and the people here seem to know what they're doing."

Laura nodded approvingly, though the gleam in her eye suggested she wasn't quite satisfied with his straightforward answer. "I'll bet it's a nice change of pace from wherever you were before. Which was?"

"Wyoming," he replied.

"Wyoming, huh?" she repeated, her curiosity clearly piqued. "Cattle country, right? Did you work ranches there too?"

Gage nodded. "Here and there. Mostly the same kind of work as what I'm doing here, fixing fences, working with the horses, cattle, whatever needs doing."

Laura's brows furrowed slightly, her smile softening into one of genuine interest. "That must've been interesting. Lots of wide-open spaces, I imagine. But what made you pack up and move to Montana?"

Before Gage could answer, Sadie interjected, her tone light but pointed. "Laura, maybe Gage doesn't want to be interrogated right now."

Laura placed a hand on her chest, feigning innocence. "Interrogated? Sadie Beaumont, I would never!" Then, with a wry smile, she added, "But come on, let a girl ask a couple of questions. New faces don't show up in Riverbend Valley every day, you know."

Gage's lips twitched into the faintest of smirks, his blue eyes meeting Laura's green ones. "Not much to tell," he said simply, his tone carrying just enough honesty to intrigue her further. "I go where the work is. The Eagle's Nest needed a ranch hand, so here I am."

"And we're glad to have him," Sadie said, her voice deliberate as she shot Laura a look that suggested she ought to ease up—or, at the very least, give Gage some breathing room.

"And how's my dear Sadie treating you?" Laura asked, slyly turning the spotlight back on her best friend. "She's not giving you too hard of a time, is she?"

Sadie groaned audibly, fixing Laura with a look of playful exasperation.

Gage chuckled softly, shaking his head. "Nothing I can't handle," he said, meeting Sadie's eyes for a split second before adding, "She knows her stuff, though, that's for sure. Keeps all of us on our toes."

Sadie felt a flicker of warmth at the compliment, though she quickly masked it with a casual shrug. "Well, someone has to make sure things get done around the ranch," she replied, though there was a faint blush creeping into her cheeks.

Laura didn't miss the subtle exchange, her sharp mind cataloging every detail for future analysis. "Interesting," she said, drawing out the word with an unmistakable air of teasing. "Very interesting."

Sadie shot her a warning glance that only made Laura grin wider. "You know," Laura continued, resting her chin on her hand as if she were settling in for a long chat, "Gage, you should come to the summer festival next weekend. The whole town shows up—live music, good food, games, and... oh! The roping competition! You strike me as someone who might enjoy a little friendly competition."

"Roping competition?" Gage repeated, raising an eyebrow.

"Oh, it's a classic Riverbend Valley tradition," Laura said with a spark of enthusiasm, tucking a stray strand of auburn hair behind her ear. "But if roping competitions aren't quite your style, there's always the dancing."

"Dancing." Gage repeated the word slowly, his deep voice carrying a faint note of amusement. "You see me as the dancing type?"

Laura tilted her head, her expression teasing as she considered him. "Well," she began dramatically, drawing out the pause, "who's to say? Even the most rugged cowboys can surprise you."

"I wouldn't count on it," Gage replied. "Not exactly my strong suit."

Mitch's voice interrupted, a little too smooth to be casual. "Well, I'd be happy to take a turn or two around the dance floor. Sadie," he added, his eyes sliding toward her, "what do you say?"

Sadie rolled her eyes in a way that was more than words could express. "Hard pass, Mitch."

Laura arched a brow, clearly catching the undercurrent of tension as her gaze darted between Gage, Mitch, and Sadie like she was trying to piece together the full picture. "Well then... Sadie, I'll definitely be expecting to see you there. No hiding out on the ranch."

A telling flush dusted Sadie's cheeks. "I don't hide," she protested. "I'm usually just... busy."

"Busy," Laura echoed with playful skepticism, drawing the word out like she was trying it on for size. "Busy writing... busy wrangling a wild horse... or busy avoiding certain situations? I think it's high time you stopped being so 'busy.' Besides, the festival's perfect—a chance to catch up." Her gaze sharpened just a touch, her voice taking on a conspiratorial edge. "Because, clearly, I've missed a thing or two happening in your life."

Sadie's blush deepened, though she tried valiantly to maintain the upper hand. "Nothing's happening in my life, Laura."

"Sure, keep telling yourself that."

Chapter 10

Sadie leaned against the porch railing, cradling a glass of sweet tea. Beads of condensation rolled down the sides, gathering in a cool pool against her palm. She gazed out over the darkened expanse of the landscape, where starlight glinted faintly off the swaying grasses. The rhythmic hum of crickets blended with the soft rustle of leaves, filling the quiet evening with the comforting sounds of home.

Laura reclined in one of the rocking chairs nearby, her own glass resting casually in her hand. Sadie had invited Laura back to the ranch after dinner, craving some much-needed girl time with her best friend. Laura's grin, the one Sadie had known since she was six years old, gave her away. Mischievous and purposeful, it all but announced that something was coming, and Sadie braced herself for it.

Laura leaned back in the rocking chair, which creaked softly beneath her weight as the cool evening breeze swept across the porch. She raised her glass of sweet tea in a mock toast, a playful glint in her eyes. "Alright, out with it. What's going on with you, Sadie... spill it?"

Sadie took a deep drink from her glass, stalling just long enough to test whether this was going to be a light dig or a full interrogation. With Laura, it could swing either way.

"What exactly am I supposed to spill?" Sadie asked, feigning innocence as she took a seat in her own rocking chair and gently pushed it into motion.

"Oh, don't play coy with me, Sadie Beaumont," Laura drawled, an eyebrow arched high as she crossed one leg over the other. "Because if we're talking spills, how about the one that happened at dinner tonight? The kind with two men, one being my brother, making squinty, laser-beam eyes at each other like it was some kind of old Western showdown?"

Sadie groaned, tipping her head back. "Laura, it wasn't that bad."

"Girl, it was that bad," Laura shot back gleefully. "If I didn't know better, I'd think my brother was about to full-on flip the table when Gage so much as asked for the salt."

Sadie groaned again, louder. "You're exaggerating."

"Am I?" Laura leaned forward, propping her elbows on her knees and flashing an all-too-knowing look. "Sadie, I've never seen my brother act like that... puff up over anyone. And don't you think for a second I didn't notice how quiet Gage was... like he was trying real hard to stay out of the way, even when he was right smack in the middle of it?"

Sadie didn't look at her as her lips pressed into a thin line. She fiddled with the rim of her glass.

"So..." Laura said, dragging out the word like she was weaving an invisible net around her friend. "Are you gonna tell me what's going on, or am I going to have to guess?"

"There's nothing to tell," Sadie insisted, but even she could hear the uncertainty in her voice.

Laura snorted, leaning back in the rocking chair with enough force that it creaked. "Oh, give me a break! I've got two eyes, Sadie. Something's happening, and if you're not ready to admit it, let me do the honors: My dear brother is sweet on you and Gage? Well, I don't think he's looking at you like he looks at a bucket of fence nails, if you catch my drift."

Sadie blinked hard, nearly choking on her tea. "Gage? He's not... no. Laura, you're entirely wrong. Mitch is... well, he's your brother" She trailed off helplessly, her words tangling in her throat like roots in a turned-over field.

"I'm wrong? Pretty sure I saw your face when Gage was staring at you during dinner," Laura said smugly. "Spoiler, you were not looking upset. And my brother, he was rather irritated."

Sadie buried her face in her hands, letting out a muffled groan of frustration. "Oh, for heaven's sake, Laura."

"Uh-huh. There is something juicy going on here." Her grin widened, her green eyes lighting up like she'd just hit treasure.

"That's not..." Sadie lifted her head, fixing Laura with as much of a glare as she could muster, though there wasn't much heat behind it. "Laura, this isn't some big romantic comedy, alright? Gage is just... a new ranch hand. A good one," she added quickly. "He's good with the horses. He's" her voice softened slightly, "different."

"And that bothers you?" Laura asked, taking a sip of her tea but watching Sadie closely over the rim of her glass.

"Nothing bothers me," Sadie replied with a touch of exasperation. "Not about him, anyway. Mitch, on the other hand—he seems determined to act like Gage showing up is some kind of personal threat."

"Well..." Laura leaned over to set her glass down on the porch floor, folding her hands together as her expression shifted into something gentler. "You can't blame him, really. Mitch seems to hope you might see him as more than 'your best friend's brother who works on your family's ranch.'"

Sadie sighed, tugging her knees toward her chest. "I know."

"And?"

"And what?" Sadie glanced over, eyebrows knit together in frustration.

"And are you thinking about him that way?" Laura asked quietly, her teasing completely gone now.

"I... Laura..." Sadie stopped, pressing her thumb to the scar on her palm. "I just don't know if I have room in my life for Mitch, or anyone, in that way right now. And honestly, I don't think I can ever consider Mitch to be anything more than your brother. This ranch is enough responsibility for me as it is. My parents are counting on me. And then there's my writing that I can barely squeeze in as it is. There's just... there's no room for anything else."

Laura hummed low in her throat, watching Sadie with an uncharacteristically serious expression. "Is that what you really think," she asked, "or is that just what you keep telling yourself so you don't have to wrestle with what you actually feel?"

Sadie glared at her, startled by the bluntness of the question.

Laura softened the blow with a small, crooked smile. "Sadie, I love you, but you've always been this way—hiding behind responsibility when what you're really scared of is being wrong or being happy."

Sadie's lips parted as if to argue, but no words came out. Finally, she slumped back, her voice small. "Maybe."

"In case you need reminding," Laura said, leaning forward again and tilting her head until she caught Sadie's eye, "life is messy. You think God blesses us with careful, comfortable, black-and-white plans? No way. He blesses big leaps of faith."

Sadie stared at her, the words settling somewhere deep in her chest like a seed looking for fertile soil.

Laura's mischievous energy returned, her grin wicked as she added, "And hey, if this leap of faith happens to include a dark-haired cowboy with a mysterious past who looks at you like you're the only person in the room, then that's between you and the Lord."

Sadie let out a startled laugh, shaking her head as her cheeks flushed. "Nothing's happening, Laura!"

"Not yet," Laura replied with a wink.

Chapter 11

Gage leaned back against the bunkhouse's rough wooden post, boots planted firmly on the edge of the porch's top step. The night stretched vast and quiet before him, a dark canvas spattered with stars so bright they could shame a city streetlamp. The Montana air was crisp—cool and dry, carrying the faint tang of hay and saddle leather. From inside the bunkhouse came the muted sounds of laughter over a round of cards being played, and the low hum of a television broadcasting some old Western. The guys, and gal, were in good spirits tonight, swapping stories like ranch hands do, but Gage didn't feel much like company.

He'd tried sitting in there with them when they first settled in for the evening, but the walls of the bunkhouse had started to close in on him. The boisterous laughter, even the teasing jabs between Ross and Julie—it was all too much. It wasn't that he didn't like them; it was just... something in him needed the quiet. Or maybe he was just trying to outrun thoughts that wouldn't stop buzzing in his head.

His gaze wandered to the main house, its silhouette distinct against the darkness of the sprawling ranch. The soft porch light warmed the front yard, and on the second-floor, one window still shone with light—long after the rest of the house had settled into sleep. He wondered if it was Sadie's. He'd noticed that same window illuminated on many late nights, and the thought sent an unbidden spark through his chest. Sadie—strong-willed, relentless, and so fiercely tied to this land—had a way of creeping into his thoughts without permission.

She was becoming a thread in the fabric of his daily life, woven tighter with each interaction. It wasn't just her fiery determination to see the ranch thrive, or the quiet strength in the way she carried herself, despite the weight on her shoulders. It was the flash of her smile when her guard slipped, the sharp humor she wielded like a whip that kept everyone around her on their toes, the way a strand of her golden hair would loosen from her braid and catch the sun at just the right moment, leaving him utterly distracted.

It unnerved him how she was getting under his skin. Her presence stirred something deep within, something he hadn't felt in years. It was faint and foreign, like the first whisper of spring through the frost, but it unsettled him all the same. People like Sadie didn't belong with people like him—roots tangled with a restless wind. He knew better than to let himself linger on her too long, but tonight, as he stared at that glowing window, the tug in his chest was harder to ignore.

He rubbed at the back of his neck, letting his calloused fingers press into the tension knotted there. "Keep your head in the game," he muttered under his breath, though the words felt flat. The problem was, Sadie wasn't just in his head, she was starting to wedge herself into his chest, too. And that? That was dangerous.

The click of the bunkhouse door breaking the stillness made Gage glance over his shoulder. Pete, the steadiest voice among the ranch hands, emerged with two steaming mugs in hand. He wasn't a man for pleasantries. If Pete said anything, it had a purpose behind it. Gage straightened slightly as the older ranch hand ambled forward, his well-worn boots creaking against the porch planks.

"Figured I'd find you out here," Pete said, his gravelly voice as unhurried as the rest of him. He handed Gage one of the mugs without waiting for a reply, then eased himself onto the porch step beside him. "You're not exactly blending in with the ruckus in there tonight."

"I'll leave the card games to Ross," Gage replied, lifting the mug in silent thanks before taking a careful sip.

"He's been dealin' for three rounds and hasn't lost a hand," Pete said, setting his own mug on the step beside him with a casual precision. "Man's due for a dose of humility, but I ain't in the mood to deliver it tonight."

Gage chuckled, but it felt more like a reflex than genuine amusement. Silence fell between them, easy and comfortable. When it stretched long enough to become companionable, Pete spoke again, his gaze fixed forward on the same dark horizon Gage had been studying.

"You've got the look," Pete said gruffly, though his tone was more curious than accusatory.

"What look?" Gage asked, though he had a feeling the older man was about to call him out on something he wasn't ready to face.

"The look of a man sittin' still, but runnin' ninety miles an hour in his head," Pete said. "Seen it plenty of times over the years—happens to al of us when somethin's weighing heavy."

Pete reached for his mug but didn't drink, letting its warmth soak into his hands instead. "So, you wanna talk about it, or you gonna keep tryin' to out-stare the stars?"

Gage smirked faintly, though it didn't quite reach his eyes. "Not much to talk about," he said after a pause.

Pete snorted, soft but dismissive, like he wasn't buying the dodge. "Suit yourself. But lemme tell you somethin'—life has a way of bendin' a man in ways he doesn't expect. It's easier to deal with when you don't carry the whole load on your own."

Gage nodded once, more out of respect than agreement. He wasn't sure what it was about Pete, but the man had a way of cutting through the layers without ever making you feel backed into a corner. It was subtle, almost like he made space for you to walk into the truth instead of shoving you toward it.

"I've been on my own so long," Gage finally said. "Ain't much I can't handle. That's just how it's always been."

"Don't make it right," Pete replied easily. "Don't make it wrong, either. But there's somethin' to be said for lettin' people in now and then—keeps a man from fencin' himself in permanently."

Gage leaned forward, resting his forearms on his knees as he stared down at the coffee. The words lingered, filling the quiet spaces in his mind. He usually liked his fences high and his gates locked, but lately... he wasn't so sure. Not with Sadie, anyway.

Pete shifted, glancing at him sideways. "And if this 'somethin' weighin' on you happens to have a name, well, just be careful, is all I'm sayin'. Tryin' to mix business with heartfelt notions doesn't always end well, especially on a ranch like this."

Gage stiffened slightly, his head turning just enough to meet Pete's gaze. The old man's eyes were sharp, direct, but not unkind. Gage didn't have to ask what Pete meant.

"Nothin's happenin'," Gage said after a long pause, though his voice carried a hint of defensiveness. "And even if it were..." He trailed off, running a hand through his dark hair. "I'm here to work. That's it."

Pete grunted, the sound somewhere between skepticism and understanding. "Ain't my place to tell you how to run your life, West. But I'll tell you this, Jack Beaumont's the kind of man who'll shake your hand or break it, dependin' on how you treat what's his. And Sadie? She's more than just his daughter. She's got a mind and a heart of her own. If you're thinkin' about makin' somethin' what it could never be, you'd best tread careful."

Pete's words settled deep, a low thrum of warning mixed with something almost protective. Gage didn't respond right away, letting the quiet stretch again. But when he spoke, his voice was softer, almost thoughtful.

"Sadie's a good woman," Pete said, his voice steady with the weight of conviction. "I may not have kids of my own, but I consider her to be family. So, whatever you do, don't go doing something reckless or stupid."

"She's not like anyone I've met before," Gage admitted, the words surprising even himself. "She's strong... stronger than most men I've met. And she's got a way of seein' things, like she's already two steps ahead of you before you've even moved."

Pete nodded slowly, taking in the earnestness behind Gage's tone. "You're right about that. Sadie's somethin' else, no doubt about it. Just make sure whatever steps you take, you've prayed on it first—or at least thought 'em through real good. God's got ways of openin' and closin' doors that you might not even see comin'. Some doors ain't meant to be kicked wide open."

"I'm not much for praying, Pete."

"Well, you might want to reconsider, son. Feels to me like there's a storm brewing ahead, and you'd be wise to bring a prayer or two along for the ride."

Pete patted his knee once before getting to his feet with a faint groan. "You'll probably thank me later," he said. "Just think on it, boy. The answers'll come when they're meant to."

With that, Pete shuffled back toward the door, leaving Gage alone again under the Montana sky.

He stared at the stars for a long moment, his mind quieter now but no less conflicted. Pete's words lingered, and though he wouldn't admit it to anyone, his thoughts strayed back to Sadie. Would it ever be more than just thoughts? He didn't know. And that terrified him as much as it fascinated him.

Chapter 12

Sadie gently patted Daisy's neck, murmuring a low "easy now" as the horse dipped her head to navigate the rocky slope toward the creek. Daisy's surefootedness was one reason Sadie trusted her on paths like this, the ones that wound through the ranch's trickier terrain. The rhythmic creak of the leather saddle and the soft scuff of hooves over packed earth and rock filled the cool morning air. Above her, the early light stretched pale blue and faintly rosy, a stark contrast to the shadows still lingering in the trees that lined the trail.

The world was quiet at this hour, save for the occasional call of a meadowlark or the distant sigh of the wind. Sadie could feel the day waking around her, not with fireworks or ceremony, but with the steady, reliable hum that mirrored ranch life itself. Everything had its rhythm here—predictable, grounded, and comforting. And yet, some days—like today—Sadie felt like she was the only piece of the puzzle that didn't quite fit.

She let out a slow breath, trying to shake off the thoughts already creeping in. Today was supposed to be about carving a little space for herself, away from the bustle of chores, from the growing and annoying interest from Mitch, and from the confusing flutter that had crept up whenever Gage was near.

"Just ride," she muttered under her breath, leaning forward to smooth a hand down Daisy's neck. The horse's ears flicked back at the sound of her voice, but Daisy kept her steady pace, winding toward Sadie's favorite writing spot.

The trees gave way as the trail opened into a clearing, and the sight of it pulled a genuine, unguarded smile to Sadie's lips. The creek was crystal clear, its surface catching flecks of sunlight as it wound lazily through the meadow. The water flow was down, but it was still gorgeous, peaceful, and calming. Cottonwood trees lined its edges, their leaves glinting silver as they swayed in the breeze. Wildflowers—purple lupines, butter-yellow balsam root, and the occasional burst of white yarrow—blanketed the edges of the water, painting the landscape in soft, earthy hues.

Beyond the creek, the mountains stood, their rugged peaks a steadfast presence against the brightening sky. Sadie's gaze drifted upward, scanning the slopes until they landed on the distant herd of wild horses that frequented this area. Their dark shapes stood out against the slopes. They moved with the easy grace of creatures untouched by human hands. They were wild, free, and utterly captivating.

She dismounted, her boots crunching softly against the pebbles near the creek as she tied Daisy's reins to a low-hanging aspen branch. "Take a break, girl," she said, giving the horse an affectionate pat before grabbing her notebook and settling onto her favorite boulder near the water's edge.

The rock was cool beneath her as she shifted, opening the notebook and running her fingers over the creased pages. This was her sanctuary, the place where she let the world quiet enough for the characters in her latest story to come alive. But as she held her pen poised over the page, her mind refused to focus.

Instead of words, her thoughts circled back to Mitch and Gage—the two names that had become increasingly tangled in her heart and her head.

Mitch had been a part of her life for so long it felt like he belonged there, as predictable and steady as the changing seasons. He was kind, loyal, hardworking—a man anyone would be lucky to have at their side. But he wasn't the man for her. No matter how much she cared about him as a friend, she couldn't picture a future where her feelings grew into something more. She didn't want to picture it. And yet, Mitch didn't seem to see that.

"I need to tell him," she murmured, her voice barely audible over the soft babble of the creek. The thought knotted her stomach, but leaving things vague would only make it worse. He deserved clarity, even if he didn't want to hear it.

And then there was Gage—an entirely different kind of knot altogether. Where Mitch's feelings had been clear, Gage was a mystery she couldn't unravel. He was quiet, steady in his own way, but with a guardedness that always seemed to keep people at arm's length. And yet, he had a way of looking at her—those dark eyes intent, like he was trying to read the pieces of her she didn't show anyone else. It unsettled her almost as much as it fascinated her. Sadie felt it in her bones—that quiet, almost unspoken energy from Gage, as if he were trying to piece her together, one careful layer at a time.

She wasn't exactly skilled in the art of flirting, much less dating. Serious relationships were unfamiliar terrain; her experiences were limited to a handful of dates that always seemed to fizzle before they sparked into something real.

The tangle of emotions Gabe stirred in her left her somewhere between curiosity and caution. Did she even want to explore what she was feeling? Or was it safer to let the questions linger, unanswered? And the deeper question—the one that gnawed at her the most—was whether the pull she felt toward him was all in her head. Could she have imagined that flicker of attraction? Or was it something too real, too undeniable, to ignore?

And yet, was it wise to even entertain those feelings, much less explore where they might lead? It was complicated, no matter how you looked at it. He was a ranch hand, and she was his employer—a dynamic fraught with pitfalls even before you factored in the Beaumont family's legacy and reputation. And her dad? She didn't even want to guess what he might think of a situation like this if it grew into something more. A tangle like that didn't just threaten livelihoods—it risked trust, respect, and the delicate balance of everything that held Eagle's Nest Ranch together.

"Why are you even thinking about him?" she asked the water, as though it might offer some divine insight. But it didn't. It just kept flowing, as consistent and unfazed as always.

Sadie sighed and finally let herself write, her hand moving over the page in an almost restless stream of thought. She didn't notice the sound of approaching hoofbeats until Daisy gave a soft whinny, making Sadie glance up.

Her father's familiar silhouette came into view over the rise. His black Stetson tipped low against the dawn light as he urged his horse into a trot. The sight of him, so steady, so completely Jack Beaumont. She raised a hand in greeting as he neared.

"Thought I saw you headin' this way. Figured I'd check on you," Jack said. He swung down from the saddle with ease, brushing a gloved hand over his jeans to knock off the dust.

"I needed a little quiet time," Sadie said with a shrug, watching as he tied his horse next to Daisy. "Didn't think anyone would come looking for me this early."

"You know me," Jack said with a faint smile. "Ranch waits for no man—or no woman, for that matter." He gestured to her notebook. "Workin' on that book of yours?"

"Trying," Sadie admitted, tucking a strand of hair behind her ear as Jack settled onto a nearby rock. "The words aren't exactly cooperating today."

"Happens... I imagine," Jack said, resting his forearms on his knees. His tone turned quieter, more thoughtful. "You know, your mama and I have been talking."

Sadie tilted her head, already wary of where this might be going. "About what?"

"About your writing," Jack said, meeting her gaze. "About how much time it takes and how maybe... maybe you oughta have a little more time for it."

Sadie blinked, stunned. "You're okay with that?"

Jack chuckled, pulling off his gloves and turning them over in his hands. "Sadie, I'd be lying if I said it won't take some getting used to. The idea of you wantin' something outside this ranch. But the truth is... you've got a gift. And I'd be a fool to try to keep you from it. It's just tough for your old dad to come to terms with the fact that the future I imagined for you isn't the one you see for yourself."

Her throat tightened, an emotion she hadn't expected creeping up fast. "Dad..."

"Now, don't get me wrong," Jack added, raising a hand to stop her. "It isn't easy. You're the best employee I got, and lettin' you pull back—it ain't somethin' I decided overnight. But I know this, God doesn't give folks gifts like yours for 'em to leave lyin' in a drawer."

Sadie's gaze dropped to her notebook, her father's words settling over her like a balm. "I wouldn't just up and walk away from everything," she said quietly. "The ranch is still home, still... everything to me."

"I know that," Jack said, his voice low and sure. "But if this is where your heart's leading you, we'll figure it out. Just... give me time to adjust and get used to the idea."

Touched, Sadie nodded, blinking hard against the sting in her eyes.

Jack smiled. "That doesn't mean you're off the hook for today, though. Speaking of which—drought's startin' to hit the north pasture real bad. Gotta get the cattle moved to the east."

Sadie chuckled, standing and brushing off her jeans. "You don't waste time, do you? One moment we are having a good father daughter talk... which I honestly didn't see coming. Then you move so easy into reality."

"Never do waste time," Jack said, pulling himself to his feet and stretching. "Now come on. Let's head back. Your mama and Madge probably got breakfast waitin', and we need to fuel up for the day ahead."

Sadie stepped closer to her father, her voice steady but tinged with emotion. "Daddy."

Jack turned toward her, concern written across his weathered face. "Yeah, baby girl?"

Without hesitation, she wrapped her arms around him in a warm embrace. "Thank you—for everything. You know I love you. But this conversation? It's not over."

Jack pulled back just enough to look at her. She could see the conflict in his eyes, but also the unwavering love he'd always held for her.

"I want to follow my dreams," she continued, her tone firm yet gentle, "but that doesn't mean I'm walking away from the ranch. It's part of who I am, and it always will be. I just need more space to focus on my writing. We'll need to figure out someone else to step in as foreman—someone who can take on the daily responsibilities. I'll still be here, filling in where I'm needed, just... in the background, more. Okay?"

Jack studied her for a long moment, his hand brushing over the brim of his hat. Finally, he gave a quiet nod. "You do what your heart's calling you to do, Sadie. You've earned that much. We'll sort everything out. Just... give your old man some time, alright?"

A smile broke through the tension in her expression, and she squeezed him again, her head resting momentarily against his chest. "Deal."

As they mounted up and rode toward the ranch, Sadie felt a renewed sense of peace, not just with her father, but with the steps she was slowly learning to take on her own. Above all, she knew one thing for sure: God wasn't done writing her story yet. And neither was she.

Chapter 13

Sadie nudged Daisy forward, the horse stepping carefully over the dry, uneven ground of the north pasture. The land stretched before her, its once vibrant grasses now brittle and sun-bleached, the rich green of summer stripped away by relentless heat and too many rainless days. Every crunch of Daisy's hooves sounded louder than it ought to, a stark reminder of just how parched the earth had become.

Her eyes swept across the scattered cattle, their movements slow and lethargic as they grazed on meager clumps of roughage that clung stubbornly to life. Even the air seemed exhausted, carrying with it the faint taste of dust and the tang of heat that left her mouth dry. Overhead, the sky hung broad and blue, mocking in its clarity, the kind of sky that should've promised a good harvest but delivered none.

Off in the distance, a small dust devil spiraled up like a warning, its swirling form skittering unpredictably across the barren patches of earth. Sadie pulled the brim of her hat lower against the glare from the sun, her heart heavy at the scene before her.

She gripped the reins as she took a deep breath, steadying herself. Moments like this called for more than just strategy; they called for faith. Quietly, as much for her own clarity as for divine intervention, she whispered a prayer into the unrelenting silence.

"Lord, show me what I'm not seeing," she murmured, her voice soft but resolute, carried away by the dry wind as if riding on its wings. "Guide us to what these cattle—and this ranch—need to endure."

She let the words settle, her eyes locking on a cluster of cattle huddled near the sparse shade of a tree. Its roots reached deep, stronger than the drought's grip, and the thought filled her with a flicker of hope. It reminded her of what her father often said: "When it dries up, dig deeper."

"Alright, everyone, listen up," Sadie called out, her voice clear and steady as she turned in her saddle to address the group of ranch hands gathered behind her. Sadie scanned the crew, her expression a mix of authority and focus. "The herd's spread thin, and they're restless from the drought. We need to move them carefully—no rushing, no spooking. These cattle are already stressed."

Pete straightened in his saddle, the brim of his hat throwing a shadow across his weathered face. He nodded with an air of calm assurance, his steady presence as much of an anchor for the group as the reins in his hands. Sadie appreciated that about him. Pete always knew when to speak and, more importantly, when not to.

"Pete," she continued, "you take the left flank. Make sure any stragglers don't peel off in that direction. Keep it tight."

Pete tipped his hat, his gruff voice low but confident. "Got it."

Sadie turned to Julie, who sat astride her bay mare. The younger ranch hand's energy was undeniable, and Sadie knew Julie would approach her task with her usual blend of spunk and determination. "Julie, you head out to the right flank. Keep your spacing and watch those prickly patches. We don't need the cattle getting tangled or spooked out there."

Julie gave a quick salute. "On it, Sadie," she said, already moving her horse into position.

Sadie's attention landed next on Gage, who sat tall and composed on his gelding, Bandit, just behind her. His expression was unreadable—calm, steady—but his stormy blue-gray eyes carried a flicker of something she couldn't quite place. Was it anticipation? Or perhaps the quiet confidence of someone who was already calculating the challenges ahead? Either way, it made her pause, though she quickly masked the hesitation behind her usual businesslike demeanor. She met his gaze for a fraction of a second longer than she intended before giving him his task.

"Gage," she said, "you'll ride mid-drive with me. We'll keep the herd together and deal with any trouble spots."

He gave a crisp nod, his voice low and steady. "Understood."

Sadie felt the faintest flicker of relief. Gage didn't ask questions or make unnecessary comments. He simply nodded and gave his word. She could work with that.

Finally, her gaze drifted toward Mitch, who was adjusting his gloves, a casual smirk playing at the edges of his mouth. He was perched confidently atop his chestnut gelding, his posture relaxed, but his eyes watchful... a little too watchful, Sadie thought, as they lingered on her a moment too long. She set her shoulders and kept her tone steady.

"Mitch," she said, her voice firm but polite, "you'll ride sweep with Ross. Follow behind and make sure the line stays tight. If anyone strays, bring them back in."

Mitch's smirk grew just a hair, but he nodded, tipping his hat with studied ease. "You got it, Sadie. Don't worry, I'll make sure no one gets left behind."

Sadie ignored the hint of insinuation in his tone and immediately refocused on the job at hand. "Alright, everyone," she said, her voice rising just enough to carry over the mumbling herd and the shuffle of hooves. "Let's move out. Stay alert and keep your spacing. The ridge ahead isn't forgiving, and we need to stick together if we're going to make this work."

With that, she turned her horse toward the restless herd and started forward, her braid swinging lightly against the back of her plaid shirt. As they moved, the sound of the cattle's low grumbles and the creak of saddles filled the steamy late morning air, mingling with the earthy scent of dust and dry grass.

Gage nudged Bandit into step beside Sadie. He kept his focus ahead, scanning the ridge where the herd would need to funnel through a narrow pass, while Sadie's attention darted from the cattle to the riders, ensuring everyone stayed on target. Together, they watched the herd converge like pieces of a moving puzzle, every section requiring care and precision.

At one point, a particularly ornery cow near the front darted sideways, threatening to draw three others along with it into a line of wild sagebrush. Sadie reacted instantly, steering Daisy sharply to block the path and redirect the cow back into the herd. Gage moved without hesitation, flanking the animal from the other side to cut off its retreat. Their movements were fluid, instinctive, and within moments, the cow was back where it belonged, the potential chaos diffused.

"Good timing," Sadie said, glancing over at Gage. Her voice carried a hint of surprise, though she tried to downplay it.

"Just doing the job," he replied, his tone even, almost detached. But there was a flicker of something undefinable in his stormy gaze when it briefly met hers—a quiet intensity that lingered, even after the moment passed.

Sadie shook her head, refocusing her attention on the herd. This wasn't about Gage West or the strange pull she felt when he was near. It was about the cattle and the ranch—the lifeblood of her family's legacy. Still, as they worked side by side, effortlessly in sync, a thought crept in despite her better judgment. With Gage riding mid-drive beside her, it felt... natural. Almost too natural, as if they were two pieces of the same puzzle, falling into place without hesitation—and that, more than anything, left her thoughts about him tangled.

The work unfolded with a steady rhythm, the kind that settled into the marrow of a ranch hand's bones, smooth and predictable like the slow sway of wild grass in the summer wind. Horses snorted softly as they moved together as a team, their hooves drumming a reliable beat into the Montana earth. The men and women working alongside one another spoke minimally now, their normal camaraderie replaced with the quiet focus that came with moving a sizable herd.

The work was grueling, requiring constant attention to the ebb and flow of the herd as the cows and calves lumbered toward their new grazing ground. Gage worked smoothly alongside Sadie, his movements as efficient as they were unhurried. Sadie couldn't deny he was good at what he did. Annoyingly good.

Suddenly, a sharp, plaintive cry cut through the air. Sadie's head whipped toward the sound just as Gage pulled Bandit to the side, stopped, and vaulted off his horse. In the midst of the dust and chaos, a lone calf, small and unsteady, had stumbled into trouble. One of its legs was caught in a rough hole in the uneven ground, leaving it precariously trapped against the barbed wire of the fence. Its mother circled nervously nearby, lowing in distress.

Sadie rushed toward the injured animal. Gage already crouched beside it, his hands gently pressing along the calf's leg to assess the damage.

"How bad is it?" Sadie asked, her brow creased with worry.

The calf's slender leg was caught deep enough in the hole that it struggled to gain any leverage, and every attempt to free itself only twisted the poor creature's leg further into the unforgiving earth. The barbed wire of the fence grazed its shoulder, leaving small streaks of blood on its light, tawny coat.

"She's stuck good," Gage said.

"Careful," Sadie warned, her jaw tight as she moved Daisy slightly to block the advancing cow. The mother's panicked bellows grew louder at the sight of Gage and her calf. Her massive frame shifting dangerously close to a full charge. But Sadie met her head-on, expertly maneuvering Daisy between the cow and Gage. She held up a hand, her voice calm but commanding. "Easy, Mama. Easy. We're helping."

The cow hesitated, her hooves pawing at the dirt as she huffed and moaned, but Sadie didn't flinch. With Daisy poised steady as a rock beneath her, Sadie diffused the moment with the kind of practiced confidence only someone like her could pull off.

"This leg of hers isn't broken, maybe a sprain," Gage called over his shoulder, relief evident in his tone. "But the more it struggles, the worse it's gonna get. She's torn up pretty bad on her backside. These scrapes from the barbwire are deep."

Relief flickered through Sadie at the news that the injury wasn't worse, but it was fleeting. The sight of the calf thrashing against the wire, its small chest heaving with exertion, wouldn't let her rest easy. "Keep her still," she said firmly, her voice steadied by experience but colored with urgency. "Do you have your fence pliers?"

Gage was already one step ahead, pulling the tool from his belt. "I need you to come hold her head."

Sadie dismounted, sliding into position at the calf's head as she silently prayed the mama cow would remain calm. She rested her hands gently on the small, trembling creature's neck, murmuring soft words of comfort. "It's alright, sweet girl," she cooed. "We've got you now. Just stay still for us, okay?"

The calf's struggles slowed by a fraction—not entirely, but enough for Gage to move in closer. With careful precision, he began cutting through the tangle of wire. Each snap brought another small lurch from the calf, but Gage's calm determination didn't waver. Sadie marveled at his focus. From the way his strong hands worked—calloused but gentle, steady but swift—she could tell this wasn't his first time managing a delicate operation like this. It was as if he'd spent years not just working with animals but understanding them.

"Hold her steady," Gage murmured, barely loud enough to be heard over the calf's labored breathing. His stormy eyes flicked toward Sadie, locking with hers for a split second.

"I've got her," Sadie assured her voice soft but resolute, fingers lightly stroking the calf's coarse coat. "She's calming down."

Gage focused on the last stubborn strand of wire. When it finally gave way with a sharp snap, he breathed out through his nose, leaning back slightly to examine his work. "There," he said, sitting back on his heels. "She's free."

Sadie shifted to give the calf some space while Gage tested its injured leg carefully. The animal didn't cry out but flinched at the touch, the pain clear despite the relief of being untangled. "She'll be sore for a while," Gage said, "but she should heal up just fine if we take care of her."

Sadie exhaled a long, slow breath. Her hand lingered on the calf's neck, her thumb brushing over the soft fur as she whispered, "Thank you, Lord."

"Let's clean these cuts before we move her," Gage said. "You got the first-aid kit with you?"

Sadie nodded, standing and moving toward her horse to retrieve the kit from the saddlebag. As she handed it to Gage, their fingers brushed, and for a brief moment, she was struck by the contrast between them—his rough, calloused hands against hers, worn from years of chores but still soft by comparison. He didn't seem to notice, his focus already back on the calf.

Together, they fell into a steady rhythm, neither speaking more than necessary as they worked to clean and dress the wounds. Sadie stole glances at Gage—at the quiet way he handled the calf, at the concentration etched across his sharp features. There was a gentle, peacefulness about him in this moment, a side she hadn't seen before.

"Where'd you learn all this?" she asked, breaking the silence as she held the bandages for him.

"Here and there," Gage answered, glancing up briefly. His lips quirked in something resembling a smile, though fleeting. "I've been around animals nearly my whole life. They teach you things if you pay attention."

Sadie tilted her head, her curiosity piqued. "And do you always pay attention?"

He chuckled, the sound low and rough but not unkind. "Always. I always pay attention. Let's just say I learn best the hard way."

She smiled, the corners of her eyes crinkling. "Well, seems to me like you've learned plenty."

Gage didn't respond right away. Instead, he tied off the last bandage with practiced efficiency, then leaned back and looked at her. "I've still got a ways to go."

Sadie, sensing the subtle shift in tone, didn't push further. Instead, she rested a hand on his arm for a brief moment.

"Whatever the road's taught you," she said, "it brought you here. This little one sure is grateful for that."

Gage met her eyes then, something unspoken passing between them—a shared understanding, perhaps, or just the quiet gratitude of two people working toward the same goal. He gave a small nod, his lips pressing into a faint smile. "Guess so."

Sadie tilted her head back, her gaze lifting to the endless expanse of sky above, where the sun blazed fiercely, casting its unrelenting heat over the land. "Let's get her back to the barn," she said, standing and brushing the dirt from her jeans. "She's had enough excitement for one day."

"I'll take her back," Gage offered immediately. "My horse can handle the extra weight."

Before she could respond, Mitch rode up, his horse skidding to a halt a few feet away. His gaze bounced between Sadie and Gage, his expression immediately tightening. "Everything alright here?" he asked, his tone sharp with concern—or perhaps something else. "Need any help?"

"Injured calf, we've got it handled," Sadie replied firmly, not missing how Mitch's gaze darted between her and Gage. "The herd still needs watching. Go back and help."

"But—" Mitch began, his voice tinged with protest.

"No buts," Sadie interrupted firmly, leveling him with a look that brooked no argument. "This is under control. Go."

For a moment, Mitch seemed poised to argue further. But something in Sadie's expression stopped him. With a tight-lipped nod, he turned his horse and rode off, his posture stiff with barely concealed frustration.

Sadie turned back to Gage, who had watched the exchange. He didn't comment, though the faintest hint of a smirk tugged at his lips as they worked together to hoist the calf onto Bandit.

"Nice way to shut him down," Gage remarked as he secured the calf with a rope. His voice carried a note of respect, though his eyes gleamed with something closer to amusement.

Sadie ignored the heat that rose in her cheeks. "Let's just focus on the calf."

"If you say so... go on back to the herd," Gage said. His closeness sent an unexpected flutter through her chest that she quickly dismissed.

"I should go with you," Sadie protested. "That leg needs proper care."

"I can handle it," he assured her, and something in his voice made her believe him. "This isn't my first injured calf."

"Give her a shot of penicillin when you get her back," Sadie instructed, fighting the urge to go with them. "Clean those wounds again, thoroughly. There should be supplies in the—"

"In the medical cabinet above the workbench," Gage finished for her, a hint of amusement in his eyes. "I found it my first day here. Some things are universal on ranches."

Sadie nodded, oddly comforted by his competence. "I'll check on you both as soon as we finish here."

"We'll be fine," he said, already mounting up carefully behind the calf. "Just trust me."

Before she could respond, he had turned his horse toward the barn and was picking his way carefully across the drought-hardened ground.

Sadie watched them go for a moment, offering another quick prayer for their safety before turning back to the task at hand.

Chapter 14

Sadie guided Daisy closer to the barn, its weathered timber frame silhouetted against the soft orange hues of the fading evening light. Normally, the sight of the structure would settle her spirit, grounding her in the familiarity of home. But this evening, after a long day of herding cattle, her chest felt tight, her nerves fluttering against the edges of calm. She dismounted with ease, tying Daisy's reins to the post with habitual precision.

From within the barn came a low murmur, too soft for her to make out the words but deep enough to carry a soothing cadence. The voice grew clearer as she walked inside toward one stall. It was Gage's deep and unhurried baritone that held a gentleness she hadn't expected, she paused in the doorway, her breath catching as the scene unfolded before her.

Gage sat cross-legged in the fresh hay beside the injured calf, his broad shoulders illuminated by the barn's overhead lights. He was hunched slightly forward, his fingers brushing idly across the calf's neck between his words. The calf, once so panicked and restless, was now nestled contentedly in the hay. Its eyes half-closed, as if lulled by the steady cadence of Gage's voice.

Sadie's gaze lingered on the clean bandages neatly wrapped around the calf's injured leg and backside, the water bucket placed just within reach, and the freshly cushioned stall.

Gage's voice rose just slightly, drawing Sadie's attention as she caught the end of his words. "... You're a tough one, aren't you? Stronger than you look, little girl."

The animal let out a soft, trembling bleat, and Gage leaned forward. His calloused hand brushed soothingly along the calf's back. Beside him sat a shallow basin of water, a clean rag draped over its edge. He shifted to dip the cloth, wringing out the excess before gently dabbing at the calf's tawny coat, his movements methodical yet tender.

"I'll admit," he continued, his voice laced with the faintest hint of amusement, "you gave me a run for my money. But we're both still standing, so I'd call that a win."

Sadie's lips twitched at his words, her chest inexplicably tightening at the unexpected softness in his manner. Here, in the quiet sanctuary of the barn, she saw a man unburdened. No judgements, no deflections. Just Gage, steady and determined, speaking softly to a creature who probably didn't understand a word but seemed somehow comforted, nonetheless.

"Looks like you made a friend," she said.

Gage turned his head toward her and his stormy gray-blue eyes met hers. His lips quirked slightly, just enough to raise the corner of his mouth. "She could use one after the day she's had," he replied.

"You did good," she said as she stepped further into the stall. "She looks better already."

Gage glanced down at the calf and then back up at Sadie, his expression guarded, though his eyes betrayed a flicker of something softer—maybe pride. "She's a little fighter," he replied simply, pushing himself into a standing position. His broad frame seemed even more imposing in the close quarters of the stall.

Sadie's gaze moved over the scene—the calf, calm and settled now; the carefully placed supplies; Gage, standing tall but slightly tousled, sweat-dampened strands of dark hair curling at his temple. Her stomach fluttered, an unexpected sensation she hurriedly dismissed.

"And you," she said, folding her arms loosely across her chest, her tone pointed yet softened with sincerity, "surprise me more and more each day. A tough and rugged cowboy, yet tender and kindhearted with animals."

Gage shrugged slightly, the motion almost self-conscious as he bent to pick up the basin of used water. "I've spent enough time around them," he said, his voice low but even. "You start to figure out what they need—and what they don't."

Sadie stepped closer, her eyes lingering on the calf's wrapped leg. "You bandaged her up well," she said, the admiration in her tone drawing Gage's attention. He looked at her then, really looked, his eyes narrowing slightly as though trying to read her expression.

"You doubted me?" he asked, the faintest hint of a teasing smirk tugging at the corner of his lips.

"I wouldn't call it doubt," Sadie countered, arching a brow. "Just...surprise. Most ranch hands don't come with a vet degree on the side."

He chuckled, the sound rumbling low in his chest. "No degree. Just practice—and maybe a little luck."

"Either way," she said, her smile easing into place, "I'm glad you're here."

A beat of silence hung between them, weighty but not uncomfortable. Gage's eyes searched hers briefly before he cleared his throat, breaking the moment as he turned to set the basin aside. "She'll need more care over the next few days," he said, his voice slipping back into something more clinical. "Keep the cuts clean, change the bandages, check for infection."

Sadie studied him for a moment longer, her hazel eyes narrowing slightly, as though she were trying to untangle the layers of thought behind Gage West's cool demeanor. How could someone who carried himself with such quiet detachment also exhibit such tenderness and skill in moments like this? She wasn't used to being caught off guard, but there was something about Gage that unsettled the usual rhythm of her thoughts—and she wasn't sure whether she found it frustrating or fascinating.

"Well," she said finally, "you did your part out here. I'll make sure she gets the rest of what she needs."

Gage gave a small nod, not looking away from her. "Glad to hear it."

Sadie crouched down beside the calf, her hand brushing lightly over the tawny fur just above the bandaged leg. The little creature stirred at her touch, letting out a weak but hopeful bleat that seemed like a quiet thanks. Her fingers lingered for a moment before moving to smooth the scruffy patch along its neck.

Out of the corner of her eye, she caught Gage still watching her, his posture relaxed but his gaze intent.

"Did you eat dinner yet?" she asked abruptly, breaking the quiet with a question that felt more practical than personal. That made it feel safer somehow.

Gage shifted slightly, his arms folding across his broad chest as he leaned back against the stall wall. "No. I've been here in the barn since I brought the calf back."

Sadie frowned, her hazel eyes narrowing just a fraction as she looked at him. "Are you hungry?"

"It's not high on my list right now," he replied evenly, glancing briefly at the calf before adding, "I'll grab something later."

Sadie stood as she processed his response. She wasn't sure why, but his answer didn't sit quite right with her. Maybe it was the offhanded tone, like he wasn't used to someone else asking about his well-being. Or maybe because it didn't seem fair that the man, who'd poured so much effort into helping the injured calf, didn't think twice about skipping a meal.

"Well," Sadie said, "if you think I'm going to let you go without dinner after all this, you've got another thing coming."

Gage lifted an eyebrow, a faint flicker of amusement playing at the corner of his mouth. "Is that so?"

She tipped her chin up with mock defiance. "Absolutely." Before he could protest, she took a step toward the stall door. "Stay here."

"You don't have to do that," Gage called after her, though his tone lacked the conviction of someone truly protesting.

Sadie paused at the stall doorway. She turned just enough to meet his gaze over her shoulder, the hint of a smile tugging at her lips. "I know I don't have to. But I want to. Stay put."

Chapter 15

"Something smells good," Gage remarked, rising to his feet and brushing hay off his knees as Sadie stepped into view. She carried a picnic basket in one hand, a thermos in the other, and had a backpack slung casually over her shoulder.

"Madge, bless her heart, outdid herself again. Roasted chicken with all the fixin's—mashed potatoes, green beans, homemade biscuits, and even peach cobbler. She was already packing food into containers when I got there. She guessed the crew down at the bunkhouse wouldn't bother coming up for dinner since it was already late, and they were likely worn out from the day's hard work. But knowing how hungry they must be after such a grueling day, she decided they deserved a hot, hearty meal to come home to. By all the food she had packed already when I walked in, you'd think she was feeding an entire battalion. Hope you've got an appetite because there's no shortage of good eating here tonight."

"Appreciate it," he said simply, moving to sit on a nearby bale of hay.

Sadie carefully unfolded a cotton tablecloth, its faded gingham pattern adding a touch of softness to the practicality of the barn stall. She draped it over a bale of hay along the stall's wall, transforming it into a makeshift dining setup that somehow felt intimate amidst the rugged surroundings. With quick efficiency, she set out an assortment of food containers.

Grabbing a sturdy paper plate, she piled it high with food—enough to satisfy even the hungriest ranch hand after a long day's work. She handed it to Gage, along with a set of silverware neatly wrapped in a napkin. "Here," she said, her voice gentle yet firm, with a touch of that no-nonsense tone that left no room for argument. "Eat."

She wasn't asking.

The corner of her lips quirked into a small, satisfied smile as she unscrewed the lid of a dented old thermos. Pouring thick ribbons of steaming coffee into two Styrofoam cups. She placed one near him, tucking it securely into the hay-covered flooring where he was sitting.

Gage sat still, his posture relaxed, but his expression distant, almost unreadable. For a moment, he simply stared down at his plate of food. His jaw tightened, and his eyes flickered with hesitation. He surveyed the meal like it was an unfamiliar object, as though the simple kindness of someone preparing a plate for him was an indulgence too foreign to accept outright.

Sadie paused, leaning her weight onto one hip as she studied him. It struck her how much of a puzzle he was—this man with his sharp edges and quiet but tough demeanor. She wondered what kind of life left a man looking at dinner as if it might disappear if he reached for it too quickly.

"Gage," she prompted. "Eat before it gets cold. You've earned it."

He blinked, snapping out of whatever thoughts had been drifting through his head, and his gaze shifted back to her. He nodded, ever so slightly.

His bites were deliberate, almost methodical, as if the act of eating was something he needed to focus on. Each forkful was measured, his chewing slow but unhurried, like a man who didn't rush through things but still carried the weight of the world on his shoulders with every bite.

The food was good—better than most of what he'd had over the years, bouncing from one job to the next. But it wasn't just the taste that made it stick in his chest; it was the fact that it was offered freely, without expectation or judgment. That, in itself, felt... strange.

Sadie busied herself with making a plate of her own. Now and then, her gaze landed on him, flitting away quickly so he wouldn't catch her watching.

"Don't forget your coffee," she said casually, nodding toward the cup sitting near his boots. Settling cross-legged in the middle of the stall floor, she balanced her plate of food on her lap. Her own cup of coffee in her hand, the rich aroma curling into the air as she swirled the dark liquid thoughtfully. After a small sip, she let its strong, bold bitterness settle on her tongue.

"I appreciate this," Gage said after a long stretch of silence. His voice was low and gravelly. He didn't over-elaborate, didn't offer a speech about gratitude or kindness—just those three quiet words.

Sadie remained silent, choosing to grant him the quiet he seemed to need. Her gaze shifted back to the calf, which lay nestled in the hay, its small sides rising and falling in a steady rhythm. The earlier tension in its wiry frame had melted away, replaced by the peace of deep, untroubled sleep. A tender smile flickered across her lips as she watched the little creature. Satisfied that it was resting easily, she turned her focus back to her dinner.

"You're not half bad at this," Gage said, breaking the silence. "Running a ranch, I mean."

Sadie looked up at him, startled by the compliment. "Well, thanks," she said, her brow quirking playfully. "I wasn't aware you were taking notes."

"Hard not to notice," he replied, shrugging, as he took another bite of his biscuit. "Not everyone can do this."

The sincerity in his tone caught her a little off guard, but she didn't let it show. Instead, she met his stormy gaze with her own steady one, tilting her head slightly as if appraising him. "And what about you, Gage? Where'd you learn to handle things so well? It's pretty obvious there are many sides to you. Hard-working cowboy, quiet and determined. Yet, you surprised me today with another side of you I didn't expect. Underneath that tough exterior, you have a gentle side."

"Guess I'll take that as a compliment," he said, the corners of his mouth twitching into a smirk.

"It is, and don't let it go to your head," Sadie said with a grin. She leaned forward slightly, her blonde braid falling over one shoulder. "But you didn't answer the question."

Gage raised an eyebrow. "And what question is that?"

"I asked... what about you? You know, tell me something about yourself. Something real. You've been here awhile now, but you're still harder to read than the weather."

Gage paused, his stormy eyes settled on hers. "What's 'real' enough for you?" he asked after a moment. "You seem to have me all figured out already."

Sadie huffed out a soft laugh, tilting her head slightly as she regarded him. "Not all figured out. Just enough to know there's more to you than what you let on. You talk when it's necessary and work twice as hard as anyone else."

Gage's jaw tightened, his gaze dropping momentarily to the floor as he considered her words. "There's not much to tell, Sadie. I've been doing this kind of work for years—traveling from ranch to ranch, picking up jobs where I can. I keep life simple."

Sadie narrowed her eyes slightly, not buying the simplicity he was trying to sell. "Simple? Maybe. But it sounds like a lonely life."

"It's just the way it is," he said. "Sometimes it's better that way."

"Better for who?" she pressed. "For you? Or for someone you left behind?"

Gage stiffened imperceptibly, her question striking deeper than she'd likely intended. A flicker of resistance crossed his face before he schooled his expression back to calm neutrality. His voice, when he finally spoke, was measured and low, a subtle edge beneath it. "I didn't leave anyone behind. There's no one waiting for me, no ties anywhere. It's just me. Always has been. I don't get attached—to anyone or to any place."

Sadie held his gaze, searching his face, as if trying to read between the lines of what he wasn't saying. His words were sharp, final, but there was a weight behind them—one that didn't sound as freeing as he made it out to be. Instead, it sounded like armor, like flimsy protection against something far deeper than wandering from job to job.

"Well," she said, "I guess you have your reasons."

"Yeah," he murmured, turning his attention back to the cup of coffee in his hands.

The calf stirred slightly, shifting in its sleep, and Gage's sharp eyes flicked to it immediately, as though he'd trained himself to look for reasons to always be on the move—to work, to fix, to distract.

"You know, I appreciate you bringing her back here this afternoon and staying with her," Sadie said, trying to lighten the mood.

Gage's lips pressed into a thin line, and he tipped his head in acknowledgment, though he didn't meet her gaze. "Couldn't just leave her here alone, injured, away from her mother?"

Sadie nodded. "No, you couldn't. It's not in you, I can tell."

That comment made him glance up, his brow furrowing slightly, as though he wasn't sure what to make of it—or her, for that matter. "And what do you think's 'in me,' Sadie?"

She tilted her head, letting her gaze linger on him for a moment longer than usual. "More than you'd like people to know."

"Everyone's got their secrets."

"Maybe," Sadie replied, leaning back slightly as she cradled her coffee cup. "But not everyone stays hidden behind them."

He looked away, leaning forward to set his empty plate on the hay floor before standing up. "Thanks for the food," he said.

Sadie studied him for another long moment before she offered a nod. "You're welcome."

"Why'd you ask me that earlier, Sadie?" Gage's voice sliced through the quiet, low, and rough like gravel underfoot. His blue-gray eyes held hers, steady yet cautious, a question lingering there like smoke. "What about me makes you want to know more?"

She hesitated. Her lips parted slightly, words escaping her at first. She thought about brushing his question off with humor, deflecting the moment with the ease of a practiced quip—but something about the way he was looking at her stopped her cold. There was a rawness in his expression, a vulnerability barely masked by the stoic set of his jaw, that tugged at the edges of her heart.

She searched his face, her hazel eyes softening as they took in the quiet tension in his posture—the way his hands flexed against his sides, like he wasn't quite sure what to do with them, and the way he stood still enough to suggest he might bolt if the answer unsettled him.

"Because you're interesting, Gage West," she said, her voice quiet but unwavering. The words seemed to surprise him, his brow furrowing slightly as though he wasn't sure he'd heard her correctly. Sadie stood and took a small step forward. "There's something about you that feels... different... important. Something that tells me you're someone worth knowing," she continued, her tone thoughtful as she let the words come. "You're not like everyone else. You carry yourself like someone who's been through millions of storms in life."

He looked away then, the brim of his hat casting a shadow over his face as his jaw tightened. Whatever emotion was working its way through him, he was wrestling to keep it contained. The silence stretched, and Sadie wondered if she'd overstepped, but she didn't back down. Instead, she stayed where she was, waiting, her heart thudding against her ribs.

When Gage finally turned back to her, his eyes shifted through countless shades of blue, like the ever-changing hues of a restless sea. "Well," he drawled, his voice low and deliberate, "you might be the first person to see me as anything other than just another ranch hand. Interesting, maybe I am. Important?" He let out a short, humorless laugh. "Not so much. Different... sure. And yeah, I've had my share of storms, more than most people."

Sadie tilted her head. "Everyone's important, Gage. Everyone matters. Even you."

"And why do you think that?" he asked, his tone rough. "Why are you so sure I matter, Sadie?"

"Because God doesn't make mistakes," she said simply. "He didn't make a mistake with you, either."

Gage's shoulders tensed. He looked away again, adjusting the brim of his hat as though it might shield him.

"I don't fit into those neat little boxes people like to put others in around here," he muttered finally, almost more to himself than her. "The good person, the honest cowboy, the faithful rancher. That's just not who I am."

Sadie smiled. "Good thing nobody's asking you to fit in a box, then," she said. "I'm just trying to get to know you—the real you." She paused, her voice softening even further. "What's underneath that hat, Gage West?"

Gage stilled.

"The calf should be fine overnight," he said, his voice tight, doused with emotion. "I'll check on her first thing in the morning."

Sadie opened her mouth to protest, but he was already moving, stepping away, the distance between them as palpable as a closing door.

"Goodnight, Sadie," he said.

Sadie swallowed hard, forcing a small smile. "Goodnight, Gage."

Sadie watched him go. There was so much he wasn't saying, so much he clearly didn't want anyone to see. And yet, she couldn't shake the feeling that underneath all that guarded strength was someone worth knowing—worth understanding.

When the barn doors creaked shut behind him, she released a slow breath, looking back at the calf snoozing peacefully. Bending down, she gently brushed the little animal's coat, her movements thoughtful as her mind churned with questions about Gage.

"Guide him, Lord. He needs you," she whispered.

Chapter 16

The rhythmic click of Sadie's laptop keys filled the quiet barn, a counterpoint to the soft rustling of hay and the occasional heart-wrenching bawl of the injured calf. Sadie sat cross-legged on an old, faded quilt, the laptop balanced precariously on her lap. Beside her, nestled in the hay, the calf shifted, its dark eyes wide and anxious.

"I know, sweetie," Sadie murmured, reaching out to stroke the calf's soft head. "Missing your momma, aren't you?" The calf let out another plaintive cry, a sound that tugged at Sadie's heart. She understood that ache, that feeling of being lost and alone.

Her fingers hovered over the keyboard, the words of her current chapter momentarily forgotten. She was stuck, the plot of the story tangled in a knot she couldn't quite unravel. "Maybe," she mused aloud to the calf, "maybe if the hero had to make a really tough choice... a sacrifice, maybe? Would that move the story forward?" The calf blinked at her, offering no immediate literary insights.

Sadie sighed, running a hand over her loose braid. Sometimes, talking through her plot problems helped, even if her audience was a bewildered bovine. It forced her to articulate her thoughts, to hear the story aloud, and often, the solution would emerge from the sound of her own voice.

She glanced at the laptop screen again. She'd been making good progress tonight, losing herself in the fictional world she was creating, a world where cowboys were noble and love conquered all, a world that often felt simpler and more hopeful than the real one.

Another soft bawl from the calf drew her attention. "Okay, okay," she soothed, offering a gentle scratch behind its ears. "Let's see if we can't find a way to get our hero out of this mess."

She was just about to refocus on her writing when a soft creak echoed from the far end of the barn. Sadie's head snapped up, her heart giving a little jump. Who would be out here at this hour? It was well past ten, and most folks on the ranch were asleep or winding down for the night.

Even in the dim light, she recognized the familiar set of those shoulders, the way he carried himself with a quiet, contained energy.

Gage.

A flicker of surprise, quickly followed by a confusing flutter in her stomach, washed over her. What was he doing out here? She hadn't expected to see him again tonight after their conversation, a conversation that had left her feeling both intrigued and unsettled.

Gage paused just inside the stall door. Surprise flickered across his features, mirroring her own. He'd probably assumed she'd be tucked away in the main house by now, not camped out in the stall.

"Sadie? Everything alright out here?"

"Everything's fine. Just... keeping the little one company. And catching up on some work." She gestured to the laptop.

"Work never stops for you, does it?" he remarked, a hint of a teasing tone in his voice.

"You know how it is," she said, shrugging.

He stopped near the calf, who let out another soft, mournful bleat. "Still missing its mother?"

Sadie nodded. "Breaks your heart, doesn't it?"

Gage's gaze flicked back to her, a hint of something unreadable in his stormy eyes. "Yeah," he said. "It does."

Sadie's eyes lingered on his face, taking in the faint lines that framed his eyes. He looked tired—more than tired, really—but there was something else there too. A quiet intensity in his expression, simmering just beneath the surface.

"What brings you out here?" she asked. "Can't sleep?"

He hesitated for a moment, his gaze flicking around the stall as if searching for an excuse. "Something like that. Just... wanted to check on things," he said, his voice casual. "Make sure everything's secure for the night."

Sadie arched an eyebrow, a playful smirk tugging at her lips. "Right. Because a seasoned ranch hand like you needs to personally inspect every latch and bolt at this hour."

A ghost of a smile touched his lips. "Can't be too careful."

"Seriously, though," she said. "Is everything okay?"

He shifted his weight, shoving his hands into the pockets of his jeans. "Yeah. Just restless, I guess." He glanced back at the calf. "Thought I'd see how the little one was doing."

"She's doing alright," Sadie said, her gaze following his. "A little lonely, but she'll be okay."

Gage remained standing, his presence filling the space. Sadie watched him, a thousand questions swirling in her mind. What was he really thinking? What was it about him that drew her in so inexplicably?

"What are you working on?" Gage asked, his gaze flicking towards the laptop.

"Just my novel," Sadie replied, a hint of self-consciousness creeping into her voice. "Trying to figure out how to get my hero out of a particularly sticky situation."

"Novel?"

Sadie tipped her head slightly, studying Gage with a playful spark in her hazel eyes. "I'm a part-time author, if you can believe that," she said, an amused lilt in her voice.

"An author? Really?"

"Mm hmm," Sadie replied, brushing a loose strand of her hair from her face. "I've got a deadline looming over me like a storm cloud. My readers are already impatient for the next book in the series."

He raised a brow. "How long have you been writing?"

Her lips quirked into a soft smile, her shoulders lifting in a casual shrug. "Long enough to know deadlines wait for no one—especially not ranchers by day and writers by night." There was a note of self-deprecating humor in her voice, as if the duality of her life amused her as much as it surprised others.

"So, do you write about cowboys?" Gage asked, a hint of mischief flickering in his eyes. He leaned casually against the wall, his posture relaxed but his gaze sharp.

"Naturally. What else would you expect from a girl raised under the wide open skies of Montana?"

"Hard life, being a cowboy," he replied.

"It's a life worth living. At least, that's how I like to tell it."

"And what's this cowboy like?" he prompted, his curiosity piqued.

Sadie hesitated for a moment, then shrugged. "He's made a mistake, a big one, and now he has to figure out how to fix it without losing everything he cares about."

Gage's gaze intensified, his eyes seeming to search hers for something deeper. "Sounds complicated."

"Life often is," Sadie replied, her gaze locking with his.

"So, what's the solution?" he asked after a moment.

Sadie sighed. "That's the million-dollar question, isn't it? I'm still working on that part." She paused, then added, "Maybe he needs to learn to trust someone. Maybe he needs to learn to let go of his pride and ask for help."

A flicker of something that looked like recognition crossed Gage's face, a fleeting shadow that was gone before Sadie could fully decipher it.

"Sometimes," he said, his voice low, "that's the hardest thing to do."

"I know," Sadie agreed. "But it's often the bravest."

The calf let out another soft bawl, a gentle reminder of their shared space and the reason Sadie was out here in the first place. Gage pushed himself off the wall, moving closer to the little creature.

"Mind if I?" he asked, gesturing towards the calf.

"Go ahead," Sadie said.

Gage knelt beside the calf, his large hand gentle as he stroked its back. The calf seemed to respond to his touch, its anxious movements calming slightly. There was a quiet tenderness in his actions, a stark contrast to his rugged exterior.

"You really are good with animals," Sadie commented, watching him.

"They're honest," he said simply. "They don't judge."

"No," Sadie agreed. "They just need love and care."

"Like people," he murmured.

The air crackled with unspoken emotion, a palpable connection that seemed to stretch between them in the quiet of the barn.

"So," Gage said, breaking the spell, his voice a little rougher now. "What happens next in your story?"

Sadie blinked, momentarily disoriented by the shift in conversation. "Well," she said, refocusing on her fictional world, "I'm thinking maybe a friend steps in, someone who sees the good in this man despite his mistakes. Someone who believes in him."

"And does that fix everything?" Gage asked, his gaze still on the calf.

"Not everything," Sadie replied. "But it gives him a chance. A chance to redeem himself, a chance to find his way back."

"Redemption," he murmured.

"It's a powerful thing," Sadie said softly. "Second chances. Forgiveness."

He looked up at her then, his blue eyes searching hers. "Do you believe in that, Sadie?"

"I do," she said without hesitation. "I believe everyone deserves a second chance. We all make mistakes. It's what we do after that matters."

"Maybe," Gage said, his voice low, "your hero needs to learn to forgive himself."

Sadie's heart ached at the vulnerability she glimpsed in his eyes. "That's always the hardest part, isn't it?" she said.

He nodded, his gaze drifting away. "So, are you going to let this friend help him?"

Sadie smiled. "I think I might. It seems like the right thing to do."

"Even if it's risky?" he asked, his eyes meeting hers again.

"Sometimes," Sadie said, her voice barely above a whisper, "the riskiest things are the ones most worth doing."

The calf nuzzled closer to Gage, its fragile frame trembling slightly as if seeking out the security it instinctively felt in his presence, a quiet solace in place of its missing mother.

"It's getting late," Gage said. "You should probably head back to the house."

"No," she replied. "I'm not ready to. I want to work out her for a little while longer."

Gage stilled, as if he weren't used to someone standing firm against his suggestions. He didn't argue, though. Instead, he shifted to sit cross-legged on the hay beside the calf. With a small, careful motion, he coaxed the animal closer until she shifted, her small, delicate head resting in his lap.

"You don't have to stay out here with us," Sadie said as she went back to typing.

Gage gave a small shrug. "I don't mind."

"She's going to be alright, you know that, right?"

"I know," Gage replied. Sadie could feel his eyes on her in a way that made her feel self-conscious. It was unsettling and comforting all at once. "I'll head out if that's what you want. But just so you know, I'm not staying here for the calf."

"Then why are you?" she asked, her voice laced with quiet curiosity.

"Because, Sadie," he said, "I enjoy being around you."

That stopped her. She blinked, momentarily surprised by the simplicity of his answer. She tilted her head, studying his face, as if trying to gauge whether he meant it as sincerely as it sounded.

After a beat, she cleared her throat as she reached for her coffee mug. "Fine, cowboy," she said. "Make yourself comfortable. Since you're in such a talkative mood, you can help me." Her lips curved into a playful smirk as she added, "I'll bounce some ideas off you. We'll see if all that ranch wisdom extends to storytelling."

Chapter 17

Sadie descended the staircase of the Beaumont house, her movements unhurried but deliberate. She rubbed at her weary eyes, stifling a yawn. The memory of the calf, nestled in the barn last night, mingled stubbornly with the lingering thoughts of a certain cowboy who had shared the quiet hours. Try as she might, she couldn't untangle her emotions—or banish the image of Gage sitting cross-legged on the barn floor. The man was a riddle she wasn't sure she how to solve. He had a way of slipping into her thoughts more and more lately.

Reaching the kitchen, she was greeted with the aroma of freshly brewed coffee, warm and steady, like a quiet promise that the day ahead could be faced. Without a word, she poured herself a cup and let the comforting scent rise like a lifeline to her senses.

At the kitchen island, Harriet stood cradling a mug in both hands. Across from her, Jack was steadily working through a hearty breakfast of eggs, sausage, and toast, his focus intent but his demeanor relaxed. Meanwhile, Madge held court at the stove, an air of easy command about her. She stood watch over a sizzling pan of sausage, humming a cheerful tune as though orchestrating a symphony of hearty flavors.

"Well, good mornin', sunshine," Madge quipped without bothering to look her way.

Jack glanced up from his plate, his thick eyebrows furrowing. "I heard you come in late last night, Sadie. Everything alright with the calf?"

"She's fine," Sadie said. "She's still shaky, but she seems calmer. She even let Gage settle her down for a bit."

"Well, I'm glad she's alright," Jack said. He set down his fork and leaned back slightly, his sharp eyes fixed on his daughter. "So Gage was with you last night? You sure you're doin' alright?"

Sadie bit the inside of her cheek and turned toward the fridge, pretending to search for something. "I'm fine, Daddy," she said, keeping her voice light. "Really. I was writing last night in the barn keeping the calf company. She was lonely and missing her momma. Gage had the same idea to check on her."

"Lonely," Madge repeated with a snort. "A calf. Lonely." She flipped a piece of sausage with exaggerated care and shook her head. "Girl, that animal will be just fine. Are you sure you weren't in that barn for other reasons?"

Sadie spun around, her cheeks coloring as she gave Madge the fiercest look she could muster—not that it had any effect on the older woman. "Madge," she said sternly, though the hint of a smile tugged at her lips. "I swear, you and that imagination. I was writing, something I do every night."

"I'm just sayin'," Madge replied with a shrug, her sly grin firmly in place.

"Oh, hush, Madge," Sadie shot back, moving to the kitchen island with her cup of coffee.

"Hmm, sounds like someone's defensive, maybe a bit flustered this morning," Harriet said, her golden-brown eyes twinkling as they flicked between her daughter and Madge.

"Mom," Sadie groaned.

Jack cleared his throat loudly enough to cut through his wife and daughter's exchange. "Got a big day ahead of us. Hope you got enough sleep," he said plainly.

"I'll be fine, daddy."

Harriet reached to pat Jack's hand affectionately, though her gaze lingered on Sadie with the kind of motherly intuition that rarely missed. "You work so hard, Sadie. I know working full time on the ranch and spending your evenings devoted to your writing is hard on you," she said gently.

Sadie softened at her mother's words. "It's not so bad, Mama," she replied. "Besides, writing helps me unwind. And last night...well, it was nice to get some quiet time in the barn."

"Quiet time in the barn, huh?" Madge teased.

Sadie's cheeks burned. "Madge, for goodness' sake."

Jack's thick brows furrowed again as he took a sip of his coffee. His sharp blue eyes flickered toward his daughter. "Couldn't have been too quiet in that barn with a ranch hand present."

"So Jack, tell me more about this new ranch hand," Harriet said, turning to her husband, hoping to sway the conversation.

Jack cleared his throat again, this time more pointedly. "Gage does his job, and he does it well. That's enough for me."

Sadie raised an eyebrow at her father's clipped tone. "Well, Daddy, not everything can be summed up in job performance, you know."

Jack didn't respond immediately, his expression carefully neutral as he speared a piece of sausage with his fork. After a moment, he said, "Just be careful, Sadie. That's all I'm saying."

"Careful?" Sadie repeated. "With what? Gage hasn't done anything to raise concern. He's hardworking, polite, and—"

"And he's a drifter," Jack interjected, his voice steady but firm. "Men like that don't stick around, Sadie. They come and go, and they don't leave much behind but questions. I've seen it too many times."

"Jack," Harriet said softly, placing a hand on his arm. "Not everyone's the same. Gage might surprise us."

Jack's jaw tightened, but he said nothing, his attention returning to his plate.

Sadie sighed, her frustration bubbling just beneath the surface. She loved her father dearly, but his tendency to judge people too quickly often left her feeling torn. She knew Gage wasn't exactly an open book, but she also sensed something genuine beneath his tough exterior.

But what did she really know about him? Gage was still a mystery, and the only thing Sadie was certain of was that unearthing that mystery might come with its fair share of risks—risks she hadn't decided yet if she was willing to take.

The back door creaked open, and Mitch stepped inside. He tipped his hat off with practiced ease and grinned.

"Good mornin', smells like heaven in here," he said.

Sadie stifled a sigh and leaned back in her chair, her mood dipping slightly.

"Well, good mornin' to you, too, Mitch," Harriet said.

"What brings you by?" Jack asked.

"Just thought I'd check in before heading down to the barn to start my day," Mitch said.

"Well, that's thoughtful of you," Jack replied.

"Mornin' Sadie, you look tired this morning," Mitch said.

"Morning, Mitch," Sadie said, her tone light as she pushed away from the table. "I'd love to stick around, but I've got work to do."

Harriet looked between her daughter and Mitch, sensing something was off.

As Sadie stepped outside, the warm morning air hit her cheeks. The ranch stretched out before her, bathed in the soft light of the rising sun. The sounds of the morning—birds chirping, the distant lowing of cattle, the rustle of leaves in the breeze—welcomed her in the way they always did, filling her with a sense of purpose and peace.

But as she made her way toward the barn, coffee in hand, her thoughts drifted back to Gage. Jack might see him as a drifter, someone who wouldn't stick around. But Sadie wasn't so sure anymore. There was something about him, something different... appealing even. And if there was one thing Sadie believed, it was that everyone had a story worth uncovering—even if it scared them to tell it.

Sadie reached the barn door and paused. Taking a sip of her coffee, she exhaled softly and pushed the door open, stepping into the familiar space.

And there he was, brushing her horse down.

Chapter 18

Gage stood beside Daisy, carefully brushing the mare's glossy chestnut coat with steady, practiced strokes. His black Stetson was tipped low over his face, casting a shadow that only added to the quiet intensity of his presence. Even with much of his expression obscured, Sadie could still make out the deep concentration in the set of his jaw and the deliberate rhythm of his movements.

Daisy leaned into his touch, flicking her tail lazily in what could only be described as pure contentment. Sadie hesitated a few feet away, taking in the scene with a small smile. There was something inherently calming about the way Gage worked with animals, as if his ruggedness had a softer edge reserved just for them. He murmured something low to Daisy, the words too quiet to catch, but whatever he said, the horse seemed to approve.

"You planning to stand there all morning, or are you waiting for applause?"

Caught, Sadie stepped into the stall, crossing her arms but wearing an unapologetic grin. "You've got some nerve, you know. Daisy's my horse, and brushing her down is my job."

Gage turned to face her, the curve of a smirk tugging at his lips. "Didn't figure she'd mind, long as someone's taking care of her. Seems to me she's not too picky about who's holding the brush."

Sadie raised a brow, walking past him to grab Daisy's mane comb from where it hung on the wall. "Maybe not," she replied, "but I'm particular about who steals my chores. You looking to take over my entire morning routine, cowboy?"

"Only if it involves coffee. Otherwise, you're on your own, Beaumont."

Sadie stepped closer. "Next time, give me a heads-up. I wouldn't want you stealing all her affection while I'm not looking," she teased.

"Seems like she's got enough for the both of us," he countered casually.

As Sadie reached for a tangled patch in Daisy's mane, her fingers lightly brushed against Gage's. The touch was brief, barely a whisper of connection, but it still managed to send a jolt of awareness straight through her. Determined not to let it show, she kept her focus on calmly combing through the knot, though the erratic rhythm of her pulse told a different story.

"Any particular reason you're up and out here so early?" Gage asked.

Sadie shrugged as she worked the knot free from Daisy's mane, her focus momentarily divided. "There's a lot to take care of today. I wanted to check on the calf first, make sure she's still doing okay. Then I need to head out to the south pasture to check on the horses. Dad's worried about the grazing conditions out that way."

Gage gave a small nod, his attention shifting back to Daisy as he brushed her sleek coat with care.

Sadie glanced toward the stall where the injured calf lay resting. "And how's our little one doing this morning?"

"She's holding steady," Gage replied. "No signs of infection in those cuts, and her leg still looks good. She's got a bit more pep than last night, that's for sure."

"That's a relief," Sadie said as she patted Daisy's neck. There was a slight hesitation in her voice before she added, her tone lighter but tinged with purpose, "You should come with me to check on the horses in the south pasture."

Gage paused in his brushing, his movements slowing as his gaze flicked to her. His jaw tightened. "Or," he said evenly, "I could head out there solo, and you could focus on everything else that needs doing."

Sadie rolled her eyes, a smile tugging at her lips. "I could," she replied, "but there's really no fun in that. I'm inviting you to come with me, Gage. Morning rides are nicer with company."

"Is that a good idea?" he asked.

"What's that supposed to mean?" Sadie tilted her head, studying him.

"You know what I mean," he said, his gaze resting steadily on hers. "The boss heading out with the new ranch hand for a ride. People might talk."

"Let them talk," she said simply. "Doesn't much bother me."

For a moment, he just looked at her, as if weighing whether she truly meant it. His eyes searched hers, questioning her sincerity—or maybe questioning himself.

"Alright," he said, "if you insist. Against my better judgment... let's saddle up."

***

The pasture unfolded before them; the horses moving effortlessly across the terrain. The landscape, though touched by the dry whispers of drought, remained breathtaking. Tufts of fading green grass mingled with stubborn wildflowers clinging to life, their colors muted but still poignant against the backdrop of rolling hills. Above it all, the mountains loomed in the distance, their rugged peaks standing steadfast beneath a sky stretched vast and endless. Even in its parched state, Montana exuded a beauty that spoke of resilience and quiet strength.

Sadie stole a glance at Gage, riding beside her. He moved with his horse as if the two were extensions of one another, his posture relaxed but controlled. The morning sunlight softened the planes of his face, and for just a moment, she let herself admire him, knowing full well that if he caught her, his wicked smirk would undo her entirely.

"So, how long have you worked on ranches?" Sadie asked, her tone casual, but her curiosity evident.

Gage glanced her way, his blue-gray eyes unreadable under the shadow of his Stetson. "Most of my life."

"Most of your life?" she pressed. "So, you were born into it?"

He shook his head. "No."

Sadie tilted her head, studying his profile as they rode side by side. "Where did you grow up?"

"Texas."

"That's quite a distance from Montana," she said. "How'd you end up here?"

"Life happened."

Sadie's gaze lingered on him, her heart tugging at the unspoken emotion in his answer. There was a story there, one he wasn't ready to tell. The set of his jaw and the quiet tension in his shoulders clarified that.

"Getting to know you is going to be quite the challenge, isn't it?" she asked.

"Sadie..." His voice held a note of warning. "There's nothing much worth knowing. I'm just a man trying to make it through each day."

"Life is meant to be more than just making it through, Gage. I want to know the real man hiding beneath that Stetson."

He turned to her, his blue-gray eyes clouded with something that looked like regret. "I can't figure out why you'd want to. I'm nothing but a simple man, Sadie. Whatever's happening between us—" he gestured vaguely between them, "—it can't lead to anywhere good. Deep down, I think you know that."

"I don't believe that for a second, Gage," she replied, her voice steady with conviction.

Their ride carried them deeper into the south pasture, where a sudden rustle broke the serene stillness. Sadie hadn't fully registered the darting shape in the tall grass when Gage surged forward, spurring his horse into a quick gallop. All at once, the source of the commotion came into view—a gangly, wide-eyed foal, stranded and separated from the herd. Its cries were shrill, a high-pitched plea that pierced the quiet morning air.

Sadie's heart clenched with an instinctive urgency. With no need to exchange words, she veered wide, angling to cut off any potential escape routes while giving Gage room to maneuver. Her pulse thrummed, adrenaline surging as their unspoken teamwork came to life. Despite the foal's erratic movements, Gage remained impossibly calm, his sharp focus clear in every deliberate motion. With practiced ease, he unfurled his lasso. The rope snaking through the air before settling neatly around the foal's neck.

He pulled it taut with confidence and turned in his saddle to glance back at Sadie. "We need to reunite him with his momma," he said.

Sadie scanned the horizon, lifting a hand to shield her eyes from the rising sun. She nodded toward a softly sloping rise ahead. "The herd might be over there," she said. "There's a creek nearby with plenty of shade trees. That's where the horses tend to linger. My guess is, this little one wandered too far."

Without further discussion, they rode together in that direction, their pace unhurried. Gage held the rope lightly in one hand, leading the trembling animal behind him.

As they crested the rise, the south pasture stretched out before them like a painting unfurling in slow, breathtaking strokes. Even in its late-summer dryness, the landscape held a quiet resilience and beauty. The grass, though faded, caught the light and glowed with a golden sheen, dotted here and there with wildflowers that refused to surrender to the season's harshness. In the near distance, the herd came into view, scattered along the shallow creek, their movements serene under the dappled shade of sprawling cottonwoods.

"There they are." She pointed to the herd and glanced back at Gage. "Let's get him to his momma."

They descended the hill at an easy pace, cautious not to spook the foal or disrupt the tranquil gathering of the herd. As they approached, the foal began to pull slightly against the rope, its cries growing louder and more insistent. Then, seemingly out of nowhere, a mare broke away from the group, her distressed whinny echoing as she galloped toward them.

"There's mama," Gage said.

Sadie's breath caught as she watched the reunion unfold. With a frantic but careful energy, the mare nuzzled the foal, her movements urgent but gentle, as though reassuring herself that her baby was truly there. The foal responded in kind, pressing close to her side, its panicked cries now replaced by soft, contented nuffs.

"That's the kind of happy ending I like," she said.

Gage dismounted, his movements slow and deliberate as he removed the rope from around the foal's neck. He stepped back as the tiny foal wobbled on its legs. With a soft nudge from its mother, the little creature turned, its movements hesitant but determined. Side by side, they made their way toward the creek.

Gage lingered a few feet away from Sadie, as if deep in thought, his posture still. He watched as the pair nuzzled each other in the golden grass, the foal's cries softening into contentment as the mother leaned down, protective and assuring.

"That is a beautiful sight," she said.

"It is," he replied.

Chapter 19

"Follow me, cowboy. I want to show you something." Sadie's eyes sparkled with mischief as she flashed Gage a grin, already turning Daisy toward the western edge of the south pasture.

Before Gage could respond, she'd urged her horse into a swift gallop, her blonde hair dancing against her back as she rode. Her laughter floated back to him on the breeze, a sound as wild and free as the Montana sky stretching endlessly above them.

Gage hesitated, watching her figure grow smaller against the backdrop of rolling hills and scattered cottonwoods. Something stirred in his chest—an instinct warning him to keep his distance, yet mingled with an undeniable pull toward this woman who was gradually working her way into his every waking moment. Getting closer to Sadie Beaumont wasn't part of his plan. Yet as he watched her ride with such natural grace and joy, his reservations began to crack a little more like spring ice on a warming creek.

"Lord help me," he muttered, shaking his head. Then he nudged his horse forward, following the path she'd taken across the wild grass.

Sadie glanced over her shoulder, satisfaction warming her chest, when she spotted Gage finally giving chase. She hadn't been sure he'd follow—that uncertainty made his decision to come after her all the sweeter. Leading him higher into the rocky terrain, she navigated Daisy through the familiar route, one she'd traveled countless times before.

"You planning on slowing down?" Gage called out, his deep voice carrying across the distance between them.

"What's wrong?" she shot back. "Afraid you can't keep up?"

His answering laugh sent an unexpected shiver down her spine. "Sweetheart, I'm just getting started."

The endearment, casual as it was, caught her off guard. Sadie felt her cheeks warm, grateful he was too far behind to notice. She focused instead on guiding Daisy up the steepening incline, where weathered rock jutted from the earth like nature's stepping stones.

As they climbed higher, the morning air grew cooler, carrying the crisp scent of pine and wild sage. The sounds of their horses' hooves against stone and soil filled the air. When they finally crested the rise, Sadie drew Daisy to a stop, turning to watch Gage's reaction as he caught up and took in the view.

Before them, the valley opened up like a secret being whispered. The creek wound its way through the rocks, its clear water catching glints of sunlight. Patches of wildflowers dotted the grass in splashes of purple and yellow, defiant against the late summer heat. And in the distance, barely visible against the backdrop of mountains, the herd of wild horses grazed peacefully.

"This is my favorite spot on the whole ranch," Sadie said, dismounting Daisy. She led the horse to a flat area near a large boulder, loosening the cinch to let her rest comfortably.

Gage followed suit, his movements deliberate as he took in their surroundings. "I can see why," he said, his voice holding a note of genuine appreciation. "How'd you find this place?"

Sadie settled onto the sun-warmed boulder, patting the space beside her in invitation. "My grandmother used to bring me here when I was little. She'd pack us a lunch, and we'd spend hours watching the wild horses." A gentle smile touched her lips at the memory. "She always said the land holds its own kind of wisdom, if we're quiet enough to listen."

Gage hesitated for just a moment before joining her on the boulder, leaving space between them. "Smart woman, your grandmother."

"She was," Sadie agreed, her gaze drawn to the distant herd. "You know what my secret dream is?" She paused, suddenly feeling vulnerable about sharing something so personal. "I've always wanted to catch one of those wild horses. Not to break its spirit, but to earn its trust. To show it that freedom doesn't have to mean being alone."

Gage studied her profile, struck by how the sunlight caught the gold in her hair, how her eyes seemed to hold the same wild spirit she admired in those distant horses. "That's quite a dream," he said. "Most folks would just want to break them, make them submit."

"That's not love," Sadie replied, shaking her head. "Genuine love gives space to be who you are, while offering a safe place to land." She turned to meet his gaze, her voice softening. "Like those wild horses— they're beautiful because they're free, not in spite of it."

Something shifted in Gage's expression, a crack in his carefully maintained armor. "You sound like you know a thing or two about wild spirits."

"Maybe I recognize one when I see one," she countered gently.

Gage looked away, his jaw tightening. The silence stretched between them, filled with the whisper of wind through grass and the nickering of horses.

"You know what I love most about my life?" he said finally, his voice rough with emotion he usually kept buried. "Every new horizon, every new place, feels like a fresh start. No expectations, no disappointments. Just..." He gestured vaguely at the vast landscape before them. "Freedom."

"But?" Sadie prompted softly, hearing the unspoken word in his tone.

"But sometimes," he admitted, "freedom starts feeling a lot like running. And sometimes..." He paused, struggling with words that felt foreign on his tongue. "Sometimes I wonder what it'd be like to have somewhere—or someone ––to come back to."

Sadie's heart quickened at his confession. She watched a hawk circle lazily overhead, gathering her thoughts. "My grandmother used to say that God gives us wings and roots, both. The trick is knowing when to use which."

"Your grandmother sounds like she was quite the wise woman."

"She was." Sadie smiled, memories washing over her. "She'd sit right here with me, telling stories about the land, about faith, about love. She always said the best stories are written in the heart first."

"Is that why you write?" Gage asked, genuine curiosity in his voice. "To tell those heart-stories?"

"Partly," Sadie admitted, touched by his interest. "But also because stories help us understand ourselves better. Like those wild horses, words remind me that beauty can be both fierce and gentle. That freedom and belonging aren't opposites."

A comfortable silence settled between them as they watched the distant herd graze. A warm breeze carried the sweet scent of sage and summer, and Sadie found herself hyper-aware of Gage's presence beside her—the subtle shift of his shoulder near hers, the quiet rhythm of his breathing.

"I never knew my grandmother," Gage said suddenly, his voice low. "Or my grandfather. Lost my parents when I was six, bounced through foster homes after that." He picked up a small stone, turning it over in his hands. "Never stayed anywhere long enough to put down roots."

Sadie's heart ached at the matter-of-fact way he delivered such pain. He was slowly revealing himself to her, each small glimpse helping her understand. Without thinking, she reached out and placed her hand over his, stilling his restless fingers. "I'm so sorry, Gage."

He stared at her hand over his, something vulnerable flickering across his features. "Don't be. Made me who I am."

"And who is that?" she asked.

"Someone who shouldn't be sitting here with you like this." He made no move to pull his hand away, though. "Someone who's got no business feeling what I'm feeling."

Sadie's pulse quickened, but she kept her voice steady. "And what are you feeling?"

Gage looked at her, his blue-gray eyes intense. "Like maybe freedom isn't everything I thought it was. Like, maybe there are some things worth hanging around for."

A strand of hair danced across her cheek in the breeze. Without thinking, Gage reached up to brush it back, his fingers lingering near her temple. The touch sent electricity through them both, and Sadie's breath caught in her throat.

"We shouldn't spend time alone together like this," Gage said, his voice rough with emotion as he pulled his hand back. "It's not safe."

"Safe for whom?" Sadie challenged gently. "You?"

"Sadie..." There was a warning in his tone, but also a plea.

"I think you're wrong," she said, standing up and brushing off her jeans. She looked down at him, sunlight haloing her hair. "I think this is exactly where we both needed to be today. Sometimes the scariest paths lead us exactly where we're meant to go."

Gage stood too, his height bringing him close enough that Sadie had to tilt her head back to maintain eye contact. "You sound pretty sure about that."

"I am." She smiled, reaching for Daisy's reins. "I have faith."

"In what?"

"In God's timing. In second chances." She paused, mounting her horse with fluid grace. "In wild things, finding their way home."

Gage's gaze lingered on Sadie for a moment, the faintest flicker of admiration crossing his expression. His lips quirked as if he were about to speak, but he hesitated, as though weighing his words. Then, with a subtle shake of his head, he rose and mounted his horse.

"You're something else, Sadie Beaumont," he said.

Sadie let out a light laugh, tilting her head to the side. "I'll take that as a compliment."

He smirked, adjusting the reins in his hands. "It was meant to be one."

As they began to ride, her smile widened, the morning air brushing against her cheeks. She glanced at him mischievously. "By the way... I liked the way you said 'sweetheart' earlier."

Gage gave her a sidelong glance, equal parts surprised and amused. "That? I said it without even thinking. Probably shouldn't have... I apologize."

"Don't apologize. I believe the things we say without thinking are the most honest. They come from a place deeper than we realize. Are you brave enough to listen?"

Gage's smirk softened into something quieter, his eyes narrowing slightly as though he were puzzling over her.

"Sadie Beaumont..." he began, shaking his head again, though his tone now held a hint of wonder, "I see these different sides of you—strong, compassionate, stubborn as a wild mare—and it's starting to make sense why you're drawn to those wild horses. There's a bit of them in you."

She chuckled, her voice tinged with bittersweet honesty. "Sometimes, I wish I had more of their wild spirit in me—free and untamed, with nothing holding me back."

"I think you've got more of it in you than you realize."

Sadie turned Daisy toward home. As they rode back across the south pasture, matching their horses' pace to walk side by side, neither could deny the change in the air between them. Something wild and beautiful had been acknowledged, like a mustang first learning to trust—cautious, yet full of possibility.

Chapter 20

The savory aroma of Harriet's pot roast and freshly baked rolls wafted through the main house. Madge bustled into the dining room, her arms cradling a steaming bowl of buttered potatoes.

"Well, if these don't smell like heaven on a plate, I don't know what does," she declared with a touch of pride, setting the bowl down with a flourish. She cast an amused glance toward Ross, her eyes twinkling. "Not that it'd matter much to this one. I'm pretty sure young Ross here would devour them even if I'd charred 'em black!"

Ross grinned from his spot at the table. "You know me too well, Madge."

Julie slid into her usual seat, elbowing Pete playfully as he eyed the food. "Easy there, cowboy. We haven't said grace yet."

Gage pulled the screen door open, the creak announcing his entrance before his boots met the wooden floor. Sadie glanced up instinctively. His dark hair was still damp at the temples, evidence of a quick cleanup after the day's work. Their eyes locked, a flash of connection that lingered far longer than either intended, before Gage moved to his usual spot at the table. The flutter in Sadie's chest, impossible to ignore.

Mitch entered just moments later, his stride purposeful as he claimed a chair that placed him squarely across from Gage. The placement didn't feel accidental. Sadie caught the subtle tightening of Mitch's jaw, that slight tell of his frustration. Without a word, she left her seat, rising to help Harriet with the last of the dishes of food, hoping to ease the tension building in the room.

The sound of Jack's heavy boots filled the space as he approached the dining room. His face, carved with lines of a life well-lived, seemed more weathered than usual. Shadows of worry lingered in the furrow of his brow and the downturn of his lips. The drought had tightened its grip on their land and, as always, on her father's shoulders. The ranch's struggles weren't just matters of soil and sky—they were woven into Jack Beaumont's very being.

It felt as though the room held its breath.

"Evenin', everyone," Jack said, his voice warm despite his obvious preoccupation. "Sorry to keep you waiting." He took his place at the head of the table, and Sadie followed. She watched as her mother reached over to squeeze his hand.

"Shall we pray?" Jack asked, and heads bowed around the table. "Heavenly Father, we thank you for this meal and the hands that prepared it. We ask for your blessing on this food and on our ranch. Lord, we especially pray for rain in these dry times, and for wisdom to steward what you've given us. Guide us in caring for this land and these animals. In Jesus' name, Amen."

"Amen," echoed around the table, followed by the immediate clatter of plates and bowls being passed.

"So, Gage," Jack said, cutting into his pot roast, "you've been with us for several days now. How are you finding Eagle's Nest?"

Sadie tried not to look too interested in Gage's response, but she held her breath slightly as he considered his answer.

"It's a fine operation you've got here, Mr. Beaumont," Gage replied, his voice steady and sincere. "It's been a pleasure working with your crew—they're a solid team, and we all seem to mesh well, pulling together to get the job done. Thank you for the opportunity to be part of it."

Sadie caught the slight softening in her father's expression at Gage's words. Jack nodded, satisfied with the response.

"Good to hear," Jack said. "We've always believed in doing things right here, even when it's not the easiest way."

Mitch cleared his throat. "Speaking of doing things right, I've been meaning to ask about those new fence posts for the north pasture. Thought maybe I could show Gage here how we like things done at Eagle's Nest."

The underlying challenge in Mitch's voice was clear, and Sadie felt her shoulders tense. But before anyone could respond, Julie jumped in.

"Hey, is anyone planning to compete in the roping competition at tomorrow's festival? I heard the prize money's better than last year."

"You bet I am," Mitch said, his chest puffing slightly. "Brought home that trophy last summer, didn't I?"

"That you did," Julie agreed, then turned her attention to Gage. "How about you, Gage? You're good with a rope."

Gage took a slow sip of water before answering. "I do all right."

"All right?" Mitch's voice carried a hint of mockery. "Step it up, cowboy. Let's see what you're really made of—not another easy little contest like last time. I'm talking about real pressure, something that tests your grit. Or... Are you afraid you'll choke in front of the whole town?"

Harriet shot Mitch a warning look. "Now, Mitch…"

But Mitch pressed on. "Just saying, might be good to see if our new hand can actually handle himself in an actual competition. Unless he's more comfortable just…"

Sadie felt heat rise in her cheeks. "Mitch, that's enough."

"It's all right, Sadie," Gage said, his eyes meeting Mitch's challenge. "Count me in for tomorrow's competition."

Madge broke the tension in the room with a laugh. "Lord, save us from men and their pride! Now, who's ready for another helping of potatoes?"

Her intervention lightened the mood, and the conversation shifted to other aspects of the upcoming festival. Harriet began describing the pie contest she'd be judging, while Julie and Ross debated which band would be playing for the evening dance.

Jack, however, remained quieter than usual, his thoughts clearly elsewhere. Finally, he set down his fork and addressed the table.

"Listen up, everyone. I know we're all looking forward to tomorrow's festival, and I want you all to enjoy it. But I need to be straight with you about what we're facing."

The table fell silent as Jack continued. "This drought's hitting us hard. Next week, we're going to need all hands on deck. We'll be rotating pastures, hauling water and feed, and doing whatever it takes to keep our stock healthy. It won't be easy, but that's why I want you all to take tomorrow evening to rest and enjoy yourselves at the festival. We'll need everyone at their best for what's coming."

"We're with you, Jack," Pete said firmly, and murmurs of agreement circled the table.

"The Lord provides," Harriet added softly, her face gentle with faith. "He always has."

"That He does," Jack agreed, then managed a smile. "Now, what time does the roping competition start? Might need to place a friendly wager."

"Competition starts at six," Mitch said.

Sadie smiled as Harriet reached across the table to touch Jack's hand. He responded with a wink and a gruff chuckle. "Looks like we'll be there. My bride deserves a night on the town."

Sadie couldn't help but admire the love between her parents. Theirs was steady, unspoken in many ways, but deeply rooted. It was the kind of love that grew stronger with each passing year, like the old oak trees that dotted the ranch.

Harriet turned her gaze on her daughter. "Sadie, you're planning on going too, aren't you?"

Sadie hesitated. "I don't know, Momma. It might be nice to stay home, have a quiet night, and work on my novel."

Before Harriet could respond, Mitch's voice cut into the conversation. "I'd like it if you came." His tone was casual but deliberate, and his glance at Gage didn't go unnoticed. "Wouldn't mind spinning you around the dance floor... you know, if Jack's alright with it, that is."

Jack, looked up from his coffee, his sharp gaze moving briefly to Mitch, then landing on Gage before finally settling on his daughter. "Sadie can decide for herself who she wants to dance with. That's not my call."

Harriet, ever the peacemaker, spoke up before any tension could build. "Sadie, I think it'd do you good to get off the ranch for a bit. Why don't you call Laura and see if she'll go with you?"

Sadie shifted in her seat. "I'll think about it."

Gage didn't say a word, but Sadie could feel his gaze, steady and unspoken, resting on her.

As dinner wound down, Sadie began gathering plates. Gage stood to help, and their hands brushed as they reached for the same dish. The contact sent a jolt through Sadie's arm, and she looked up to find his eyes fixed on hers.

"I got these," he said.

"Thanks," she replied. "And good luck tomorrow. Not that you'll need it."

A hint of a smile played at his lips. "We'll see about that."

Madge watched their interaction with knowing eyes, exchanging a glance with Harriet. The two women shared a subtle smile before turning back to their tasks.

Jack, however, remained watchful of his daughter, fully attuned to the simmering tension brewing between Gage and Mitch. He couldn't shake the certainty that Sadie was at the heart of it.

***

The ranch hands gradually dispersed into the crisp Montana night, their laughter, and footsteps fading into the quiet hum of crickets outside. Sadie was on her way upstairs, eager to retreat to the solitude of her room, when her father's voice stopped her at the bottom of the staircase.

"Sadie," Jack called, his tone making it clear this wasn't a casual request. "Come sit with me for a bit on the front porch."

She hesitated, her hand resting on the banister as the exhaustion of the day pulled at her, but the look in her father's eyes—steady, yet lined with something unspoken—made her pause. With a small nod, she stepped away from the stairs and followed him out the front door.

Chapter 21

Sadie settled into the wooden rocking chair beside her father on the wraparound porch, the familiar creak of the boards beneath them a comforting sound in the evening air. Together, they watched the ranch hands make their way toward the bunkhouse, their silhouettes long in the fading light.

Jack's weathered fingers drummed a slow rhythm against the arm of his chair. "How's the south pasture looking? Horses doing okay?"

"The land's pretty parched, Daddy." Sadie's voice carried a note of concern. "I'm worried about how dry it's getting out there."

Jack's gaze drifted toward the horizon, his expression thoughtful as he continued his steady tapping against the chair's worn wood.

"Daddy," Sadie said, studying her father's troubled expression. "Something's bothering you. And I know it's more than just the drought."

Jack shifted in his chair, his weathered face softening as he met his daughter's gaze. "Sadie, you're grown now, and Lord knows you've earned the right to make your own choices. But understand this—I'm your father. That job doesn't end, not ever. And as long as I'm breathing, I'll be looking out for you."

Sadie's heart squeezed at the emotion in her father's voice. "I know that, Daddy."

"I see what's happening," Jack said quietly. "Between you and Gage. I've noticed the tension between you and Mitch. And it's clear he's got feelings for you, too."

"I've been meaning to talk to Mitch."

Jack's knowing look made her cheeks warm. "Sweetheart, I wasn't born yesterday. I've watched you grow up on this ranch. I know you inside and out. I know your heart and can see it's pulling you in a certain direction."

"Daddy—"

"Let me finish," he said gently. "Gage is a good worker. Strong, capable. But like I said before, he's also a drifter, Sadie. Men like that... they've got restlessness in their bones. They don't always stay, and it'll break my heart to see you upset if he leaves."

"If he has a reason to stay, he might not leave."

"Maybe," Jack conceded. "But that's a mighty big risk to take with your heart, child." He paused, his voice softening. "And then there's Mitch."

"What about Mitch?"

"He's solid, dependable. Known him since he was knee high to a grasshopper. His roots run deep here, just like yours."

Sadie stood, moving to lean against the porch railing. In the distance, a coyote called out to the rising moon.

"Daddy," she said finally, turning to face him. "I know you want what's best for me. But my heart... it's not something I can just direct where others think it should go. Even if that direction seems safer."

"I know that, baby girl. Just... be careful." Jack said, understanding in his eyes. "I feel ashamed, in a way."

"Why Daddy?" She asked confused.

"Sadie, I've spent years dreaming of you taking over this ranch. Lately, it's been weighing on me—this life, this place, it's been all you've ever known, and I'm partly to blame for that. You've never really had the chance to explore the world beyond these fences, to experience the kind of carefree youth most people your age should have. You've never traveled far from home, never dated much, never had the freedom to spread your wings and see life on your own terms. And for that, darlin', I feel like I've let you down."

"Oh, Daddy," Sadie said softly, her voice catching as she looked at him, emotion brimming in her hazel eyes.

Jack raised his hand. "Let me finish. You deserve more than just duty and tradition. You deserve to be young, to feel free, and to find your own joy. I want that for you, Sadie—more than anything. When it comes to love, honey, I know it's only natural to want a partner to share your life with. But be careful. Men—well, they can be a complicated bunch. Trust your instincts, but more importantly, pray. Pray on what you're feeling and on all the things we both see happening right now. Take the time to listen—to your heart and to God. Whatever path you choose, know that your momma and I are here for you, every step of the way."

Sadie nodded.

"Never forget this, sweetheart: hold your head high and stay steady in your convictions. Stand firm for what's right, no matter the cost. And if you let a man into your heart, make sure he knows—without question—that you are to be cherished, respected, and loved whole-heartedly."

Jack rose from his chair, wrapping his arms around Sadie in a warm, steady hug. His embrace spoke volumes—love, pride, and a quiet reassurance that only a father can offer. Without a word, he released her and headed inside, the screen door creaking softly before clicking shut behind him.

Sadie lingered on the porch long after he was gone, the cool night air wrapping around her like a bittersweet memory. The vast Montana sky sprawled above, endless and speckled with stars that blinked with a quiet rhythm. She sat on the porch step, her elbows resting on her knees, her hands cradling her chin as her thoughts wandered in a tangle of emotions—hope and uncertainty, longing and resolve.

The soft chirping of crickets filled the stillness, their song blending with the faint rustle of the wind through the drought ridden grasses. It was a melody she'd heard countless times before, but tonight it felt different, heavier somehow. Should she risk letting someone like Gage West—wounded, complex, and magnetic—inch closer to the guarded places she rarely let anyone see?

Sadie released a slow breath. Out here, beneath the vastness of the heavens, it was easier to believe what her grandmother used to say—that God's plan always unfolded in its own time, no matter how the heart fretted. For now, she let the night hold her questions, her hopes, and the faintest flicker of something new—something wild and profoundly beautiful—taking root deep within.

Chapter 22

The buzz of excitement rippled through the crowd as Sadie and Laura made their way toward the roping arena at the Riverbend Valley Summer Festival. Children darted between food stalls, their faces sticky with cotton candy, while the scent of kettle corn and grilled hamburgers drifted on the early evening breeze. The announcer's voice boomed through the speakers, testing the system and calling out preliminary instructions to competitors.

"I still can't believe you almost didn't come," Laura said, linking her arm through Sadie's as they navigated through the crowd. "The summer festival's roping competition is practically a town holiday."

"I had plenty of work to do on the ranch," Sadie replied, though her eyes were already scanning the competitors' area where cowboys adjusted saddles and checked their ropes.

Laura nudged her playfully. "Sure, and it has nothing to do with avoiding certain people?"

"Laura—"

"Or maybe watching certain people?" Laura wiggled her eyebrows, nodding toward where Gage stood with his horse, checking his gear.

Heat crept up Sadie's neck. "I came to support everyone from Eagle's Nest."

"Mm-hmm." Laura's knowing smile spoke volumes. "Well, let's find a good spot. I want to see everything."

They found a place along the fence where the worn wooden rails provided a perfect vantage point. The arena stretched before them, freshly raked dirt creating a clean slate for the competition ahead. Sadie noticed Mitch on the far side, leading his horse in small circles, his movements more animated than necessary.

"Ladies and gentlemen," the announcer's voice rang out, "welcome to the 47th Annual Riverbend Valley Summer Festival Team Roping Competition!"

The crowd cheered, and Sadie felt the familiar thrill of anticipation. She'd watched this competition every year since she was a little girl, perched on her father's shoulders until she was old enough to stand on her own.

"First up," the announcer continued, "we have the Miller brothers from Sweet Grass County!"

As the first team took their positions, Laura leaned closer to Sadie. "So, are we going to talk about what's going on?"

"What do you mean?"

"Oh, please."

"Laura," Sadie said. "It feels strange talking about this. Mitch is your brother, and while I've never given him any reason to think we could be more than friends, his jealousy toward Gage is getting out of hand. I just don't know how to handle it anymore."

"Do you want me to say something to him?"

"No, I'll handle it. It's childish to get someone else involved. I just... thought he'd pick up on the signals and ease off on his own."

"Okay, fair enough. But what about Gage? Let's talk about him."

"Gage... I don't even know where to start. It's like he showed up out of nowhere and suddenly, he's taking up all this space in my mind, in my heart... in my life," she said, her voice tinged with vulnerability. "I've never felt anything like this before—not with anyone. It's overwhelming, Laura. And it scares me because... it's all happening so fast. Too fast."

"Sadie, you know I've loved you like a sister for as long as I can remember," Laura said, her tone softening, her hazel eyes brimming with understanding. "So trust me when I say this—I only want what's best for you. Always."

Sadie gave a tentative nod, her gaze fixed on the dirt beneath her boots. Laura reached out, giving her arm a gentle squeeze, the kind of unspoken reassurance only a lifelong friend could offer.

"And what I think is best right now?" Laura continued with a sly smile. "It's simple: go for it. Whatever this is between you and Gage, whatever it could be—explore it. What's the worst that could happen? If it doesn't work out, you'll pick yourself up and go on. But if it does... Sadie, it could be something amazing."

Sadie hesitated, her lips parting as if to protest, but Laura cut her off with a playful nudge.

"And just so you know," Laura added, her voice dropping into a more serious tone, "I've never seen a man look at you the way he does. There's something in his eyes when he looks at you... like a flicker of heat that can't be faked. It's this mix of fire and peace, like he's found something he didn't even know he was searching for. Honestly, Sadie, I don't think Gage came into your life by chance."

The crowd's collective gasp drew their attention back to the arena, where the Miller brothers had just completed a clean run. The announcer called out their time as the next team prepared to enter.

"It's complicated," Sadie admitted. "Mitch has been there my whole life for me, you know? And now "

"And now there's Gage," Laura finished. "Who, by the way, looks mighty fine checking his saddle over there."

Sadie couldn't help but look. Gage moved with an effortless grace that made even the simplest tasks seem spectacular. As if sensing her gaze, he glanced up, their eyes meeting across the arena. The smile he gave her sent her heart stuttering.

"Oh my word," Laura whispered gleefully. "You've got it bad, girl."

Before Sadie could respond, Mitch approached. "Ladies," he greeted them, though his eyes fixed solely on Sadie. "Came to watch the competition?"

"Wouldn't miss it," Laura replied cheerfully. "Good luck out there!"

Mitch's confident grin didn't quite reach his eyes. "Thanks, but I don't need luck. Been practicing some new techniques that'll make last year's performance look amateur."

"I'm sure you'll do great, Mitch," Sadie said sincerely, though she noticed his gaze drift toward where Gage was warming up his horse.

"Well, we'll see who's the better man today, won't we?" Mitch's tone carried an edge that made Sadie uncomfortable. He tipped his hat and strode away, his shoulders set with determination.

Laura waited until he was out of earshot before whispering, "Was it just me, or did that feel like he was marking his territory?"

"Laura!" Sadie scolded, but she couldn't deny the accuracy of her friend's observation.

The competition progressed steadily, each team showing their skills in the intricate dance of header and heeler, working in perfect synchronization. The afternoon sun beat down across the arena as the announcers called out times, and the crowd responded with appreciative cheers and groans.

"Next up," the announcer's voice boomed, "Mitch Monarch and Pete Lewis from Eagle's Nest Ranch!"

The crowd erupted in supportive cheers, and Sadie watched as Mitch guided his horse into position. Pete, steady and focused as always, took his place as the heeler. The steer burst from the chute, and Mitch's horse sprang into action. His loop flew true, catching the steer's horns in a textbook catch. Pete's timing was perfect, and together they completed a clean run.

"Seven point two seconds!" The announcer called out. "That puts them in the lead!"

Mitch circled back, making sure to pass by where Sadie stood. His chest was puffed with pride as cheers and whistles followed him out of the arena.

"That was impressive," Laura admitted. "Don't look now... your cowboy's up next."

Sadie's breath caught as Gage rode into position. He sat easily in the saddle, his movements fluid and natural. Ross, his heeling partner, nodded ready from the other end of the arena.

The steer exploded from the chute, and Gage moved like he could read the animal's mind. His loop sailed through the air with devastating accuracy, and Ross's follow-up was lightning quick. The crowd fell silent as the flagman dropped his flag.

"Six point eight seconds!" The announcer's excitement was contagious. "Ladies and gentlemen, that puts Gage West and Ross Sanderson in the lead!"

The crowd erupted, and Sadie clapped harder than anyone. Laura elbowed her ribs gently.

"Could you be any more obvious?"

"Oh, hush," Sadie replied, but she couldn't keep the smile from her face.

As the competition continued, the tension mounted. Teams were eliminated until only two remained for the final round. Both Mitch and Gage had qualified, and the energy in the arena was electric.

Mitch's determination was visible in every line of his body as he waited for the signal. The steer burst out, and Mitch's horse leaped forward. His loop was perfect—almost too perfect, as if he was performing for the crowd rather than focusing on efficiency. The extra flourish cost him precious seconds.

"Seven point five seconds!" The announcer called. "A strong run from Monarch and Lewis!"

Mitch's frustration was visible as he guided his horse out of the arena, his jaw clenched tight. Sadie felt a pang of sympathy for her childhood friend.

"Last up, Gage West and Ross Sanderson!"

Sadie's hands gripped the wood rail as Gage rode into position. The arena fell quiet, the only sound the soft snort of horses and the creak of leather.

"I'm nervous," Sadie whispered.

Laura squeezed her arm. "Girl... you and me both."

The steer burst from the chute, and Gage moved with the same confidence he brought to everything he did. His loop seemed to float through the air in slow motion before settling perfectly around the steer's horns. Ross's heeling shot was equally precise, and they brought the steer down with practiced ease.

"Six point five seconds!" The announcer's voice rang with excitement. "Ladies and gentlemen, we have our winners! Gage West and Ross Sanderson take first place in this year's team roping competition!"

The crowd erupted in cheers, and Sadie was caught up in the excitement, clapping until her hands stung. Laura's knowing grin went ignored as Sadie watched Gage dismount with characteristic grace, accepting congratulations with humble nods.

"Go congratulate him," Laura urged, giving Sadie a gentle push.

"I don't know—"

"Sadie Beaumont, if you don't go over there right now, I'm going to start singing 'Kiss the Girl' from The Little Mermaid at the top of my lungs."

"You wouldn't dare."

Laura took a deep breath, and Sadie quickly held up her hands in surrender. "Okay, okay! I'm going!"

She made her way through the crowd, her heart picking up speed with each step. Gage was just finishing securing his horse when she approached.

"Congratulations," she said, proud that her voice came out steady.

He turned, and the smile that crossed his face made her breath catch. "Thanks. Glad you came to watch."

"I wouldn't have missed it."

"Felt like I had a guardian angel in my corner," he said.

Heat bloomed in Sadie's cheeks.

Mitch appeared beside them, his expression tight but controlled.

"Nice roping," he said to Gage, though the words seemed to cost him. "I want a re-do in the near future."

"Mitch," Sadie warned, but Gage held up a hand.

"You rode and roped well, Mitch. That first catch of yours was something else."

The simple praise, delivered without condescension, seemed to take some of the fight out of Mitch. He nodded once, then turned to Sadie. "Save me a dance later?"

"Probably not a good idea," she replied carefully.

Mitch's lips pressed into a thin line, but he walked away without another word.

"Thank you, Sadie," Gage said

"For what?"

"Just for being here," he said. "For coming over and congratulating me. I'm not used to that."

Someone called Gage's name for the award presentation. He stepped back, tipping his hat with a slight smile, and moved toward the gathering crowd.

Laura materialized at Sadie's side, practically vibrating with excitement. "Well? What happened? What did he say? Why are you blushing?"

"I'm not blushing," Sadie protested, but she could feel the warmth in her cheeks.

"Sadie," Laura said, "I've never seen you look at anyone the way you look at him."

"I'm scared, Laura," Sadie admitted quietly. "He's never had a stable life. What if I get too close? What if... what if he leaves? That's what cowboys like him do, isn't it? What if he breaks my heart?"

"And what if he doesn't?" Laura said.

Chapter 23

The festival lights blazed bright against the deepening navy sky as Gage and Ross stood at the center of attention, their horses beside them, while an enthusiastic audience snapped picture after picture. Even Gage, who mostly tried to stay out of the spotlight, couldn't suppress the smile tugging at his lips. The crowd's energy was electric, surging through him as he held the championship trophy in his hands. For the first time in years, he felt a spark of pride and belonging—real and undeniable.

Ross leaned on his saddle horn beside him, his grin wide. "Alright, Gage, which one of these fine folks do you think is going to paint our heroics across the front page of tomorrow's paper? That pretty lady in the red dress looks like she's ready to write us straight into local legend history."

Gage chuckled, tipping his hat toward the woman, who immediately blushed and looked down at her notepad. "Not sure if I'm cut out to be a legend, Ross. Might be more your speed."

"Don't sell yourself short, partner," Ross shot back, adjusting his hold on his reins. "After that run we just had, there's probably a little boy out there naming his stuffed horse after you as we speak."

"You're full of it," Gage replied, shaking his head, though the corners of his mouth curved into a wider smile.

The announcer waved for another round of applause, and more cameras clicked and flashed as Gage shifted uncomfortably on his feet. His gaze wandered over the crowd, naturally honing in on familiar faces from Eagle's Nest Ranch. Jack and Harriet stood off to one side, Jack giving him a subtle nod of approval while Harriet beamed with pride. Laura was laughing at something Sadie whispered into her ear, but it was Sadie herself who drew his full attention.

She was radiant. Her blue summer dress catching the light as she clapped along with the crowd. Sadie's smile reached him like the first warm rays of sunlight after a bitter winter, piercing straight through the shadows he'd carried for so long. It wasn't just her beauty that struck him—though she had a way of lighting up a room without trying—it was the calm assurance in her eyes, the quiet strength in the way she moved through the world as if she belonged to it and it to her. Gage's chest tightened, unfamiliar but undeniable, a pull so sharp it almost took him by surprise.

He didn't do permanence; he didn't do "staying." Always, there had been the next town, the next job, the next empty horizon to chase. But tonight, standing there under the festival lights, all he could think about was stepping closer, closing the space between them. For the first time, the idea of staying still didn't feel like confinement; it felt like freedom—because it meant staying near her.

"Alright, cowboy, time's up," Ross said with a nudge to Gage's arm. "They're gonna want us off this stage eventually, and I don't think standing here lost in thought is gonna charm anybody."

Snapped out of his daze, Gage nodded and turned toward the festival organizers. He handed off the trophy for safekeeping and gave a few polite thank-yous before leading Bandit toward the path out of the arena. Ross followed close behind as they moved toward the stables.

"You were quiet back there," Ross remarked as he swung his leg over and dismounted. His boots hit the ground with a solid thud. "That trophy too heavy, or was the crowd just too much for the ever-aloof Gage West?"

Gage smirked, but didn't take the bait. "Just not the type to soak up attention, that's all."

"Uh-huh. So... what's the deal with you and Sadie?"

Gage shot him a half-hearted glare as he guided Bandit into a stall. "Drop it, Ross."

Ross raised his hands in mock surrender. "Alright, alright. But in case I haven't said it in a while, Gage—when it comes to women, playing it cool isn't always the winning hand."

Gage muttered something about knowing his own business, but before Ross could needle him further, the sound of approaching boots interrupted their banter.

"Evenin', boys." The voice was deep and smooth, with just the right amount of polish to make it clear the speaker wasn't your average ranch hand. Gage turned to see a broad-shouldered man striding toward them, his boots freshly shined and his silver tie clip glinting under the stable's lantern light.

He tipped his wide-brimmed hat and extended a hand, first to Ross, then to Gage. "Clayton Brant. Watched the competition and figured I'd come congratulate the two top-notch cowboys who stole the show."

"Appreciate it," Ross said.

Clayton's smile was confident. "I don't believe in missing an opportunity to connect with talent when I see it."

Gage raised an eyebrow. "That right?"

"Sure is." Clayton's gaze shifted between both of them. "You boys mind if we talk? Got a little business proposition I believe you'll want to hear."

Ross glanced at Gage, his curiosity clearly piqued. Gage gave a small nod and leaned back against the stable wall, crossing his arms over his chest but saying nothing, signaling the man to go on.

Clayton wasted no time diving in. "I run the Triple 8 Ranch, which neighbor's the Eagle's Nest Ranch on the north." His movements were deliberate as he brushed invisible dust from his jacket sleeve. "We've been growing steadily over the past few years—best cattle contracts in the region, not to mention state-of-the-art equipment. And none of that's possible without good cowboys. Folks like you two. Name your skill. We've likely got a better way to make sure it's used—and compensated—properly."

Ross let out a low whistle. "State-of-the-art equipment, huh? Sounds expensive."

"It is." Clayton's voice didn't miss a beat. "But that's where our edge lies. We're not afraid to invest in the best—and reward the best for getting the job done right."

"What exactly are you proposing?" Gage asked, his voice calm but measured. He wasn't one to bite on a hook without knowing exactly how sharp it was.

"I want both of you," Clayton said simply. "Full-time positions at Triple 8. You'll each make a good salary—probably a good twenty percent more than what you're making at Eagle's Nest. On top of that, you'll have access to year-end bonuses, four-day work weeks, and an air-conditioned bunkhouse for when the summer heat gets too unbearable."

Ross blinked and let out a laugh, shaking his head as he muttered, "An air-conditioned bunkhouse? You're definitely playing cards I've never seen on the table before."

Clayton flashed a grin. "Just wait until you see the operation in person. It's ranching like you've never known it."

Gage stayed quiet, his instincts warring with each other. On the one hand, the offer would've been a no-brainer for him not long ago—better pay, more perks, fewer strings attached. But since coming to Eagle's Nest, something had shifted in his way of thinking. He didn't know what to call it, or maybe he was too afraid to name it, but he knew that leaving Eagle's Nest ranch wouldn't be easy, no matter how sweet the deal.

"You make it sound like paradise," Ross said, though his tone had turned serious. "But what's the catch? Every job's got one."

Clayton gave a half-shrug, the picture of casual sincerity. "No catch. Just a fair paycheck for honest work. My one rule? Commitment. I run a tight ship, and I need to know the people on it are loyal to see it succeed."

"Loyalty's earned, not bought," Gage said, his voice low. He kept his arms crossed, and while his posture was calm, there was an unmistakable edge to his tone.

Clayton met Gage's gaze, his smile not faltering, but his eyes narrowing slightly. "And as an honest man yourself, Mr. West, I think you'd see I've earned more than most. But hey, no rush to decide. Both of you are welcome to come out to Triple 8 anytime. Say Sunday afternoon—I'll give you the full tour."

"Generous offer," Ross said, ever the diplomat. "We'll give it some thought."

"You do that," Clayton said, slipping two business cards from his pocket and offering one to Gage, then Ross. "When you're ready, call me."

With a final tip of his hat, Clayton strode out of the stable, his polished boots crunching against the dirt as he disappeared into the night.

Ross let out a low breath, studying the card in his hand. "Well, that's somethin' you don't get every day."

"Nope," Gage replied simply, slipping the card into his pocket.

Ross turned to him, his expression wry. "Got any thoughts?"

Gage shrugged. "Seems slick. A little too slick."

"Fair." Ross nodded, then added, "But higher pay is higher pay. And air conditioning."

Gage smirked, closing Bandit's stall gates. "You can survive summers without air. People been doin' it for generations."

Ross fell into step beside him, eyeing him sideways. "You're deflectin'."

"Not really."

"Uh-huh. Just promise me you'll actually think about it. No harm in takin' a tour." Ross slapped Gage on the back before splitting off toward the festival lights. "If nothing else, maybe they'll feed us real well during the visit. Fancy ranches like that always do."

The old Gage would've jumped at the offer without hesitation, eager for the freedom to drift somewhere new. But now? Now there was Sadie. Her laughter. The way she looked at him, like she saw something more than just a cowboy passing through town.

Chapter 24

The twang of fiddles and steady thrum of guitars filled the evening air as Sadie watched her parents sway together on the makeshift dance floor. Her father held her mother close, whispering something that made Harriet throw her head back in laughter, their decades of love evident in every shared movement and secret smile.

"Your dad's still got those two-stepping skills down pat," Laura remarked, bumping Sadie's shoulder playfully. "Who knew Jack Beaumont could be such a smooth operator?"

Sadie smiled as she watched. "They've been dancing together since high school. Mom says Dad used to practice in the barn when he thought no one was watching."

"Now that's dedication," Laura said, her eyes twinkling. "Though I bet he wasn't the only Beaumont practicing dance moves in that barn."

Heat crept up Sadie's neck. "I have no idea what you're talking about."

"Oh please, I caught you more than once trying to perfect your line dancing form when we were teenagers. What was it you said? Something about proper footwork being essential to—"

"To maintaining dignity during social functions," Sadie finished, laughing despite herself. "I was fifteen and had just read Pride and Prejudice for the first time."

"And now look at you," Laura gestured toward the dance floor. "Standing here while perfectly good music goes to waste."

Sadie's gaze drifted across the festival grounds, unconsciously searching for a certain tall figure in a black Stetson. "I'm just enjoying the atmosphere."

"Mm-hmm. The atmosphere. That's what we're calling him now?"

Mitch appeared beside them, his boots clicking against the wooden platform. "Evening, ladies."

"Hey, big brother," Laura greeted him.

"You look real nice tonight, Sadie," Mitch said, his voice carrying an undercurrent of something possessive that made her shoulders tense. "That blue dress suits you."

"Thank you, Mitch." Sadie's reply was polite but measured.

"You know, I was thinking about that roping competition earlier," he continued, shifting closer. "Sure, West may have won this round, but I've been working on some new techniques. Next time—"

"Mitch," Laura interrupted, "maybe we could talk about something other than roping? The band's actually playing one of your favorite songs."

Mitch's attention remained fixed on Sadie. He extended his hand, a confident smile playing at his lips. "How about a dance?"

Sadie hesitated, her stomach knotting. Over Mitch's shoulder, she caught sight of Gage making his way through the crowd, and her heart skipped.

"I appreciate the offer, Mitch, but—"

"Come on, Sadie," he pressed, reaching for her hand. "Just one dance."

She pulled back instinctively, just as Gage reached them. His presence seemed to change the very air around them, and Sadie felt herself relax slightly.

"Evening, folks," Gage said.

Mitch's jaw tightened.

"Mitch," Laura warned, but he was already reaching for Sadie's hand again.

"How about that dance now?" His tone had lost its earlier charm, replaced by something harder.

Before Sadie could step back, Gage moved smoothly between them. "I believe the answers no, Mitch."

The tension crackled between the two men, and Sadie held her breath.

Laura moved in, her small hand wrapping firmly around her brother's arm.

"That's enough," she said, her voice carrying unusual authority. "Mitch, you're embarrassing yourself. Come on—you and I need to have a talk."

For a moment, Mitch looked like he might argue, but Laura's grip tightened. "Now, brother."

As Laura led Mitch away, Sadie released a shaky breath. "Thank you," she said.

Gage turned to face her, his expression softening. "You okay?"

"Yes, I just..." she gestured vaguely at the retreating siblings. "I hate things are awkward with Mitch. We've been friends forever, but lately..."

"He wants more than friendship," Gage finished. His blue eyes studied her face carefully. "Can't say I blame him."

The band struck up another slow tune, and Gage's lips curved into a smile as he extended his hand to Sadie.

Sadie placed her hand in his, trying to ignore how perfectly their hands seemed to fit together. "I thought you couldn't dance?"

"Maybe I just need the right partner."

He led her onto the dance floor, and to Sadie's surprise, his movements were sure and graceful as he pulled her into his arms. They fell into step with the music, and Sadie relaxed into his embrace.

"You've been holding out on me, Mr. West," she said, looking up at him. "Where did you learn to dance like this?"

"Foster mom number three. She taught ballroom dancing, said every gentleman should know how to lead a lady properly." He spun her in a smooth turn. "Course, I wasn't much interested in being a gentleman back then."

"And now?"

His arms tightened slightly around her. "Now I'm seeing the appeal."

Sadie could feel the curious glances from other dancers, could practically hear tomorrow's gossip spreading through town, but she didn't care.

"I'm still trying to figure you out, Gage West. Every time I think I have you pegged, you surprise me."

"Is that a good thing?"

"I'm thinking it might be." She smiled up at him. "Though I have to admit, finding out you can dance is a bit shocking. What other hidden talents are you keeping secret?"

His laugh rumbled through his chest. "Well, I make a mean apple pie over an open campfire, but if you tell anyone, I'll deny it completely."

"A cowboy who can bake? Now I know you're just making things up."

"Cross my heart," he said, his eyes twinkling. "Though fair warning—my crust is nowhere near as good as Madge's."

"Whose is?" Sadie chuckled. "I think she has some secret recipe passed down through generations."

The song drew to a close, but neither of them moved to step apart. Around them, the festival continued in full swing—children darting here and there with sparklers, couples sharing funnel cakes, teenagers trying to win prizes at game booths. But in that moment, it felt like they were in their own world.

They moved in perfect harmony, swaying effortlessly to the gentle melody of the band's next song.

Chapter 25

The barn was already bustling as the first streaks of daylight edged the Montana sky. Sadie stood at the center of the activity, clipboard in hand, her pencil tapping lightly against its edge as she scouted the operation. Everyone was moving with purpose, the brisk tempo of boots on dirt and the occasional thud of hay bales dropping into place underscoring the urgency of the day. Dust hung in the air, but Sadie scarcely noticed as her mind ran through the list of tasks before her.

"All right, listen up, everyone!" Her voice carried above the commotion, pausing most movement in the yard. "Drought conditions make this one of those all hands on deck days. We've got livestock in every pasture depending on us for feed and water, so teamwork is key."

She glanced around, meeting each set of eyes—tired, maybe, but attentive. Ranch hands were like that, she'd discovered over years of working alongside them. Direct, responsive, and always willing to give their best when rallied. Her father had taught her early that a team worked best when it trusted the person giving orders. And so, she took a steadying breath and channeled the confidence she hoped would keep morale high.

"Pete, I need you on the water truck all day," she said. The older ranch hand adjusted his hat and nodded.

"The rest of us will focus on hay. Mitch, Gage, Ross, Julie—you four are on loading duty. We'll all work the pastures together, starting with the east and moving clockwise to hit them all. Once we finish a pasture, we head back here to reload. Got it?"

There was a chorus of acknowledgments, Ross tipping his hat with a playful wink.

Sadie rolled her eyes but smiled despite herself. "Rusty, keep them honest," she said to the dog, whose tail wagged furiously at being included in the day's strategy.

The ranch hands scattered, each taking their assignments in stride, and the thunder of work resumed at a feverish pace. Sadie tucked the clipboard under her arm and headed toward the barn to double-check the hay supplies, her mind already skipping ahead to how they'd conserve water between pastures.

As she passed one truck, a thrumming hum tickled the edge of her awareness. It wasn't the sound of machinery or the workers, but something closer. Mitch's low whistle cut through the shuffle of her thoughts.

"Sadie, got a minute?" His tone was tame, almost casual, but there was an undercurrent that told her the conversation wasn't about hauling hay bales or filling water troughs.

Sadie turned, spotting Mitch leaning against the trailer hitch with his hands shoved into his jean pockets. She hesitated. There was work to do, but she wasn't hard-hearted enough to brush him off, not when his expression spoke more to someone looking for a lifeline than a fight. "Sure," she said, folding her arms loosely and standing just far enough to signal her boundaries. "What's on your mind?"

Mitch sighed, kicking lightly at the dirt beneath his boots, and for a moment, the normally self-assured man looked almost boyish. "Look, I owe you an apology—for the festival. I acted like a fool, and I know I embarrassed you."

Sadie arched her brows, surprised by his straightforwardness. "You're right, you did." She didn't soften her words, though her expression remained calm. "So why did you act that way?"

He rubbed the back of his neck, the corner of his mouth twitching downward. "I guess... I don't know. Maybe I was jealous. It felt like you were slipping away from the way things used to be. Like..."

"Like what?" she pressed, her voice gentle but firm.

"Like maybe you've already made a choice, and it's not me," he admitted, glancing up at her, vulnerability flickering in his eyes.

Sadie's heart ached for him—not with romantic longing, but with the sting of knowing you couldn't give someone what they wanted. "Mitch," she began slowly, "we've known each other a long time. And that history means a lot to me. But whatever you're hoping for or thinking might happen? That's not us. I need you to understand that."

He gave a hollow chuckle, then nodded. "I get it. It just—it's hard, you know? You're... well, you're Sadie. Everyone—"

"Stop." She held up a hand. "You can't see me as some ideal you're chasing. Whatever version of me you're holding to does not exist. I'm just Sadie. And you're Mitch. And the friendship between us still matters, but only if we respect what it really is. Just friends."

He exhaled sharply, his shoulders losing some of their tension. Then he extended a hand, managing a faint smile. "I won't ever put you in that position again. Deal?"

Sadie clasped his hand with a firm shake. "Deal."

Mitch lingered a beat too long before nodding and stepping away.

Sadie turned back toward the barn, her gaze catching on Gage, standing framed in the doorway. A bale of hay rested effortlessly on his broad shoulder, his stance half-shrouded under the barn's overhang. His hat was tipped low over his brow, and his sleeves were rolled up against the day's heat, revealing sinewy forearms.

But it wasn't just the rugged ease of him that made her steps falter—it was the way his deep, unreadable eyes locked onto hers. There was a grin tugging at the corners of his mouth, subtle and unspoken, yet impossible to miss. And as warmth rose to her cheeks, Sadie knew there was no mistaking the effect he had on her.

Mitch, however, wasn't quite finished gathering forgiveness or stirring trouble. With Sadie's clear refusal still fresh in his mind, he approached Gage with the swagger of a man trying to mask his bruised pride.

"You got a second?" Mitch asked, strolling over as Gage dropped the bale of hay on the trailer. Wiping the sweat from his brow, Gage turned fully, meeting Mitch's steely expression with one that was perfectly neutral.

"Sure," Gage replied.

"Look, I didn't mean to come across so... aggressive at the festival last night. Sometimes a man gets ahead of himself," he said.

Gage merely nodded, his hands resting casually at his sides as he waited for what was coming. He didn't have to wait long.

Mitch's voice carried an edge, his smugness barely concealed as he leaned in just enough to close the gap. "Sadie's been in my life for as long as I can remember," he said, his eyes narrowing. "If you treat her wrong, you'll answer to me. You get that?" He glanced over his shoulder, scanning the area until his gaze landed on Sadie, his stance shifting slightly. When he turned back, his tone softened, though the tension lingered beneath the surface. "I was out of line last night. Let's call it water under the bridge, yeah?" His smile didn't quite reach his eyes, the apology as much about appearances as anything else.

Gage's lips twitched. "No hard feelings on my end, so long as you do the same."

There, in the loaded silence that followed, the difference between the two men seemed to stretch like the banks of the winding river near the ranch: one, trying to force respect where it hadn't yet been earned; the other, letting character speak louder than words.

As Mitch stalked off, Gage returned to the barn to grab more hay, his jaw set.

Chapter 26

As dusk painted the sky in hues of amber and rose, the ranch hands and the Beaumont family gathered behind the barn for a well-earned meal. The aroma of sizzling burgers and grilled vegetables wafted through the air as Madge worked skillfully over the propane grill and griddle, her laughter peppering the lively conversations around her. The crew, dusty and weary from the day's labor, was eagerly filling their plates with seconds before settling back onto hay bales or at picnic tables with a shared sense of camaraderie.

Sadie stood next to Gage, resting against the wooden fence, their elbows brushing just slightly as they gazed out at the horizon.

"Long day," she murmured, more to herself than him.

"Long but good," he replied, his voice steady. "We got done what needed doing."

"Tell me something," Sadie said. "Do you enjoy working here? Really like it, I mean?"

Gage shifted his weight, his arms crossing over the top rail as he glanced at her. "Why do you ask?"

"Because I need to know," Sadie replied, her voice steady but laced with something unspoken—a mix of uncertainty and hope. She turned to face him, her blonde hair framing her face in the fading light. "There are changes coming in the future here on the ranch. Some big ones."

His brow furrowed. "Changes?"

She nodded, hesitating for a moment before continuing. "I can't say too much just yet—there's a lot my parents and I still need to figure out. But what I can tell you is... we're building toward something different. And I guess I just need to know where you stand."

Gage's focus shifted back to the pasture, where the faint silhouettes of horses grazed beneath the sprawling opulence of the night sky. Her question wasn't just about work. He could hear it—the need for clarity, not just about the ranch, but about him.

"Do I enjoy working here?" he said. "Yeah, I do. Eagle's Nest isn't just a typical job. It's different from any place I've ever been. You... your family... this land..." He trailed off, flexing his hands against the wood as he searched for the right words. "It's got a hold on me."

Sadie studied him, her hazel eyes soft but unwavering. "Do you see a future here?" she pressed gently. "Not just for the ranch... but for yourself?"

Gage swallowed hard. All his instincts—the ones that had told him for years to keep his guard up, to avoid getting tethered down—kicked in. He thought of Clayton Brant's offer, the promise of a bigger paycheck and an easier life. But then his mind drifted back to moments like these: the quiet pride in Jack's eyes, the warm meals cooked by Madge, Harriet humming an old hymn as she cooked and cleaned alongside Madge. And Sadie—always Sadie. The thought of her brought a pull in his chest he couldn't ignore.

"I don't have all the answers, Sadie," he admitted, his voice low. "But I know this much. Working here? Being here? It feels more right than I ever thought it could. And that's saying something for a man who's spent most of his life running from anything that looks like roots."

The corner of her mouth pulled into a faint, hopeful smile. "That's something, at least."

He glanced sideways, catching the way her fingers toyed with the edge of her turquoise pendant, a familiar gesture he'd come to recognize as her working things out in her mind. "You said there'd be changes. What kind of changes are we talking about?"

Sadie hesitated before letting out a quiet laugh, shaking her head. "You know, you're not the only one trying to figure things out, cowboy. I wish I had it all mapped out—what the ranch will look like in ten years, where I'll be, even who I'll be. But right now, all I know for sure is this place needs to change if it's going to survive. And so do I."

Her honesty unraveled something inside him. "If I've learned one thing since getting here, it's that this ranch has a way of pulling people closer, to the land, to the work, to each other. Whatever changes may be coming, I'm sure they'll be for the better."

Sadie turned toward him fully, the distance between them as slight as the breeze rustling the nearby aspen trees. "Well," she said, a hint of playfulness returning to her voice, "if you're planning on sticking around a little while longer, I'd say you're already a part of that pull."

The way she looked at him just then—with a mixture of strength and tenderness that mirrored everything he admired about her—called to a part of him he hadn't known existed until that moment. He reached over and rested his calloused hand on hers.

Her breath hitched at the contact, and she didn't pull away.

Sadie's smile turned playful as she teased, "Careful, Gage. Stick around much longer, and you might just find yourself putting down roots."

"Maybe roots aren't such a bad thing after all," he said.

"Sadie, Gage," her father called out from behind them.

Sadie reluctantly drew back from Gage, her smile softening as she turned to face her father.

"Yes, Daddy?" she asked, brushing a strand of hair from her face as the warm evening breeze teased it.

Jack gave Gage a measured look before turning his focus fully to his daughter. "Mind if I have a quick word with you, sweetheart?"

Gage, ever observant, tipped his hat with an easy, respectful gesture. Without a word, he turned and walked away.

Jack turned his attention to his daughter, his expression equal parts pride and concern. "It's been a long day, Sadie. You handled everything well. What's the plan for tomorrow?"

Sadie shifted her weight, brushing a stray strand of hair behind her ear. "Well, Daddy, we're running low on hay and feed, and the whole county's in the same boat. The delivery truck can't make it out until later this week, so I'm planning to drive into town with the truck and trailer to pick up a load. I'll probably have one of the ranch hands follow me with another truck and trailer so we can bring back as much as possible."

Jack nodded thoughtfully. "Smart plan. This drought's got me worried, though. I haven't seen one this bad since you were just a little girl."

Sadie reached across the table and gave his hand a reassuring pat. "We'll manage, Daddy. Lord willing, we'll get through this."

Jack squeezed her hand gently, his mind already working through details. "Alright, here's what I'm thinking. You take Gage with you in one truck, and Mitch and Ross can run the other. Make sure both trailers are loaded to the limit. While you're gone, Pete, Julie, and I will take the feed and water trucks out to the herds. We'll keep things running on this end."

Sadie nodded, her steady hazel gaze meeting his. "Sounds like a plan. I'll leave first thing in the morning."

Jack stared at her for a moment, pride flickering in his tired eyes. "You're your mother's daughter, through and through. Always one step ahead."

Sadie smiled softly. "I learned from the best."

"While you're in town, make sure to grab some lunch before heading back. I want you ready to hit the ground running afterward," he said, his voice firm but kind.

"Got it, Dad," Sadie replied.

Jack studied her for a long moment, his silence carrying the weight of unspoken thoughts. "Have you thought about who's going to step in as foreman once you're ready to step back?"

She hesitated briefly before answering. "I'm working on it. I've got two ranch hands in mind, but nothing's set in stone yet."

Jack crossed his arms, his gaze steady. "And who might those two be?"

Sadie turned the question back to him, her tone gentle. "Actually, I'd like to hear your thoughts first, Dad. Who do you think would be the right fit?"

Jack rubbed his chin thoughtfully, his weathered features creasing in a way that showed both pride and deliberation. He glanced over toward the barn, where the faint glow of a lantern outlined the bustle of the ranch hands finishing their chores. "Well," he began, his voice steady but introspective, "Pete's been here the longest. He's solid.

Always dependable, knows how to rally a team without raising his voice. There's a steadiness about him folks respect."

Sadie nodded, her father's assessment aligning with her own thoughts. "True. Pete's got the experience, and he's good with people. But he has mentioned before he likes his job and has no interest in moving up in position."

Jack nodded. "He's told me that in the past as well, but a man can change his mind. What about Gage? There's something different about Gage. Strong. Determined. I have a good feeling about him. Even so, his history of moving job-to-job bothers me. Nevertheless... he's different."

Her attempts at a neutral expression faltered slightly, but she quickly recovered. "Different how?"

"He's green when it comes to how we run things here—not a fault of his, mind you, just a fact. But the way that boy works? Grit in spades. And there's something in his eyes, something I can't quite name... like he's been carrying a heavy load on his back for a long time and is finally starting to put it down. That kind of struggle teaches a man resilience. I've seen him out in the fields with the horses and cattle. He has a quiet touch that goes deeper than skill—it's instinct. That's rare."

Sadie felt her heart knot at her father's words. Gage had indeed started to ease into life at Eagle's Nest, though his pace wasn't always as quick or polished as Pete's. Still, her dad wasn't wrong—there was a presence to Gage, a silent intensity that spoke of wounds healing and strength being forged through fire. An intensity that demanded respect. He had the qualities of a leader.

Jack turned his attention back to her, his sharp eyes searching hers like he was looking for something more than just her response. "But here's the thing, Sadie. A foreman's not just about hard work, instinct, or even loyalty. It's about trust—trust that they'll stick through the lean seasons, through the fights with suppliers, through tough calls that might rub people wrong. And trust that they care about this place as much as I do." His voice softened just slightly. "My question is, do you think Gage West could find that kind of belonging here? Because once I step back and retire, you'll be the one he'll need to answer to."

Sadie hesitated, her father's question reverberating in her mind. Did she believe in Gage? Could he see Eagle's Nest not as just another stop in his journey, but as a place to plant roots?

"I think he could, Daddy," she said. Her voice grew more confident as she met her father's gaze. "But he's never had a place like this before—a place worth staying for. If we help him see it, if we give him the space to believe it's where he's meant to be... then yes, I think Gage could grow into a role like that."

Jack studied her a moment longer, then nodded gruffly, his approval subtle but unmistakable. "Alright, Sadie. I trust your instincts on this. Just make sure you take your time and think it through. Foreman or not, a man like Gage might need more than a job to keep him tethered."

Sadie felt her cheeks heat as she brushed a stray lock of hair from her face.

"I'll think it through," she promised.

"Have you given much thought to how the other ranch hands might take your final decision?"

"I have," Sadie replied, her brow furrowing slightly. "Honestly, Pete's the kind of guy who'll take it in stride, no matter who is chosen. He's steady and level-headed—he won't kick up dust over it. Julie's still green and learning the ropes, so I don't think she'd have any reason to protest, either. And as for Ross," she paused, a small smile tugging at the corner of her mouth, "well, he's a good hand, but he's still got some maturing to do. He's a bit too carefree right now to take on the responsibility of foreman."

"And Mitch?" Jack asked, his tone shifting to something more serious.

Sadie sighed, her expression darkening just a little. "Mitch is the thorn in all this. He's got the experience, sure, and he works hard, but his arrogance, and that need to be the center of attention, rubs many people the wrong way. It drives me up a wall sometimes, especially when he gets competitive with the other hands. I can't deny he's capable, he's a good worker, but..." her voice softened, "if Gage were chosen, I can see Mitch raising a fuss. His jealousy as of late is an issue, and... well, it's been hard to ignore."

"Well, let's start setting things in motion," he said with a nod. "Tomorrow, after you return from picking up supplies in town, radio me to let me know you're back. Then we'll have a quick meeting in the bunkhouse. I'll inform everyone about the upcoming changes here on the ranch. Let's get things rolling."

Jack offered her a smile, giving her shoulder a gentle pat before heading back toward the others.

"That's it, Daddy?" she called after him, a mix of curiosity and surprise in her tone. "No more advice or thoughts on this?"

He stopped mid-step, glancing back with a knowing smile. "No need for any, cowgirl," he said, his voice steady and full of quiet confidence. "You've already got it figured out."

Chapter 27

Sadie shifted in her seat at the Bluebird Café, trying to rub some of the day's exhaustion out of her shoulders. Across from her, Mitch ate his meal in silence. Gage relaxed, calm and cool, sat beside her, lost in his thoughts. Ross, meanwhile, was as boisterous as ever, tearing into his cheeseburger like he hadn't eaten in days. "I don't know how Lillian keeps up with all those customers," he muttered through a bite of food. "I'm flat-out exhausted just watching her. I wish I had half her energy."

Sadie nodded, her fork pausing halfway to her mouth. "Honestly? Same here."

Lillian appeared at their table, her coffee pot poised. She practically danced into their quiet lunch scene, her bright red bandana tied snugly over her curls, and a knowing twinkle in her eyes.

"Well, well," she said, pouring more coffee into Mitch's cup first. "I don't think I've ever seen y'all this quiet. And judging by the look on your faces, I'd say the ranch is feeling the burn of this dry spell, just like the rest of us."

"It's not just our ranch, Lillian. It's all the ranches in the area." Sadie said.

"Saw on the news early this morning, the good Lord might send us some rain soon. They're calling for storm clouds by the end of the week," Lillian said.

Across the table, Mitch let out a low, disbelieving grunt. "Well, we've all seen storms tease the valley and change their minds, so I'll believe it when I see it."

Lillian set the pot down with a little more force than necessary, fixing Mitch with a playful glare that only she could pull off. "I might not hold a degree in meteorology, sweet pea, but I've been right about the weather more times than your boots have been scuffed. And I dare say my prayers might have a little pull."

Sadie chuckled. The heat of the past few weeks had pressed down on the ranch like a hand squeezing dry soil, and it was hard not to feel a nagging sort of doubt about relief ever arriving.

"Even if it comes," Mitch said cautiously, "Will it be enough? Pastures are getting harder to rotate, and the creeks are running low."

"We'll figure it out," Sadie replied firmly. "One storm won't fix the county's drought, but it'll give us something to work with."

Lillian smiled, admiration in her gaze. "That's the Beaumont way—always thinking a step ahead. That's why your family's been the heart of this valley since before half of us were born. You remind me a lot of your granddaddy, so much, you know."

Sadie blushed, deflecting the praise with a soft laugh. "Thanks, Lillian. But it's going to take more than one family to keep this valley afloat. We may all have to band together and help one another whenever possible."

"True enough," Lillian agreed, pouring the last of her pot into Gage's cup. "Y'all enjoy your lunch."

She winked and disappeared.

The cafe door swung open, and a tall figure strode in, commanding attention not with volume but with presence. Clayton Brant.

Everything about him seemed designed to catch the eye—the crispness of his shirt, the polished boots, the confident way he adjusted his hat as his gaze scanned the room. The moment Gage spotted him, Sadie noticed his jaw tighten, the knuckles around his coffee cup white for just a second before he forced himself to relax.

Ross was less subtle. He froze mid-bite, his fork hovering in the air like he'd just seen the prize bull escape its pen.

Sadie's curiosity was immediate. "Alright, what's got you two looking like a pair of raccoons caught in the henhouse?"

Gage glanced briefly at Ross, who looked like he might choke on his burger before finally leaning back, hands raised in theatrical surrender. "Don't look at me. He's all yours, cowboy."

That earned him a sharp glare from Gage, but Sadie cut in before it went any further. "What?"

For a beat, Gage said nothing, his expression unreadable. Finally, he set his cup down and leaned in toward her, his voice low enough to keep their conversation between the four of them at their table. "He made us a job offer."

Sadie blinked, her mind working to process the sudden shift in information. "Clayton Brant... made you both a job offer?"

Ross coughed dramatically, clearly hoping to derail the conversation. "It's really not that big of a—"

"Ross!" Sadie shot him a warning look, her hazel eyes narrowing.

"Alright, alright!" he relented, throwing his hands up. "It was after the roping competition at the festival. He caught us off guard, said we did good work, and threw some other fancy words our way. But it's not like we said yes."

"No," Gage added firmly, his voice calm but serious. "We didn't say yes. But I should've said something to you sooner."

Sadie stared at him, a thousand questions bubbling under the surface. She could see the regret in his face, hear the sincerity in his voice, yet there was still that nagging sense of betrayal. "Why didn't you?"

Gage exhaled, his gaze steadfast on hers. "Because I didn't want you thinking I'd jump ship. I meant what I said, Sadie. I like working here. I didn't want to risk losing your trust."

Her brow furrowed, still conflicted. "Trust isn't something you protect by keeping secrets, Gage. You either Ross. You both should have come to Dad or me when Mr. Brant, that little weasel, tried to poach you with job offers."

"I know," Gage admitted, leaning back slightly. "And that's why I'm telling you now. No excuses."

Ross, sensing the tension, jumped in. "Sadie, we're still here working our tails off, aren't we? That's gotta count for something."

Sadie's lips twitched. "I suppose it does."

Clayton strode up to the table with his usual swagger. "Afternoon, boys," he greeted, a toothy grin spreading across his face as he tipped his hat toward the group, making a deliberate show of ignoring Sadie's presence.

Sadie arched a brow as her hazel eyes flicked upward to meet his. Standing with deliberate calm, her blonde waves catching the light in the cafe as she straightened to her full height.

"Well, isn't this a surprise," she said, her voice cool but laced with unmistaken resolve. "Nice to see you, Clayton."

Clayton's grin faltered, if only slightly, as his gaze darted toward her. There was a flicker of something behind his eyes that might have been embarrassment—or perhaps irritation. "Sadie," he finally said, drawing her name out slower than necessary. "Didn't see you there."

"Oh, I'm sure you didn't," she replied smoothly, folding her arms and tilting her head. "I suppose there's just too much to notice in one afternoon, huh?"

A low chuckle came from Gage's direction, and Clayton's gaze shifted to him, darkening slightly. Gage leaned back in his chair, a faint smirk playing on his lips. He didn't say a word, though—he didn't need to.

Clayton cleared his throat, shifting his stance. "So, Sadie," he said, plastering the charm back on like a second skin. "How's the ranch?"

Sadie's eyes narrowed ever so slightly, though her expression remained composed. "Everything's just fine, Clayton." She allowed a polite smile to rest on her lips—a smile that didn't quite make it to her eyes.

Clayton opened his mouth, likely to issue some retort, when Gage finally spoke, his tone unhurried but carrying a quiet authority that was impossible to ignore. "You need something, Clayton? Or are you just here to enjoy the scenery?"

The subtle jab prickled at Clayton, a muscle tightening in his jaw as he looked away momentarily before feigning disinterest. "Just passing by," he said, his voice clipped. "Thought I'd check in on you boys. See how y'all are doing."

"Well," Gage said, his smirk growing wider, "you've checked in."

Clayton's eyes snapped toward Gage, the faintest hint of a flush creeping up his neck. Before he could fire back, Sadie stepped in again, her voice cutting through the tension like the crisp sound of a whip cracking.

"Clayton," she said smoothly, her tone a masterclass in politeness layered with steel, "You can leave now."

It was a dismissal, plain and simple, though delivered with such grace that Clayton couldn't openly argue without appearing petulant.

So instead, he tipped his hat again—this time with a little less gusto—and forced a tight smile. "Of course. Always a pleasure, Sadie."

She nodded, her arms still folded. "You take care now."

Clayton hesitated for a second longer, his gaze flicking between Sadie and Gage, as though weighing whether there was anything more to say. But when Gage leaned forward ever so slightly, his smirk fading into something more serious, Clayton thought better of it. With a sharp turn on his heel, he walked off.

Gage chuckled and shook his head. "That one's full of hot air, isn't he?"

Sadie shrugged. "Men like Clayton only have as much power as you let them think they do." Her lips curved upward then, her expression brightening. "I've had plenty of practice with him."

"Sadie," Gage said.

"Yeah?" she asked.

"Never lose that fire in you," he said, his voice low but firm, each word weighted with sincerity. She was a paradox he couldn't help but marvel at, a steady breeze when calm was needed, a decisive leader when chaos arose, and, at her core, as untamed and breathtakingly bold as a wild mustang. Every moment with her revealed another layer, and each one left him in awe.

Chapter 28

Gage leaned against the dining room wall in the bunkhouse, arms folded, his gaze steady as he watched Pete, Mitch, Julie, and Ross settle at the long wooden table. Pete thumbed through a well-worn deck of cards, shuffling absentmindedly, while Julie sat next to him, her hands wrapped around a steaming mug of coffee.

Mitch sat slightly apart from the rest, his chair angled back on two legs, boots propped on the edge of the table. His eyes flickered with impatience, the set of his jaw revealing a simmering agitation.

Sadie stood in the doorway, the sunlight catching in her blonde hair and casting a halo around her.

"Any idea what this is about?" Julie said to Pete, her eyes darting toward Sadie.

Pete shrugged, his expression unreadable. "Could be anything. Best to wait and see."

Before the speculation could grow, Jack Beaumont stepped inside. The soft conversation among the ranch hands ceased instantly.

"Afternoon, folks," Jack greeted, his deep voice filling the space. He removed his hat, dusting off a hint of dust before settling it on the peg by the door.

"Boss," Pete replied, the other hands echoing the sentiment with nods and murmurs.

Jack moved to the head of the table, his presence commanding yet calm. Sadie took a place beside him, her posture straight, hands clasped in front of her.

"I appreciate you all gathering here on short notice," Jack began, his gaze sweeping over each face. "I've got some important news to share, and I wanted to tell you altogether."

Jack continued, his tone steady. "As you know, Sadie's been the full-time foreman here for some time now—keeping things running smoothly, making sure we stay on track. She's balanced her responsibilities here with her passion for writing, which is no small feat."

Sadie glanced down modestly, a faint blush coloring her cheeks.

"I'm proud to say that Sadie's writing career has really taken off," Jack said, a note of pride evident. "So much so that she's decided to step back from her full-time duties here at the ranch to focus more on her writing. Her mama and I support her decision."

There was a ripple of surprise around the table. Gage's gaze shifted to Sadie, his expression unreadable, while Mitch straightened abruptly, his boots thudding to the floor.

"It wasn't an easy decision," Sadie added, her voice clear. "But it's one I feel called to make. I'll still be around, just not in the same capacity."

Jack nodded. "With that in mind, we'll need to appoint a new foreman. It's a role that requires dedication, knowledge of the land, and respect for the family we have here. After careful consideration, I've come to the decision to offer the position to one of two people."

Mitch leaned forward, anticipation alight in his eyes.

"Pete," Jack turned toward the seasoned ranch hand, "you've been with us the longest. Your experience and steady hand have been invaluable. It's only right that I offer the position to you first. You deserve it."

All eyes shifted to Pete. He set the cards down, meeting Jack's gaze squarely. "I appreciate that, Jack. Truly, I do. But I'm content where I am—don't have a hankering for the extra responsibility. I'd rather keep doing what I do best."

Jack inclined his head, respect clear in his eyes. "I understand. Your contributions as they are mean a great deal to me."

Mitch's fingers drummed impatiently on the tabletop, his gaze flickering between Jack and Sadie.

Jack turned his attention to Gage. "That brings me to you, Gage." He paused, his words settling among the ranch hands. "You've proven yourself to be a hardworking, capable hand. Your skills with the livestock and your leadership qualities haven't gone unnoticed. I believe God put you here on my ranch for a reason. I have faith in you and believe you'd make a good foreman."

Gage straightened, surprise flashing across his features. "I... appreciate that, sir."

Before he could say more, Mitch shot up from his seat, his chair scraping loudly against the wooden floor. "Hold on just a minute," he snapped, his voice edged with irritation. "You're offering the foreman position to him?"

"Mitch," Sadie interjected, a warning note in her voice.

He ignored her, his gaze fixed on Jack. "With all due respect, I've been here longer than Gage. I know this ranch inside and out. If anyone's earned that position, it's me."

Jack regarded Mitch calmly. "I value your hard work, Mitch, but this isn't just about tenure. It's about who's the best fit for the role."

Mitch's eyes flashed. "Best fit? We barely know anything about him! He blows in from who-knows-where, and suddenly, he's foreman material?"

"That's enough." Jack's tone brooked no argument.

"I don't want to cause any trouble. If this is going to be an issue—" Gage said.

"No trouble at all," Jack asserted, cutting him off. "My decision is made."

Mitch scoffed, his gaze searing into Gage. "Of course it is. Isn't that convenient?"

Sadie stepped forward, her eyes locking with Mitch's. "What exactly are you insinuating?"

He turned to her, bitterness creeping into his voice. "Oh, come on, Sadie. Don't play coy. Everyone can see how chummy you two have gotten. Maybe that had a little something to do with Dad's decision."

A stunned silence fell over the room.

"Careful, Mitch," Jack warned, his tone dangerously low.

Mitch threw his hands up. "It's the truth! We're all thinking it. Gage waltzes in here, gets the plum assignments, and now he's being handed the top spot."

"Stop it!" Sadie's voice rang out, firm and unwavering. "This isn't about you, or some twisted idea you have about favoritism. Dad made his decision based on merit."

Mitch's jaw tightened, his eyes glistening with a mix of anger and hurt. "You're blind, Sadie. Blind to what's right in front of you."

Julie stood, placing a hand on Mitch's arm. "Let's step outside, cool off."

He jerked away from her touch. "Don't. Just... don't."

Ross, who had been uncharacteristically silent, cleared his throat nervously. "Maybe we should all take a minute."

Jack's gaze hardened. "Mitch, if you can't accept this decision respectfully, perhaps you need to reconsider your place here."

"You'd like that, wouldn't you?" Mitch spat. "Fine. Maybe I will."

With that, he stormed out of the bunkhouse; the door slamming shut behind him.

An uncomfortable silence settled over the group.

Pete sighed heavily, rubbing the back of his neck. "Well, that went south in a hurry."

"Are you alright?" Sadie asked Gage, her eyes searching his.

He nodded slowly. "I'm fine. But I don't want to be the cause of division here."

Jack shook his head. "This isn't on you, Gage. Mitch has been struggling with some things lately. He'll need to sort them out himself, and if he can't, then I'll ask him to leave my ranch."

Julie offered a small, supportive smile. "For what it's worth, I think you'll make a great foreman, Gage."

Ross added his agreement. "Yeah, man. You've got my vote."

Gage looked around at the faces of his colleagues—some offering encouragement, others still processing the rapid turn of events. "I appreciate the confidence," he said sincerely. "But I'd like to take some time to think it over."

Jack nodded. "Of course. Take a couple of weeks. Meanwhile, you'll shadow Sadie more closely. She'll be transitioning out of her role, starting immediately. When you're not with her, work with me or Pete. No rush to make a final decision."

"Understood," Gage replied.

Jack glanced around the room. "I know this is a lot to take in. Change can be difficult, but it can also bring new opportunities. I have faith in each of you and in this ranch. Now, let's get back to work."

Pete stood, slipping his hat back on. "Thanks boss, for the consideration. It means a lot."

One by one, the ranch hands filtered out of the bunkhouse until only Sadie, Jack, and Gage remained.

Jack clapped a hand on Gage's shoulder. "Keep up the good work, son. I'm confident the foreman position is a good fit for you."

"Yes, sir."

With a final nod, Jack left the bunkhouse, leaving Sadie and Gage alone.

"I'm sorry about Mitch," she said.

"It's not your fault. He's got his own demons."

She studied him, noting the way his eyes reflected a mix of resolve and uncertainty. "What are your thoughts on stepping into the foreman position?"

He met her gaze, a subtle warmth in his eyes. "I've never been one to back down from a challenge."

A small smile tugged at her lips. "That much I know."

He took a slow breath. "But I meant what I said—I need to think about it. This ranch... it's become more than just a job to me. And that's unfamiliar territory."

She nodded understandingly. "Take all the time you need."

He hesitated, then added softly, "Thank you—for believing in me."

"You've earned it."

Gage gazed deeply into Sadie's eyes, his heart pounding in his chest. Gently, he brushed a stray lock of hair from her face, tucking it tenderly behind her ear. "Sadie Beaumont," he murmured, his voice barely above a whisper, "you've awaken feelings in me I've never known before. Regardless of my decision, I want you to know—I'm all in."

He turned and walked toward the door, retrieving his Stetson from the peg on the wall. Placing it on his head, he glanced back at her, his eyes softening as a grin spread across his face.

"All in? What do you mean?" she asked, her voice tinged with hope.

"With you," he replied simply.

She watched as he stepped out the door, her emotions swirling.

"Lord," she whispered, "guide us both."

A smile played on her lips as she followed him outside.

Chapter 29

The next morning, Gage rose before dawn, unable to sleep any longer. The air was crisp, carrying the promise of a new day. After coffee and a quick breakfast, he headed to the stables, where he found Pete already at work, brushing down a speckled gray stallion.

"Mornin', Pete," Gage greeted.

Pete looked up, his lined face breaking into a friendly grin. "Mornin', Gage. You're up early."

"Couldn't sleep," Gage admitted. "Figured I'd get a head start on the day's work."

Pete nodded knowingly. "Got a lot on your mind, I reckon."

Gage picked up a brush and started brushing the horse as well. "You could say that."

"Listen," Pete said after a moment. "I think you'll do right by this place as foreman. I hope you really are considering the job. If I were your age again, I'd jump on it."

"Appreciate that," Gage replied.

"Being foreman isn't just about giving orders. It's about listening, learning, and respecting the land and the people working it," he said.

Gage nodded thoughtfully. "I understand that."

"And as for Mitch," Pete continued, "he's a good worker, but he lets his pride get the best of him. Don't take his outburst yesterday personally."

"I'm trying not to."

"What are you going to do about that situation?" He asked.

"I figure the best way to calm him down is by having a good long talk with him. I don't enjoy working around others that have a thorn in their side, and I'm obviously his thorn."

"Talking makes sense," Pete said, nodding. "And I agree... I think you are the thorn that is pushing his buttons lately. Mitch can be a hot-headed fool every so often. The way I see it lately... he obviously has his sights set on Sadie. He's letting his testosterone overrule his common sense."

"We can't work well together if this continues..."

"No, we surely can't."

"Morning, Pete, Gage," Jack called as he entered the barn.

"Morning, sir," they said in unison

"You boys are at it early this morning," Jack said.

"Tryin' to beat the heat of the day... and the incoming storm they're predicting," Pete said.

Jack nodded as he looked over at Gage.

"I've been doing some thinking, sir," Gage began. "I'd be honored to accept the foreman position, I really would. But I need to work things out with Mitch first. I won't work with a man who has a chip on his shoulder against me. If the offer still stands, that is."

A smile spread across Jack's face. "It does."

"I won't let you down," Gage promised.

"I know you won't," Jack replied, patting him on the shoulder.

Gage hesitated before speaking again. "I intend to talk to Mitch today. See if we can smooth things over."

Jack regarded him thoughtfully. "You don't owe him that, but it's a noble gesture."

"I think it's important," Gage insisted.

Jack nodded. "Very well. I won't stand in your way. Can't guarantee how he'll respond, but I admire your willingness to try."

"Thank you."

As Gage strode out of the barn, Jack added, "Oh, and Gage?"

He turned back. "Yes, sir?"

"Welcome to the family."

"Means a lot to hear you say that, sir."

***

Gage surveyed the area, noticing Mitch's truck parked near the bunkhouse. Nearby, Mitch was prepping the water tanker, filling it up to haul out to the pastures. As Gage neared, Mitch caught the sound of his approach and glanced over, his expression giving nothing away.

"Mornin'," Gage called out.

Mitch gave a brief nod, eyes fixed on his work.

Leaning against the truck's flatbed, Gage said, "We can't keep working like this, Mitch."

"No, we can't," Mitch replied. "Maybe it's time you hit the road again, Gage."

"That's not gonna happen," Gage stated firmly.

"Sure thing, cowboy," Mitch shot back. "I'm a patient man. You'll be on your way soon enough, no doubt about it."

Gage took a steadying breath, his gaze fixed on Mitch. "Look, Mitch, we need to work this thing between you and me out."

"Got nothing to say to you," Mitch replied curtly, tightening the valve on the tanker.

Gage stepped closer, but not too close—respecting the unspoken boundary between them. "I'm not here to cause trouble. I just want us to find a way to work together."

Mitch spun around, his eyes flashing with suppressed anger. "Work together? That's rich coming from you. You're a drifter. You found your way to this ranch. For some reason, the foreman's job was thrown your way. You've snuggled up to Jack and Sadie—you think you can just walk in here and everything will go your way? Take over everything?"

"It's not like that," Gage said calmly. "I didn't plan any of this. Jack offered me the position because he believes it's what's best for the ranch. He believes I can do the job."

"Funny how what's best for the ranch seems to line up with what's best for you," Mitch retorted.

Gage clenched his jaw, resisting the urge to fire back. "This isn't about me. It's about all of us. The ranch is going through changes, and we need to stick together."

Mitch shook his head, a bitter laugh escaping his lips. "Save the speeches for someone who cares. I see right through you."

"What's that supposed to mean?" Gage asked, a hint of frustration creeping into his voice.

"You think I don't notice how you look at Sadie? Or how she looks at you?" Mitch narrowed his eyes. "You're not just after the foreman job—you want her too."

"Yes, I am attracted to Sadie. I know you are as well. I think that's where the real problem between us is." Gage paused, choosing his words carefully. "But, Mitch, whatever's between Sadie and I is our business. It's none of yours."

"It's my business when it affects me," Mitch snapped. "You waltz in here, turning everything upside down."

"I'm not trying to take anything from you," Gage said evenly. "But I will not apologize for being here."

Mitch took a step forward, his fists clenched at his sides. "Maybe you should."

Gage held his ground. "I'm not looking for a fight, Mitch."

"Could've fooled me."

They stood in tense silence, the air heavy with tension. Finally, Gage broke the silence. "If you can't find a way to work with me, at least don't stand in the way of progress."

Mitch's gaze hardened. "The only progress I see is you muscling into Sadie's life."

"Think what you want," Gage replied firmly. "But I'm here to stay. I'm not going anywhere. I intend to date Sadie properly and see where it leads."

"See where it leads? That's rich coming from you," Mitch scoffed. "Here's what's going to happen: you'll stick around a bit longer, charm your way deeper into Sadie's heart. Then things will get old, or they'll get tough. You'll get that restless itch to move on. Then you'll leave her—break her heart. And guess what? I'll be right here waiting, cowboy."

Gage shook his head. "There's no talking to you man to man, is there?"

Mitch's glare hardened, his shoulders tense. "There's no talking because there's nothing to say," he snapped.

Gage shook his head slowly. "Suit yourself," he replied, his voice steady. "But just know that my door is always open if you change your mind."

Mitch scoffed, turning his back to Gage as he climbed into the truck. "Don't hold your breath," he muttered before slamming the door shut. The engine roared to life, and with a cloud of dust, he drove off toward the pastures.

Gage watched him go, a mixture of frustration and disappointment settling in his chest. He had hoped to find some common ground, but it was clear that Mitch wasn't ready to meet him halfway. With a heavy sigh, he turned and made his way back toward the main barn.

Chapter 30

The air was thick with anticipation, a charged stillness that had settled over Eagle's Nest Ranch like a held breath. Sadie stood on the porch of the main house, her eyes fixed on the horizon where dark, tumultuous clouds gathered, rolling over the distant mountains like a tide of ink. A low rumble of thunder reverberated through the valley, the sound both ominous and hopeful.

"Looks like the storm's finally moving in," Harriet remarked, joining Sadie with a steaming mug of chamomile tea in hand. Her brown eyes scanned the sky, a mix of apprehension and relief etched across her lined face.

Sadie nodded, her fingers unconsciously toying with the turquoise pendant resting against her collarbone. "We've prayed for rain, and it's almost here. Just hope it's not more than we can handle. Whatever's coming toward us looks horrible."

Her mom gave a reassuring pat on Sadie's shoulder. "The Good Lord doesn't give us more than we can bear, honey. But it doesn't hurt to be prepared."

"Exactly what I was thinking," Sadie replied, her mind already racing through the checklist of tasks that needed to be done before the storm hit. "I better round up everyone to secure the ranch."

"Your dad and Pete are already in the north pasture, reinforcing the fences," she informed her. "Julie and Will are gathering the smaller livestock into the lower barns."

"Thanks, Mom. I'll get Gage and see to the equipment and the horses." Sadie took a deep breath, steeling herself for the hours ahead.

As she descended the porch steps, the wind picked up, rustling through the aspen trees and carrying the scent of approaching rain. She found Gage near the stables, tightening the straps on a tarp covering a stack of hay bales.

"Gage!" she called out over the increasing gusts.

He looked up, his blue eyes meeting hers beneath the brim of his worn Stetson. "Storm's rolling in faster than we thought," he noted, pulling the final strap taut.

"Yeah, we need to move quickly," Sadie agreed. "Can you help me secure the equipment and make sure the horses are sheltered? The old barn might not hold up if the winds get too strong."

He gave a quick nod. "Already on it. I moved the tractors into the machinery shed and started bringing the tools inside."

Their eyes held for a moment longer than necessary, a silent understanding passing between them.

"Great minds think alike," she said with a smile.

"Or maybe I've just learned to anticipate your orders," he teased lightly, his eyes crinkling at the corners.

Sadie felt a warmth spread through her despite the cooling air. "Well, I won't argue with that. Let's divide and conquer. I'll check on the mares, and you handle the rest of the horses?"

"Sounds like a plan." He adjusted his hat and headed toward the paddocks.

As they worked, the ranch buzzed with focused energy. Clouds swallowed the sun, casting an eerie twilight over the land. The wind whipped through the trees, leaves torn free to dance erratically before settling onto the dry earth.

In the stables, Sadie moved from stall to stall, soothing the anxious mares with soft words and gentle strokes. Daisy nickered nervously as Sadie approached.

"Easy, girl," Sadie murmured, running a calming hand down the mare's neck. "We'll get through this just fine."

She secured the stall door and double-checked the latches on the windows, ensuring they were fastened tightly. As she moved to the next stall, she caught a glimpse of Gage outside, leading a restless stallion toward shelter. His movements were deliberate and assured, a steady presence amidst the growing chaos.

A sudden clatter drew her attention back inside. One of the younger mares kicked at her stall door, eyes wide with fear.

"Whoa there," Sadie approached cautiously. "It's okay."

The mare tossed her head, nostrils flaring.

"Having a bit of trouble?" Gage's voice came from behind her.

She turned his way, a mild grin on his face despite the situation. "Just a little," she admitted.

"Mind if I give it a try?"

"Be my guest."

Gage stepped into the stall, his movements slow and measured. He whispered soothingly to the mare, his voice barely audible over the rising wind. Within moments, the horse began to calm, her tension easing as she responded to his quiet confidence.

Sadie watched, a mix of admiration and something deeper stirring within her. "You have a way with them," she said softly. "A horse whisperer..."

He glanced at her over his shoulder. "Just takes patience. And a bit of understanding."

Their eyes met, and for a heartbeat, the world outside faded—the storm, the ranch, all of it seemed distant compared to the magnetic pull between them.

"Sadie!" Mitch's voice shattered the moment, sharp and insistent.

She blinked, stepping back as reality rushed in. "I'll be right there," she called out, her tone neutral.

Gage's jaw tightened almost imperceptibly at the sound of Mitch's approach. "I should finish up outside," he said, breaking the eye contact.

"Right. Thanks for your help." Sadie forced a smile before turning to exit the stable.

Mitch strode toward her, his expression a mix of irritation and concern. "I've been looking all over for you," he said curtly.

"I'm a bit busy, Mitch," Sadie replied, her patience already wearing thin. "What do you need?"

"We need to talk," he insisted, lowering his voice.

Sighing, Sadie crossed her arms. "Can it wait? There's a storm coming, in case you hadn't noticed."

"It's about the storm—and other things." He gestured toward the side of the barn, away from prying ears.

Reluctantly, she followed him. "What is it?"

Mitch took a deep breath, struggling to find the right words. "I don't like how close you're getting to Gage."

Sadie stiffened. "Excuse me?"

"You heard me," he pressed on. "He's not the kind of guy you should be around. He's a drifter, Sadie. No roots, no ties. He'll be gone as soon as the wind changes."

Anger flared within her. "Who I choose to spend time with is none of your business, Mitch."

"It is when it affects the ranch," he argued. "And when it affects you."

She shook her head, disbelief and frustration mingling. "This isn't about the ranch. This is about you not respecting my choices."

"Can't you see I'm trying to protect you?" His voice rose, desperation creeping in. "I've known you my whole life. I care about you. Doesn't that mean anything?"

Sadie took a step back, her gaze hardening. "I appreciate your concern, but I don't need protecting—not from Gage, and certainly not from my own decisions."

Mitch's expression hardened. "You're making a mistake."

"That's not for you to decide." She squared her shoulders. "You're walking a thin line, Mitch. Now, if you'll excuse me, I have work to do."

She turned abruptly, leaving him standing in shock. Her heart pounded with a mix of anger and an unsettling sense of foreboding. Mitch's jealousy was becoming more of a problem, one she couldn't ignore much longer.

As she headed back toward the main house, fat drops of rain began to splatter against the dry earth, the storm finally making good on its promises. The first roll of thunder echoed across the valley, a deep rumble that seemed to resonate within her chest.

"Sadie!" Harriet called from the porch, waving urgently. "We need to get the windows secured. The wind's picking up fast. A flash flood warning just came over the radio."

"I'm on it, Mom," Sadie replied, quickening her pace.

Together, they moved through the house, closing windows, latching indoor shutters and drawing curtains. The rain intensified, pelting against the windows with a relentless rhythm. The sound was both alarming and oddly soothing—a long-awaited reprieve from the drought but carrying the threat of destruction.

"Have you heard from your father?" Harriet asked, concern etched in her features.

"No," Sadie answered, trying to keep her worry at bay. "They should be heading back soon, I would imagine."

"I hope so. This storm is worse than we anticipated."

Sadie nodded, her thoughts turning to Gage and the others still out in the elements. She grabbed her rain slicker and headed back outside; the wind tugging at her clothes as she made her way toward the barns.

Chapter 31

Lightning forked across the sky, illuminating the ranch in stark relief. Gage emerged from the equipment shed, his coat drenched, but his movements purposeful.

"All the animals are secured!" He shouted over the roar of the storm.

"Good," Sadie called back. "Have you heard from my dad?"

He shook his head. "Not yet."

Just then, Will came running up, his hat clutched tightly to his head. "Sadie! Gage! There's trouble!"

Her heart lurched. "What is it?"

"Got a call over the radio. The bridge near the east creek is washed out, and some of the horses are trapped on the other side. The water's rising fast."

"Where's my dad?" Sadie demanded.

"He's still out there with Pete," Will said, worry clear in his eyes. "They might be trying to get to the horses."

Sadie didn't hesitate. "We have to help them."

Gage grabbed her arm gently. "It's too dangerous."

She pulled free, determination blazing in her gaze.

He searched her face, then gave a resolute nod. "I'm coming with you."

They quickly gathered what they needed—flashlights, ropes, and a medical kit—before saddling two of the sturdiest horses. The storm battered them with relentless fury as they rode out, the rain lashing against their faces and the wind threatening to unseat them.

The path toward the east creek was treacherous, mud sucking at the horses' hooves and visibility reduced to mere feet. They pushed onward, driven by urgency and a shared resolve.

"Stay close!" Gage shouted, his voice barely carrying over the storm.

"I'm right behind you!" Sadie replied, her voice firm despite the fear gnawing at her.

A sudden flash of lightning illuminated the landscape, revealing the swollen creek ahead. The bridge—or what remained of it—was a mangled mess of wood, half-submerged in the churning waters. The force of the river that fed the creek had been too much.

"There!" Sadie pointed toward a cluster of trees where she spotted movement.

They dismounted, tying the horses securely before approaching on foot. As they waded through the raging, fast-moving creek, through the sheets of rain, they could make out the silhouettes of several horses, huddled together and clearly panicked.

"Easy now," Gage murmured soothingly as they drew nearer.

"Do you see my dad?" Sadie asked anxiously.

Gage scanned the area, squinting against the rain. "No sign of them yet."

Sadie's heart clenched. "We have to get the horses to higher ground."

They worked quickly, moving from horse to horse, attaching lead ropes and speaking in calm tones despite the raging storm. The animals were skittish, eyes rolling with fear, but Gage and Sadie's steady presence began to soothe them.

Just as they were preparing to lead the horses away, a loud crack split the air. Sadie looked up just in time to see a large branch snapping from an overburdened tree plummeting toward her.

"Sadie, watch out!" Gage yelled, lunging forward.

He shoved her aside, the force of his movement sending them both sprawling into the mud as the branch crashed down where she had stood moments before. Pain shot through Gage's shoulder as he landed hard, a sharp gasp escaping his lips.

"Are you okay?" Sadie scrambled to her knees, reaching for him.

He grimaced, clutching his shoulder. "I'm fine."

"You're hurt!" she exclaimed, worry flooding her voice.

"It's nothing," he insisted, though his pallor suggested otherwise.

Before she could argue, another figure emerged from the storm. "Sadie! Gage!"

"Pete!" Sadie cried out in relief as the older ranch hand approached.

"Your dad's up ahead," Pete shouted. "He's got a busted leg. We need to get him out of here."

Sadie's blood ran cold. "Where is he?"

"About fifty yards that way," Pete pointed. "But the ground's unstable. Mudslides are starting. The rains coming too fast. The grounds parched and can't soak up the rain."

Gage pushed himself to his feet, wincing but resolute. "Take the horses," he told Pete. "We'll get Jack."

Pete hesitated, glancing between them. "Are you sure?"

"Go!" Sadie urged. "We'll follow as soon as we can."

Pete nodded sharply, leading the horses upward, away from the rising creek that looked more like a river now.

Sadie turned to Gage, concern etched across her features. "Can you move it?"

He tested his arm, gritting his teeth. "I'll manage."

They pushed forward, navigating the treacherous terrain. The rain pelted them mercilessly, each step a battle against the elements.

"Over here!" Sadie shouted, spotting the faint glow of a flashlight.

Jack lay at the base of a small slope, his face pale but determined. "Sadie!" he called out. "What are you doing out here?"

"Saving you, apparently," she replied, forcing levity into her tone as she knelt beside him.

"You should be back at the ranch with your mama. She's probably worried sick."

"Hush. What happened?"

"Ground's slick. The rain came too fast and the ground can't absorb it fast enough," he explained tersely. "My horse slipped, and I got trapped under him for a bit when he came down. Think my leg's broken."

Gage surveyed the situation quickly. "We need to get him out of here before the slope gets worse... or collapses."

Sadie nodded. "I'll support his left side. You take the right."

They maneuvered Jack carefully, his weight adding to the already strenuous conditions. Progress was slow, each step fraught with danger.

Without warning, the ground beneath them began to shift. A rumbling indicating an imminent landslide.

"Move!" Gage yelled.

They surged forward as the earth gave way behind them, a cascade of mud and debris sweeping down.

They reached a more stable area, panting and soaked to the bone. Jack leaned heavily on them, his breaths ragged.

"Can't... go much... further," he managed.

"We're almost there, daddy, just hang on," Sadie assured him, though she wasn't certain how much more any of them could take.

Gage's face was etched with pain, but he didn't falter. "Just a bit further."

Lightning struck a nearby tree, the impact sending splinters flying. Sadie ducked instinctively, her heart pounding. The storm was relentless, a primal force that seemed intent on testing their limits.

As they crested a small rise, the faint outline of the ranch came into view through the veil of rain.

But fate had one more trial in store. A swollen tributary, normally a gentle stream, now raged between them and the path home.

"It's too deep," Jack observed grimly. "Moving too fast."

"We'll have to find another way around," Gage said.

"There isn't time. It'll only get worse," Sadie argued.

Gage assessed the situation, his mind racing. "I'll cross first, see how strong the current is."

"No," Sadie protested. "It's too risky. Let's move together through the water and brace each other."

He met her gaze, his eyes steady. "Trust me."

Without waiting for further argument, he stepped into the water, the frigid current pressing against him with formidable strength. He moved slowly, testing each step, until he reached the opposite bank.

"It's manageable," he called back. "But you'll have to be careful. Currents strong."

With a mixture of apprehension and hope, Sadie and Jack began to cross, Gage reaching out to guide them.

Halfway across, the ground shifted beneath Sadie's feet, the current pulling at her with sudden force.

"Sadie!" Gage lunged forward, grasping her arm as she slipped.

Her foot found purchase on a submerged rock, and she steadied, gripping his hand tightly. "Gotcha!" He yelled, relief clear.

They made it across, collapsing onto the muddy bank, exhaustion threatening to overtake them.

"Let's keep moving," Jack urged after they had all caught their breath, his voice weak. "This is tornado type weather. Not safe to be out here."

They struggled onward; the ranch drawing closer with each agonizing step. Faint lights shone through the darkness—beacons guiding them home.

At last, they stumbled onto the porch. Harriet and Madge rushed out to meet them.

"Jack!" Harriet cried, her hands flying to her mouth. "Oh, thank heavens!"

"Get him inside," Gage instructed, his tone authoritative despite his weariness. "He needs medical attention."

Harriet and Madge moved to assist, supporting Jack as they ushered him into the house.

Sadie turned to Gage, her eyes shining with gratitude and concern. "You're hurt badly," she said, noticing the pallor of his skin and the strain etched on his face.

"It's nothing," he repeated.

"Don't give me that," she chided gently. "Come inside."

He didn't argue, allowing her to lead him into the warmth of the house.

Inside, the chaos of the storm outside faded to a distant roar. Harriet fussed over Jack in the living room, while Madge barked orders, her years of experience in crises taking over.

Sadie guided Gage to the kitchen, where the light was brighter, and the energy calmer.

"Sit," she directed, pulling out a chair.

He complied, too drained to protest.

She fetched the medical kit, setting it on the table before carefully peeling off his soaked jacket.

He winced as she examined his shoulder.

"It's dislocated," she observed.

"I figured," he managed, attempting a wry smile.

"We need to pop it back into place."

"Go ahead."

She met his gaze, appreciating the trust he placed in her. "Alright. On the count of three."

He braced himself.

"One... two..." She moved swiftly on two, pulling and rotating his arm in a practiced motion.

There was a sharp jolt, followed by a dull ache as the joint realigned.

He exhaled shakily. "You said on three."

She gave him a small smile. "I find it's better this way."

"Can't argue with results."

Silence settled between them, filled only by the muffled sounds of the storm and the distant voices in the other room as Pete and Will entered the house.

"Where'd you learn to do that?" he asked, his breath still uneven.

"Pete," she replied softly, her eyes meeting his. "Believe it or not."

He looked at her quizzically, a mix of curiosity and admiration in his gaze.

"It's a ranch, Gage. We've had our share of injuries around here," she said, her voice gentle. "Pete took a bad fall years ago when I was out riding with him. It was just the two of us. He told me what to do, and I followed his instructions."

"Well, thanks to Pete," he said with a grateful smile. "I figured I'd have to drive into town after the storm to have my arm setback in place."

Sadie moved a little closer, a soft smile playing on her lips. "Yeah, thanks to Pete. You'll be fine now," she whispered.

They lingered in the moment, the adrenaline still coursing through them as she leaned in slightly more, their faces just inches apart.

"Thank you," she said softly, her eyes reflecting a depth of emotion that words couldn't capture.

"For what?" he asked, his gaze unwavering.

"For helping my father. For everything."

He reached up, his fingertips grazing her cheek. "I'd do it again. A thousand times."

"Gage..."

He lowered his hand, uncertainty flickering across his features. "Sadie, there's something I need to tell you."

She held her breath; the world narrowing to the space between them.

"All my life, I've been running," he began, his voice barely above a whisper. "Never staying in one place long enough to get attached. But being here, with you... It's different. You make me want to stop running."

Emotion welled within her, tears threatening to spill.

"You are worth it, Sadie," he said, his eyes searching hers. "This place, this feeling... I've found something I didn't even know I was looking for."

Their proximity charged with unspoken promises. "You're not alone anymore," she whispered.

He reached for her hand, his fingers entwining with hers.

The moment hung between them, ripe with possibility. His gaze dropped to her lips, and she felt her breath catch in anticipation.

Just as he leaned in, the kitchen door swung open.

"Sadie! We need more towels for your father," Madge announced, bustling in with her usual vigor. She stopped short, taking in the scene with a keen eye.

"Oh! I didn't realize you two were in the middle of something," she said, a mischievous twinkle in her eye.

Sadie stepped back, cheeks flushing. "It's okay, Madge. I'll get the towels."

Gage cleared his throat, a faint smile ghosting across his lips. "I should check on the others."

Madge watched him exit, then turned to Sadie with a knowing grin. "Well, isn't he just the hero of the hour?"

Sadie busied herself gathering kitchen towels, avoiding Madge's gaze. "He certainly helped us out there."

"Mm-hmm," Madge replied, her tone dripping with implication. "Seems to me there's more than just gratitude going on."

Sadie paused, clutching the fabric in her hands. "It's complicated."

"Life always is, sweetheart." Madge softened, placing a gentle hand on her arm. "You have a good head on your shoulders and a strong heart. Trust yourself... and buckle up for the ride, 'cause I have a feeling... it's gonna be a good one."

A smile broke out on Sadie's lips. "Thanks, Madge."

"Anytime, dear." She patted her arm before heading back toward the living room. "Now, let's tend to that father of yours."

Chapter 32

Sadie stood on the porch, arms wrapped around herself as she surveyed the ranch. Fences lay toppled, sections of the barn roof were missing shingles, and debris was scattered across the fields. The storm had been fierce, testing their resolve and resources. Yet, in the soft light of dawn, there was a strange beauty to the disarray—a testament to what they'd endured and a reminder of the resilience required to rebuild.

She sipped from a steaming mug of coffee; the warmth seeping into her cold fingers. Her gaze drifted to the bunkhouse, where the ranch hands were moving around outside, beginning the cleanup process. Even from a distance, she could spot Gage among them, his tall frame unmistakable. He moved with purpose, despite the sling cradling his injured shoulder—a tangible reminder of the previous night's peril.

Her thoughts wandered to the moment in the kitchen when they'd nearly crossed the line from friendship into something deeper. The memory sent a flutter through her heart, equal parts excitement and apprehension. She had slept little, her mind replaying the look in his eyes, the vulnerability he'd shown. But with daylight came doubts. There was so much left unsaid between them, so many uncertainties.

"You're up early," Harriet's gentle voice interrupted her reverie.

Sadie turned to see her mother stepping out onto the porch, her own mug in hand.

"Couldn't sleep," Sadie admitted. "Too much to process. How's daddy?"

"Resting," Harriet replied. "He'll be out of commission for a while, but he's tough. You know how he is. Doc set his leg last night and your dad grumbled the whole time. We finally made it home around 2 this morning."

Sadie smiled softly. "He's stubborn as a mule."

They both laughed as Harriet looked out across the ranch. "It looks daunting now, but we'll get everything back in order. We always do."

"I know. It's just... a lot." Sadie hesitated. "Dad's injury, the state of the ranch, and... other things."

Her mother gave her a knowing look. "Other things, hmm?"

Sadie offered a faint smile. "You always could read me like a book."

"Comes with the territory of being a mother." Harriet rested a hand on Sadie's shoulder. "Life is full of complications, honey. It's how we navigate them that defines us." Harriet squeezed her shoulder gently.

"Gage is something else, mama. I don't know what we would've done without him yesterday."

Harriet reached over, placing a gentle hand on Sadie's. "You care for him."

It wasn't a question, but Sadie nodded nonetheless. "I do."

Harriet squeezed her hand. "Your father and I have noticed. He's a good man. He seems smitten with you."

"I think he is," Sadie said softly. "But there's so much I don't know about him."

"Sometimes taking a chance is worth it," Harriet advised. "Your father and I took a chance on each other. It wasn't easy, but it was the best decision we ever made."

Sadie looked into her mother's eyes, finding reassurance. "Thanks, Mama."

The sound of footsteps drew their attention. Gage approached, his expression neutral but his eyes searching.

"Morning," he greeted, nodding to both women.

"Good morning, Gage," Harriet replied warmly. "How's the shoulder?"

He adjusted the sling slightly. "It'll be fine. I've worked through worse."

Sadie frowned. "You shouldn't push yourself for the next few days. There are plenty of us to handle the repairs around the ranch."

"I'm not one to sit around while others do the heavy lifting."

Harriet took a discreet step back. "Well, I'll leave you two to discuss the day's plans. Plenty to do." With a parting smile, she headed back inside.

An awkward silence settled over them. Sadie cleared her throat, struggling to find the right words. "Thank you again for everything you did last night."

He shook his head lightly. "Just did what anyone would have."

"Not everyone would risk themselves like you did," she insisted.

He looked out over the ranch, his jaw tightening. "How's your father?"

"Resting." She paused, studying his profile. "You should be resting, too."

"I'm fine."

"Stubborn," she murmured, a hint of a smile tugging at her lips.

He glanced at her, the corner of his mouth lifting slightly. "Takes one to know one."

She smiled and shook her head as she set her coffee mug down. "How about we get started accessing the damage on the ranch together? Two sets of eyes are better than one."

He nodded. "I'd like that."

They spent the morning walking the property, noting fences that needed mending, trees that had fallen, and areas where the soil had eroded. Despite the work ahead, there was a peacefulness in the air—a sense of renewal.

As they walked, Sadie opened up to Gage about her life on the ranch, her hopes for its future, and memories from her childhood.

"You really love this place," he observed.

"With all my heart," she affirmed. "It's not just land or buildings. It's part of who I am. I've never wanted to leave or go anywhere else. This is home."

He looked thoughtful.

"You've never had a place to call home until now," she said gently.

He hesitated before answering. "Not really. Moved around a lot. Never stayed anywhere long enough to put down roots."

She stopped walking and turned to face him. "I think it's time you do."

He met her gaze, vulnerability flickering in his eyes. "It is."

"I want you to know whether or not you take the foreman position. I want you here. I want this to be your home."

In the distance, the sound of a vehicle approaching broke the moment. They turned to see a truck kicking up dust along the driveway.

As the truck drew closer, Sadie's expression shifted to one of apprehension. "That's Deputy Gillman's' truck."

Gage's demeanor changed subtly, a guarded look replacing his previous openness.

The truck came to a halt near them, and a tall man in a sheriff's deputy uniform stepped out, adjusting his hat.

"Morning, Sadie," Deputy Gillman called out as he approached.

"Morning, Deputy. Everything alright?" she asked.

"Got word there was some trouble here last night with the storm," he said. "Just making sure everyone's okay."

"Dad broke his leg. The rest of us are fine," she assured him. "Had a few close calls, but nothing we can't handle."

Deputy Sanders glanced at Gage, his eyes lingering. "And you are?"

"Gage," he replied evenly, extending his hand.

The deputy shook it firmly. "Don't think we've met before. You're new in town."

"He's been working here at the ranch for a while now," Sadie interjected, a hint of defensiveness in her tone.

"Yep... Mitch mentioned that." The deputy's scrutinizing gaze didn't waver.

"Is there something I can help you with?" Gage asked calmly.

Deputy Sanders shifted his stance. "Just doing my rounds. Making sure everyone's safe. You never know who's passing through these days."

Sadie bristled. "Gage has been a great help to us."

"Good to hear," the deputy replied, though his tone suggested otherwise. "Well, if you need anything, don't hesitate to call. And Gage, I don't want any trouble around here. I keep a close watch on everything in this town... including new people."

With that, he tipped his hat and headed back to his truck.

As the dust settled behind the departing vehicle, Sadie turned to Gage. "I'm sorry about that. He can be... protective, and obviously Mitch must be running his mouth about something."

Gage gave a small shrug, wincing slightly from his shoulder. "It's alright. He's just doing his job."

But there was a shadow behind his eyes.

"What is it?" she pressed gently.

He sighed, running his hand through his hair. "There's... there's a lot about my past I haven't told you. And if Mitch and that Deputy are close, which it appears they are... some of Mitch's comments lately are starting to make sense."

She waited patiently.

"I haven't always made the best choices," he admitted. "Got mixed up with the wrong crowd after my parents passed. Did some things I'm not proud of."

"Like what?" she asked.

He looked away. "Ran away from my foster homes several times when I was younger. I got involved in some petty crimes. Nothing violent, but enough to get me in trouble. Got in a few fist fights that I shouldn't have. Spent time in jail."

Sadie reached out, placing a reassuring hand on his arm. "Everyone has a past, Gage."

He met her gaze, searching for judgment but finding none. "I've done my best to put that life behind me. I'm not that person anymore. But I know that my past might cause problems here. People talk. Rumors spread."

Sadie was silent for a moment before speaking. "I have a feeling you're right about Mitch. He'll use whatever he's dug up as fuel for the fire."

"I don't want to cause any trouble."

She took a deep breath. "What matters is who you are now, and the choices you make today. Give yourself a little grace. Forgive yourself for the things you've done in the past. You've proven yourself to be a good man, Gage—kind, hardworking, and brave. That's what I see when I look at you."

"You don't know how much that means to me."

She smiled softly. "You're not alone anymore, Gage."

He looked into her eyes, gratitude, and affection evident in his gaze. "I don't deserve you."

"Maybe not," she teased lightly. "But I'm glad you're here anyway."

They both laughed, the tension easing.

"Now," she said. "How about we go check on the horses? I think they could use some attention. And then I think we need to go have a talk with Mitch and set a few things straight."

"Lead the way."

Chapter 33

As they headed toward the stables, the sun peaked higher in the sky. The horses neighed softly upon seeing them, their gentle eyes reflecting trust.

Sadie approached her favorite mare, Daisy, running a soothing hand over her mane. "Hey, girl. Rough night, wasn't it?"

Gage leaned against the stall door. "She's a beauty," he remarked. "And so are you."

Sadie smiled. "She's been with us since she was a foal. Strong-willed but loyal. Kind of like someone else I know."

Gage chuckled softly. "Are you comparing me to a horse now?"

"Only the best qualities," she teased. Her expression turned more serious. "Gage, about Mitch—are you sure you're up for this? We don't have to confront him today."

He met her gaze steadily. "He's causing trouble. It's better to address it sooner rather than later."

She nodded. "Alright. We stand together on this, right?"

"Yes, together. Let's go."

As they made their way to the equipment shed where Mitch was, Sadie couldn't help but feel a mix of anxiety and determination. Gage walked beside her, his presence steadying.

They found Mitch sharpening tools, his posture stiffening as he noticed their approach. "Well, look who it is," he drawled, not bothering to hide the disdain in his voice.

"Mitch, we need to talk," Sadie began calmly.

"About what?" he replied tersely. "I'm busy."

"About some things you've been saying," Gage interjected. "It's time to clear the air."

Mitch set down the tool with a clang. "Folks have a right to know who they're working with, Gage."

Sadie stepped forward. "Mitch, that's enough. Gage has been nothing but helpful since he arrived. My family trusts him, and so do I."

Mitch scoffed. "Of course you do. But leopards don't change their spots."

Gage took a deep breath. "I won't deny I have a past, Mitch. You've obviously done some research. Deputy Gillman came out for a visit earlier."

"Did he now?" Mitch nodded. "He's a good man."

"I want a fresh start, Mitch. I want to be a part of this ranch and a part of this community. I won't deny I've done some things in my life that I'm not proud of. If you wanted to know anything about my past, you could have asked. I would have been honest."

Mitch eyed him skeptically. "A fresh start? Or a chance to take advantage of decent folks?"

Sadie's eyes flashed with anger. "That's unfair, and you know it. Gage risked his life for this ranch last night, which I might add, you were nowhere to be found during the entire storm. If you can't accept that Gage is a part of this ranch now, then maybe you don't belong here anymore."

There was a tense silence. Other ranch hands nearby had paused their work, sensing the confrontation.

Mitch glanced around, realizing he was outnumbered in sentiment. His expression wavered before hardening again. "Fine. But don't say I didn't warn you."

"Mitch, look at me," Sadie said sternly.

He turned to face her, avoiding eye contact with Gage.

"I want you to take a week off. I'll let dad know I've ordered you time off with pay. Now go home and get your head on straight. And no more trying to cause problems. What you did involving Deputy Gillman was uncalled for."

He grabbed his tools and stalked away, leaving Sadie and Gage standing amidst the quieted whispers of the others.

"You didn't have to do that."

She looked up at him. "Yes, I did. Consider it foreman training 101. You're part of this ranch, part of our family now. We stand up for each other... and I want you here."

He nodded, a weight seeming to lift from his shoulders. "I won't let you down."

"I know you won't," she replied with a reassuring smile. "Now, let's get back to work. We've got a lot of rebuilding to do."

Chapter 34

Gage sat on the steps of the bunkhouse, the night air cool against his skin. Stars pierced the velvet darkness, indifferent to the turmoil below.

He couldn't shake the memory of last night in the kitchen with Sadie. The way her eyes had softened when she looked at him, the gentle curve of her smile—it all made his heart swell in a way he hadn't felt in a long time. He'd been so close to crossing that line he'd kept between them, a line he'd long avoided for reasons he wasn't sure he understood anymore.

But today had thrown everything into turmoil. Mitch's actions, his biting words—they gnawed at him like a persistent ache. He wanted to be the man Sadie saw when she looked at him, strong and unflinching. Yet doubts and fears clung to him, whispering that he wasn't enough. They wouldn't let go, no matter how much he wished they would.

"Mind if I join you?" Pete's gravelly voice interrupted his thoughts.

Gage nodded. "Be my guest."

They sat in companionable silence for a while before Pete spoke. "Beautiful night."

"Yeah."

"What's going on in that head of yours?"

Gage huffed a quiet laugh. "Is it that obvious?"

"I've been around long enough to recognize when a man is wrestling with himself."

Gage stared out into the darkness.

Pete watched him. "Sadie?"

He glanced over, surprised.

"Son, I've been where you are before."

"I doubt that," Gage said.

"My parents were killed in a plane crash when I was fifteen. I was already working on this ranch... back then, it was run by Jack's father, Luther." Pete paused for a moment, looking up into the sky. "Ole Luther took me under his wing. He and his wife and their kids were the only people I had in this world. They let me stay here and continue working on the ranch. They became my legal guardians. Not only that, but they became my family. But back then, I felt like the odd man out. Like I literally was all alone in this world. I've been where you are, Gage. Years went by, and I found myself smitten with Luther's niece. She came for a visit during the summer I was 20 years old. Her parents were going through a divorce. That little gal had my heart the day she stepped foot on this ranch."

Gage watched Pete as he spoke, a faraway look in his eye.

"And?" Gage said.

Pete looked at him. "I messed up. I should have followed my heart, Gage. Instead, I made the biggest mistake I've ever made in my life. I let her go. Oh... we had a great summer. We talked about a future. I asked her if she'd stay here. If she'd marry me. She said she would. I even bought her a ring. Then, like a fool, I talked myself out of it. Kept telling myself I wasn't good enough for her. What kind of life could a ranch hand give a fine city woman like her? I worried I was asking too much of her. I worried I was taking her away from her dream of going to college and becoming a teacher. I let her go, Gage. I broke off our short engagement and started avoiding her. Then a few days later, I watched her leave."

Pete looked Gage straight in the eye and said, "Don't be like me. I'm a lonely old man that could have had more. I probably could have had a wonderful life with a wife and kids. Instead, I let self-doubt grab a hold of me. I thought too much about what ifs... what if this happened... or what if that happened? I let the only woman I ever loved walk away. And you know something?"

"What?"

"I should have run after that woman. I should have got myself on a Greyhound bus headed for Boston. I should have found her and begged for forgiveness. But I didn't."

Gage sighed. "Sadie's an incredible woman. I just don't want to hurt her. I don't want to mess up."

"Then don't."

"It's not that simple."

"Why not?"

He hesitated. "I've got a past. Baggage. I've done things I'm ashamed of. I don't know how to be what she needs."

"None of us are perfect," Pete replied. "Don't make the same mistake I did, trust me. And how do you know what she needs?"

"I don't... I honestly don't have a clue what she needs. Women have always been a mystery to me. But Sadie... there's something about her. She's got a hold on me I've never experienced before. What if I mess this up?"

"Gage, if things go south in the future... and they will, trust me, then you face it together. That's what relationships are all about—embracing both the good and the bad," Pete said.

"I don't know how to love someone like her," Gage admitted, his voice barely above a whisper. "I don't know if I know how to love anyone."

Pete shook his head. "I think you're mistaken, son."

Gage glanced at Pete, uncertainty clouding his eyes.

"Love is in here," Pete said, placing a hand over his heart. "Not up here," he added, tapping his temple. "You're thinking too much."

"I'm gonna mess this up... I can just feel it."

"Oh... quit. Man up. Everyone makes mistakes," Pete replied. "But love means working through them together. It means not giving up at the first sign of trouble."

Gage looked down at his hands.

"Love isn't something you can figure out like a puzzle, Gage. It's a journey you share with someone, one step at a time."

He stood up, stretching his muscles, and turned to head back into the bunkhouse. Before closing the door, he paused and looked back. "Life's too short to carry regrets, Gage. Whatever's eating at you from your past, forgive yourself and move forward."

Chapter 35

Gage stood at the base of the main house steps, his Stetson in hand, fingers nervously tracing the brim. He took a deep breath, the crisp morning air filling his lungs as he steadied himself.

He climbed the steps and knocked firmly on the heavy oak door. Moments later, it swung open to reveal Madge, her eyes twinkling beneath a cascade of graying curls.

"Well, good morning to you, Gage," she greeted warmly, wiping her hands on a floral apron dusted with flour.

"Morning, Madge," he replied with a polite nod. "I was hoping I could speak with Jack if he's available."

She arched an eyebrow, a smile tugging at the corners of her mouth. "He's in the living room, grumbling over the books like a bear with a sore paw. This broken leg has him all out of sorts."

Gage managed a small chuckle. "I can imagine. Mind if I come in?"

"By all means," Madge stepped aside, ushering him into the foyer. "And Gage?"

"Yes?"

"It's good to see you," she said.

"Thank you."

Jack Beaumont sat in his leather armchair, a pile of ledgers and receipts strewn across the coffee table that had been moved to the side of the chair to make it easier for the injured man to reach everything. His leg was propped up on an ottoman, encased in a cast and resting on a stack of cushions. He glanced up as Gage entered, his rugged face etched with lines of frustration and restlessness.

"Gage," Jack acknowledged, his tone neutral. "What brings you by this morning?"

"Morning, Jack," Gage began, shifting his weight slightly. "I wanted to talk to you about the foreman's position."

Jack set down the ledger he was holding, giving Gage his full attention. "Have a seat."

Gage sat down in the leather armchair opposite Jack, the leather creaking softly as he settled in.

"So, you've made a solid decision?" Jack prompted, his gaze steady.

"Yes, sir," Gage replied, meeting his eyes. "I'd like to formally accept the position, if the offer still stands."

Jack studied him for a moment, his expression unreadable. Then a hint of a smile brushed his lips. "It does. I'm glad to have you on board in a larger capacity."

"Thank you," Gage said earnestly. "I appreciate the opportunity. This ranch—it's become more than just a place to work. It feels like home, and that's something I'm not used to, sir."

Jack nodded thoughtfully. "That's good to hear," he said, pausing as his eyes narrowed slightly. "You understand that family comes first on this ranch? The animals here are part of our family, and I expect you to care for this land as if it were your own."

"I understand," Gage affirmed. "I intend to give it everything I have."

Jack leaned back, his fingers steepled under his chin. "There's something else I'd like to discuss."

Gage tensed slightly. "Alright."

"Sadie," Jack stated plainly.

Gage felt his pulse quicken. "What about her?"

Jack's gaze was penetrating. "My daughter means the world to me. She's strong, independent, and she cares deeply for this ranch and for the people in her life."

"I know," Gage agreed.

"I reckon I know the look of a man who's got intentions toward a woman," Jack continued.

Gage swallowed hard, choosing his words carefully. "Mr. Beaumont, I won't deny it. Sadie is... she's remarkable. I've never met anyone like her."

Jack's expression remained guarded. "What are your intentions?"

Gage took a deep breath, sitting up straighter. "I care about your daughter—a great deal. Honestly, I'm in love with her. I have been since the moment we met, I just didn't realize it at first. I didn't expect it, and I know I don't have much experience with... with this sort of thing. But my feelings for her are genuine."

Jack studied him, the seconds stretching into what felt like minutes. "Love is a serious thing, Gage."

"I understand that," Gage replied earnestly. "And I don't take it lightly. I know I don't come from much. My past isn't exactly spotless, but I'm committed to making a good life here. For myself, and—if she'll have me—for Sadie."

Jack sighed, his gaze softening ever so slightly. "What's your plan, then?"

Gage hesitated for a moment before pressing on. "First, I wanted to be upfront with you—out of respect. I intend to tell Sadie how I feel, but only if you approve. I believe in doing things the right way."

A faint smile tugged at the corner of Jack's mouth. "Old-fashioned of you."

"Maybe so," Gage admitted, a hint of a smile in return. "But I think some traditions are worth keeping."

"Let me tell you something, Gage. My daughter is precious to me. I've watched her grow into a strong woman, capable and kind. She puts others before herself more often than not. She deserves someone who will cherish her, support her dreams, and stand by her no matter what."

"I want to be that man," Gage said firmly. "I may not have all the answers, and I know I'll make mistakes, but I'm willing to learn and to try my best every day."

"Will you be joining us for church services on Sundays?"

"Yes, sir, I'll be there."

"Will you do your best to invite God into your relationship? Strive to be a man of God and follow His teachings?"

"Yes, sir, I'll try. This is new territory for me, so I may stumble along the way."

Jack regarded him thoughtfully. "You've proven yourself to be hardworking and dependable since you came here. You've saved my skin more than once, and for that, I'm grateful. But being part of this family—it's a commitment beyond the ranch work."

"I realize that," Gage assured him. "And I'm ready to make that commitment."

Jack was silent for a moment, then he nodded slowly. "Alright. I'll give you my blessing to pursue a relationship with Sadie. But know this—if you hurt her, there won't be a place on this earth far enough for you to hide."

Gage managed a wry smile. "Understood, sir."

Jack extended his hand, and Gage rose and moved toward him, grasping his hand firmly. "Welcome to the Eagle's Nest family—officially."

"Thank you," Gage replied, relief and gratitude washing over him.

"Now, sit back down," Jack said, leaning back again. "There's someone else who should be part of this conversation."

He raised his voice slightly. "Harriet! Would you mind joining us for a moment?"

From the kitchen, Harriet called back. "Be right there!"

A few moments later, Harriet appeared in the doorway, wiping her hands on a dish towel. Her eyes flicked between the two men, curiosity evident. "What's going on?"

"Have a seat, darling," Jack gestured to the chair beside Gage.

She settled in, looking expectantly at her husband. "Is everything alright?"

"Better than alright," Jack assured her. "Gage here has accepted the foreman's position."

Harriet's face lit up. "Oh, that's wonderful news! Congratulations, Gage."

"Thank you, ma'am," he replied with a shy smile.

"But that's not all," Jack continued, casting a glance at Gage.

Gage cleared his throat, suddenly feeling the weight of the moment. "Mrs. Beaumont, there's something I'd like to tell you."

Harriet's expression softened. "Go on, dear."

"I've fallen in love with your daughter," he confessed, the words tumbling out more smoothly than he anticipated. "From the moment we met, she's had an effect on me that I can't quite put into words.

She's... she's changed the way I see the world, the way I see myself. I intend to tell her how I feel, with your and Mr. Beaumont's blessing."

Harriet's eyes glistened with unshed tears, a gentle smile spreading across her face. "Oh, Gage, that's the most heartfelt thing I've heard in a long time."

Jack chimed in, his tone lightening. "He came to me first, just like a gentleman should."

Harriet reached out, placing a hand over Gage's. "You're a good man, Gage. I've seen the way Sadie looks at you when she thinks no one's watching. I believe the feeling is mutual."

Gage's heart skipped a beat. "You think so?"

Harriet exchanged a knowing glance with her husband. "A mother knows these things."

Jack nodded in agreement. "She's her own woman, capable of making her own choices, but it's clear to us that she cares for you."

Gage felt a surge of hope. "I plan to speak with her as soon as possible."

"Well, she's out in the south pasture checking on the cattle," Harriet informed him. "Why don't you take some time this morning and wander out that way?"

"I think I will," Gage agreed, rising from his seat.

"Gage."

"Yes, sir?"

"Remember what I said," Jack reminded him, though his eyes held a hint of warmth. "And good luck."

Gage extended his hand toward Harriet. Harriet pushed his hand away as she too stood up. "None of that, Gage," she said, embracing him.

Gage, startled by her embrace, didn't resist. "Thank you, ma'am," he replied.

He then turned and walked toward Jack, and they shook hands. "I believe in you, Gage. Now go find my daughter and be a good man," Jack said.

Gage tipped his hat. "Thank you—both of you."

He stepped outside and headed to the barn, his thoughts a whirlwind of emotions—nervousness, anticipation, and a burgeoning joy he hadn't ever felt.

Behind him, inside the house, Harriet turned to her husband with a satisfied smile. "Well, that went well."

Jack grunted softly. "I suppose it did."

"You're pleased. Admit it," she teased gently.

He shrugged, a softness creeping into his expression. "He's a good man. Rough edges, sure, but who doesn't have those?"

"Exactly," Harriet agreed. "And our Sadie deserves someone who sees her for who she is."

Jack reached for her hand, squeezing it affectionately. "Seems our family is growing."

She chuckled. "It's about time."

Chapter 36

Gage swung himself onto Midnight's back, the black gelding shifting beneath him with restless energy. A tremor of anticipation coursed through Gage's veins as he guided Midnight out of the barn.

He'd left the saddle behind. There was no need for it, and besides, he'd always felt more connected to a horse without the leather and stirrups between them. It seemed fitting for what he was about to do—a gesture as honest and unguarded as the feelings he'd finally embraced.

The south pasture stretched out before him, a patchwork of rolling hills and grazing cattle. Gage urged Midnight into a steady canter, the wind whipping through his hair. His thoughts churned with rehearsed words and half-formed sentences, but none of them seemed adequate. How did a man who'd spent his life running find the right way to tell a woman like Sadie Beaumont that she'd become his reason to stay?

As he crested a small rise, he spotted her. Sadie sat astride Daisy, her posture relaxed as she conferred with Pete, Will, and Julie. The trio of ranch hands listened attentively, their faces lit with easy camaraderie. The sight tightened something in Gage's chest—a mix of longing and gratitude that he could barely comprehend.

He slowed Midnight to a walk as he approached; the others turning to regard him with curiosity.

"Mornin'," he called out, tipping his hat.

Surprise flickered across Sadie's features before settling into a warm smile. "Mornin', Gage. Where have you been?"

He swallowed, hoping his nerves didn't show. "I was wondering if you'd join me for a ride."

Her eyebrows lifted slightly. "A ride? Now?"

He nodded, holding her gaze. "If you've got the time."

Pete glanced between them, a knowing gleam in his eye. "We can handle things here, Sadie."

Will suppressed a grin. "Yeah, we've got it covered."

Sadie hesitated, curiosity evident. "Well, I suppose I could."

"Good. Would you mind riding with me?"

She tilted her head, a playful glint in her eye. "On your horse?"

"That's right."

Her gaze flickered to Midnight, then back to him. "No saddle?"

He shrugged lightly. "You'll be safe with me."

A faint blush colored her cheeks, but she didn't look away. "Alright, then."

Sadie swung her leg over and dismounted Daisy with ease. She led her mare to Pete, handing him the reins. "Would you mind taking care of her for a bit?"

Pete accepted the reins with a nod. "Not at all." As she turned away, he shot Gage a subtle wink. "Go get 'em, cowboy."

Gage felt heat rise to his face, but couldn't suppress the grin that tugged at his lips. Julie watched with open fascination, her eyes darting between Gage and Sadie like she was witnessing the start of a fascinating story.

Will was already on the move. He dismounted his horse and stepped forward. "Let me give you a hand, Miss Sadie."

She smiled appreciatively. "Thank you, Will."

Will clasped his hands together, creating a makeshift step. Sadie placed her boot in his grip, and with a light boost, she settled astride Midnight, just ahead of Gage. The warmth of her back pressed against his chest sent a jolt through him, but he steadied himself, focusing on the reins.

He glanced back at the trio, watching them. "We'll be back after a while."

"Take your time," Pete called out, his tone congenial.

Gage tipped his Stetson in farewell, then nudged Midnight into an easy trot. The horse obeyed willingly, sensing the significance of the moment. They rode in comfortable silence for a few minutes; the ranch falling away behind them.

Sadie shifted slightly against him. "Are you going to tell me where we're going?"

He leaned forward, his breath close to her ear. "Just wait. Enjoy the ride."

She laughed. "You do like your secrets, don't you?"

"Only the good ones."

They continued on, the landscape unfolding in familiar patterns—the sway of prairie grasses, the distant line of cottonwoods marking the creek's path. The sky was a brilliant blue, unmarred by clouds, as if the world itself conspired to make this day perfect.

As they approached the creek, Sadie began to understand their destination.

"I thought you might like to visit your favorite spot," Gage said.

She turned her head slightly, her eyes meeting his. "You remembered."

"Hard to forget something that means so much to you."

They arrived at the clearing where the creek whispered over smooth stones; the water catching the sunlight in dazzling glints. The wildflowers were in bloom, splashes of color amidst the green. Gage brought Midnight to a halt beneath the shade of an old elm tree.

He swung his leg over and dismounted, then extended his hand up to her. "Careful now."

She accepted his help, her fingers slipping into his. As she slid down, she was momentarily pressed against him, their closeness sending a charge through the air. Neither hurried to create distance.

"Thank you," she said softly, her eyes searching his.

"Anytime," he replied, holding her gaze a moment longer before stepping back.

He tied Midnight's reins to a low branch, patting the horse's neck in silent gratitude. "Ready?"

Sadie nodded. "Lead the way."

They made their way up the gentle slope, the path familiar but no less enchanting. The slight rocky ledge led to the flat boulder overlooking the creek—a natural perch offering a panoramic view of the ranch in the far distance and the mountains beyond.

Sadie settled onto the stone, drawing her knees up as she gazed out. "It's even more beautiful today."

Gage sat beside her. He followed her gaze to the wild horses grazing on a distant hillside. Their silhouettes were graceful against the rugged backdrop—a picture of unrestrained freedom.

"They're out early," he observed.

She smiled wistfully. "I could watch them for hours. They remind me of everything wild and untamed."

He glanced at her; the wind tousling a strand of hair across her face. "They remind me of you."

She looked at him, surprised. "Me?"

He nodded, a softness in his eyes. "Strong, spirited, impossible to tame. You move through this world with a grace that's all your own."

A blush rose to her cheeks. "I'm not sure everyone would agree with you."

"Well, not everyone knows you like I'm beginning to."

She held his gaze; the moment stretching between them. "And how is that?"

He took a steadying breath. "As someone who's shown me kindness when I didn't deserve it. Someone who's challenged me to be better, to see more in myself than I ever thought possible."

She looked down, her fingers tracing patterns on the stone. "Gage..."

He shifted closer, his voice earnest. "Sadie, there's something I need to tell you."

She met his eyes again. "What is it?"

He hesitated, the weight of his emotions pressing against the confines of his usual restraint. "I've spent my whole life running—never staying in one place too long, never letting anyone get too close."

"I know," she said gently.

"But since coming here..." He gestured vaguely at the land surrounding them. "Something changed. You—your family—this place, it's all changed me. You did something to me."

She smiled softly. "How so?"

"I used to think freedom meant being on my own, no ties, no obligations. But now..." He shook his head, a hint of a smile playing at his lips. "Now I realize that true freedom is finding a place where you can be yourself completely, where you're accepted—faults and all."

Her eyes searched his, hope flickering in their depths. "Gage, are you saying..."

He reached out, taking her hand in his. His thumb brushed lightly over her knuckles, the simple touch grounding him. "What I'm trying to say is that I've fallen in love with you, Sadie Beaumont."

A breath escaped her parted lips, her eyes glistening.

"With everything that I am, I have fallen deeply in love with you," he affirmed. "I know I'm not perfect. I've got a past that's rough around the edges, and I've never been one to settle down. But with you, I want to be the man you see in me. I want to build a life here—with you—if you'll have me."

Tears gathered in her eyes, but her smile was radiant.

He squeezed her hand gently. "I spoke to your parents this morning. Told them how I feel about you. They gave me their blessing to pursue a relationship with you."

Her eyes widened in surprise. "You did?"

He nodded. "It seemed like the right thing to do. They deserve to know my intentions are honorable."

She laughed softly, a tear slipping down her cheek. "You amaze me. You are something else."

He brushed the tear away with a calloused thumb. "Is that a good thing?"

She leaned into his touch. "It's a very good thing."

A moment of quiet enveloped them, the sounds of the creek and distant birdsong filling the air. Gage felt a peace he'd never known—a sense that he was exactly where he was meant to be.

"So," he ventured, a hint of uncertainty creeping in. "How do you feel about all this?"

She gave him a playful look. "I thought it was obvious."

"Maybe I need to hear it," he admitted.

"Gage West, I've been falling for you since the day you rode into my life. Your strength, your kindness, the way you see the world—it's changed me too."

His heart swelled, relief and joy coursing through him. "You've got no idea how happy that makes me."

She smiled mischievously. "I might have some idea."

He chuckled, the sound rich and unguarded. "So, where do we go from here?"

She tilted her head thoughtfully. "Well, we could start by enjoying this beautiful day together. And then, we'll take things one step at a time."

He nodded, contentment settling over him. "I like the sound of that."

They sat side by side, watching as the wild horses moved gracefully across the hillside. Gage felt the weight of his past lift, replaced by the hope of a future he never dared to imagine.

"Thank you," he said quietly.

She glanced at him. "For what?"

"For showing me what it means to belong. For giving me a place to call home."

She squeezed his hand. "You've always had a place here, Gage. You just had to let yourself see it."

He looked into her eyes, the depth of his feelings reflected back at him. "I see it now."

She rested her head on his shoulder, a contented sigh escaping her. "Good."

They remained that way for a while, wrapped in the simplicity of being together. The barriers between them had crumbled, leaving only the promise of what lay ahead.

After a time, Sadie sat up slightly. "You know, the wild horses might get jealous."

He raised an eyebrow. "Oh? Why's that?"

She grinned. "They've had my heart for a long time. But now, it seems someone else has claimed it."

He chuckled, warmth spreading through him. "Well, maybe we can share."

She laughed, the sound like music to his ears. "I think they'd be alright with that."

He stood, offering his hand to help her up. "We should probably head back before they send a search party."

She took his hand, rising gracefully. "You're probably right."

They made their way down the slope, the path easier now with their burdens lightened. Gage untied Midnight and prepared to mount.

Sadie hesitated. "Wait."

He paused. "What is it?"

She stepped closer, her eyes luminous. "I just wanted to do this." She rose onto her toes and pressed a soft kiss to his cheek.

He felt heat rise to his face, a smile tugging at his lips. "You keep that up, and we might never get back."

She laughed lightly. "Is that a promise?"

He shook his head in playful exasperation. "You're going to be trouble, aren't you?"

"Definitely."

Gage enveloped Sadie in his arms and softly whispered, "Let's do this properly now." He leaned in and kissed her with every ounce of his being. The world around them seemed to melt away.

Chapter 37

Madge's eyes danced with delight as she stood on the front porch, watching Gage, Sadie, and the rest of the ranch hands ride toward them. "There they are!"

Harriet nodded, a satisfied expression on her face. "I've got some fresh lemonade waiting inside. Come on—all of you," she called out to the group.

Sadie turned to glance at Gage, her fingers intertwined with his. "You ready for this?"

Gage grinned. "Yes ma'am. I am."

She squeezed his hand, her eyes softening.

Inside, the familiar warmth of the Beaumont kitchen enveloped them. Gage, Sadie, Pete, Will, and Julie gathered around the large oak table that had hosted countless meals and memories. Madge moved effortlessly between them, pouring glasses of lemonade, the ice clinking softly against the sides.

Jack cleared his throat, sitting at the head of the table. His weathered face bore a broad smile. "Well, it seems we've got some celebrating to do," he began, his voice rich with emotion. "Gage here is officially our new foreman, and from what I gather, there's another reason to be pleased."

All eyes turned to Gage and Sadie. She looked at her father, affection evident in her gaze. "Yes, there is. Gage and I have decided to see where this road takes us."

Harriet beamed, her hands clasped together. "I am so happy for you both."

Jack raised his glass of lemonade. "To new beginnings and strong partnerships—both in work and in life."

They all lifted their glasses, the clinking symbolizing a shared hope for the future. "Hear, hear!" echoed around the table.

Will grinned, his eyes twinkling mischievously. "Does this mean we have to start calling you 'boss' now, Gage?"

Gage chuckled, shaking his head. "Only if you feel like it, Will. I reckon things won't change too much around here."

Julie leaned forward, her chin resting in her hand. "Well, I, for one, am looking forward to seeing how you two lead the ranch together."

Sadie laughed. "Let's not get ahead of ourselves—one step at a time. Gage is the foreman now. Once Daddy's leg heals, and he's back working on the ranch, I'll devote more time to my writing. But for now, I'll follow Gage's lead and his direction on the ranch."

Pete raised his glass again. "To Gage and Sadie—may your journey be filled with happiness."

Madge wiped her hands on her apron, her eyes glistening. "You kids have no idea how much this warms my heart."

Harriet reached over to squeeze her friend's hand. "It's a blessing, indeed."

Gage glanced around the table, a profound sense of belonging settling over him. "I want to thank all of you. You've made a drifter feel like he finally has a home."

Jack met his gaze, his voice steady. "You're part of this family now, Gage. Don't ever question that. We've all seen how hard you've worked and the goodness in your heart. We're proud to have you here."

Will leaned back in his chair, balancing it precariously on two legs. "Just don't go getting a big head now."

Sadie rolled her eyes playfully. "As if we'd let that happen."

Madge clucked her tongue at Will. "Keep all four legs of that chair on the ground, young man, before you go toppling over."

He grinned sheepishly, settling back down. "Yes, ma'am."

Harriet stood, smoothing her skirt. "How about we move this celebration outside? It's too beautiful a day to be cooped up indoors."

"Wonderful idea," Madge agreed. "I've got some cookies cooling that would go perfectly with this lemonade."

They all made their way to the expansive porch that wrapped around the house. The view overlooked the rolling pastures, where horses grazed lazily under the afternoon sun.

Gage and Sadie settled on the porch swing, its gentle creaking melding with the sounds of the ranch. The others gathered around, some seating themselves on the steps or chairs, others leaning against the railing.

"So, Gage," Julie began, "what's the first order of business as our new foreman?"

He exchanged a glance with Sadie before replying. "Well, I was thinking we could start by fixing that section of fence along the east pasture that was damaged in the storm."

Pete nodded approvingly. "Solid plan. I've got the supplies ready whenever you give the word."

Will took a swig of his lemonade. "Just as long as we don't have any more run-ins with wicked storms. My ribs are still sore."

Everyone chuckled, remembering the storm that had them all scrambling.

Madge appeared with a tray piled high with cookies. "Here we go. Fresh from the oven."

"Madge, you're spoiling us," Sadie said, taking one and biting into it with a satisfied sigh.

"Someone's got to keep your strength up," Madge teased, her eyes twinkling. She handed a cookie to Gage. "And you, young man, you always take care of my girl, you hear?"

"Yes, ma'am," Gage replied with a grin.

As the afternoon light mellowed into a golden hue, the conversation flowed easily. They shared stories, joked about past mishaps, and discussed plans for the ranch's future.

At one point, Harriet nudged Jack gently. His expression growing contemplative. "If I may," he said, drawing everyone's attention. "I'd like to say a few words."

The group fell silent, a respectful hush settling.

Jack took a deep breath. "We've been through a lot together—good times and tough ones. But through it all, we've held on to what's most important: our faith, our love for this land, and our commitment to one another. Today, we're not just celebrating a new chapter for the ranch, but also the beginning of something beautiful between Gage and Sadie."

He looked at each of them, his gaze settling on the couple holding hands on the swing. "I'd like us all to join hands."

One by one, they formed a circle, hands linking together. The warmth of touch and the unity it symbolized brought a profound sense of connection.

Jack bowed his head. "Heavenly Father, we come before You with hearts full of gratitude. Thank You for the blessings You've poured out upon this ranch and each person here. We ask for Your guidance and wisdom as we move forward. Guide Gage on his journey to follow You. Bless him with peace and understanding as he embarks on a life devoted to Your word. Bless Gage and Sadie as they embark on this new journey together. May their love be a reflection of Your love—patient, kind, and enduring. Strengthen our bonds as a family, and help us to support one another in all things. In Jesus' name, Amen."

"Amen," echoed softly around the circle.

The group remained still for a moment, the weight of the prayer settling gently among them. As hands were released, conversations began to stir once more.

But Sadie and Gage didn't let go. Their fingers remained entwined, a silent promise passing between them.

She turned to him, her eyes shimmering with emotion. "Did you ever think life would lead you here?"

He shook his head slightly, a soft smile playing on his lips. "Not in my wildest dreams."

"Funny how things work out," she mused.

"Funny, indeed," he agreed, his thumb brushing lightly over her knuckles.

Around them, the sounds of laughter and chatter faded into the background. The world seemed to narrow until it was just the two of them.

"You know," Gage began, his voice barely above a whisper, "I've been thinking a lot about something one of my foster mother's used to say."

"Oh?" Sadie tilted her head inquisitively.

"About how God gives us wings and roots. I've carried those words with me for years," he continued. "I spent so much time using the wings, I forgot about the roots."

She smiled. "And now?"

He met her gaze steadily. "Now I've found a place to plant them."

Emotion welled in her chest, words catching in her throat. Instead of speaking, she leaned in, her lips meeting his in a tender kiss.

It was as if time stood still. The kiss was soft, filled with unspoken words and a depth of feeling that transcended any declaration.

A cheer rose from the others, pulling them back to the present. "Finally!" Will whooped, clapping his hands.

"About time," Pete added with a chuckle.

Julie sighed dramatically. "I've been waiting for this moment."

Madge dabbed at her eyes with the corner of her apron. "You two are going to make me cry."

Harriet's smile was radiant. "Couldn't be happier for you both."

Jack nodded approvingly. "Looks like everything is as it should be."

Sadie and Gage parted slowly, their foreheads resting together as they laughed softly. The sound was pure joy—a melody that echoed the song in their hearts.

"Think they noticed?" Gage joked.

Sadie glanced around at the beaming faces of their family and friends. "Just maybe."

He chuckled. "Guess the cat's out of the bag."

"And I wouldn't have it any other way," she replied, her eyes shining.

"How about some music?" Madge suggested, disappearing into the house before anyone could respond.

Moments later, the soft strumming of a guitar drifted through the open windows, a familiar country tune that spoke of love and home.

Will stood, offering his hand to Julie. "May I have this dance?"

She giggled, accepting, as they moved to a flat patch of grass in the yard.

Pete tapped his foot, humming along. Harriet and Jack sat beside each other, holding hands.

Gage stood, extending his hand to Sadie. "Care to dance?"

She placed her hand in his. "I thought you'd never ask."

They joined Will and Julie in the front yard and moved together effortlessly, the world around them fading once more. The music, the laughter, the gentle breeze—it all blended into a perfect harmony.

"We're in this together." Sadie said.

He reached up to tuck a stray strand of hair behind her ear. "Together," he echoed.

She leaned into him. "Feels right, doesn't it?"

"More than anything I've ever known."

Their lips met once more, a kiss that spoke of promises kept and a future unfolding.

When they parted, she rested her head on his shoulder. "Think we're ready for what's ahead?"

He smiled, a contented sigh escaping him. "As long as we're side by side, I believe we can handle anything."

"Good," she whispered. "I love you."

Gage smiled softly. "I love you more."

Leave A Review

If you enjoyed this book, please consider leaving an honest review on Amazon or Goodreads.

Visit Our Website:

www.tarabaisden.com

Visit Our Amazon Author Page HERE

Find Us On Social Media:

Facebook

Facebook Author Page

Instagram

TikTok

Threads

BlueSky

About The Author

Tara Baisden is a Contemporary Christian Inspirational Romance author who proudly calls the beautiful state of West Virginia her home. Nestled on a sprawling mountainous property, she is surrounded by the peace and serenity of nature. Her days are happily spent in the quiet of country life, writing heartwarming stories of love, faith, and second chances. Tara also enjoys quilting, working in her garden, tending to her beloved pets, and soaking in the beauty of her surroundings.

With deep roots in West Virginia, family is everything to Tara. One of her favorite pastimes is gathering on the front porch with loved ones, sharing stories, laughter, and enjoying the simple, meaningful moments that life offers. When she's not crafting her novels, Tara can often be found exploring the rich history of her home state, visiting local historical sites, and, of course, stopping by every bookstore she passes! Her passion for reading and discovery always fuels her next adventure.

Tara is the author of the Laurel Ridges series of novels, as well as the Riverbend Valley series of novels, of which have been beloved by fans of inspirational romance. Her novels reflect her love for faith, family, and the timeless beauty of the world we live in.

Known for her sweet and clean romances, she creates characters that feel like family and settings that make readers want to visit again and again.

You can find out more about Tara and her latest releases at www.tarabaisden.com or follow her on social media for updates and behind-the-scenes glimpses of her writing process. Stay connected—you won't want to miss the heartfelt stories of love and family she has in store!

Also by Tara Baisden